FAITH

by Donald Herion, Jr.

FAITH

Published by The Sorcerer's Workshop
11850 Riverside Drive, 124, Valley Village CA 91607

ISBN-10: 0578315556
ISBN-13: 978-0-578-31555-3

For permission requests to reproduce or transmit, write to the publisher at the address below:

The Sorcerer's Workshop
11850 Riverside Drive, 124
Valley Village CA 91607

Back Book Cover Design by The Sorcerer's Workshop
Front Book Cover Original Design by The Sorcerer's Workshop

For So Many...

Chapter I

Faith, someone told Charlie Walker, can come in all sizes and shapes. For him, Faith's size was about five-foot-five and approximately one hundred and thirty pounds (she would insist one twenty six); and her shape was quite lovely to the eyes. She sported long black hair that danced like a waterfall whenever she liberated it from her favorite yellow scrunchy. Later, after she got married, she would shorten her hair. A woman does not mind snipping a few inches after it has done its job, getting the right guy to commit. Her well-formed oval face angled down to a firm, dimpled chin. She had wide-set brown eyes (she said they were hazel, but Charlie refused to use that word). She had a nice nose; not too big or too small. She boasted an engaging mouth, wide and honest when smiling, and devastatingly effective when frowning. Fortunately, Faith was generally a happy person, so she saved those frowns for rare, special moments.

The first time Charlie met Faith, she literally danced up to him. It happened on a Saturday afternoon that had interrupted his one real addiction—weekend golf. She glided so lightly, so effortlessly toward him that he half suspected she could walk over wet sand and scarcely leave an imprint. Her body was lean and toned, as one would expect from a dance instructor.

Charlie marched into that dance studio not in the best mood. His golf game was going great, having broken eighty-five the last three outings. He was hoping to crack eighty that fine day but his responsibilities as best man came first. Learning how to dance rather than making a thirty-foot putt seemed like a complete waste of time. After all, couldn't the bride and groom schedule this on a Tuesday or Wednesday night? No one does anything of importance on those days. However, he learned a valuable lesson from Ryan, the soon to be groom, that day. What the bride wants, she gets. Happy wife, happy life, someone said once. A married woman likely spoke those words, Charlie surmised. However, Ryan appeared, at the time, to be very content with the deal. Charlie wondered how long that contentment would last.

Of course, agreeing to be the best man compelled Charlie in ways that taxed his patience. He thought his only responsibilities were going to be interviewing strippers for the bachelor party, not losing the ring in a poker game and making a stale, very forgettable toast at the reception. However, there were other equally-important responsibilities. So here he was, the condemned Best Man, spending a beautiful Saturday cooped up in a small dance studio, not far from his university, waiting for his turn to dance into something called 'The Sway;' or was it 'The Slow Dance'? Turn, step, turn, step.

"Your turn, Best Man," Faith said. She hooked her index finger in a come-hither motion that was both authoritative and enticing.

Charlie stepped out feeling oddly vulnerable. Despite being a fine athlete, dancing came in a distant last, right after skiing, as an activity he actually enjoyed. He met Faith in the middle of the dance floor. The Maid-of-Honor, Beth, was running late again, so Faith had to fill in for her. Everyone else was fiddling with their phones or practicing off to the side.

"Stop looking so depressed, Best Man. You might actually have some fun," she said, observing his discomfort. Her voice twanged musically. He was not sure he liked it. It did not seem to suit her.

"He'd rather be on the golf course," quipped Amy.

The bride went back to her phone and argued with the caterer about the main course as if the fate of the world depended on chicken or filet mignon.

"Golf? I play a little golf," Faith confessed, as she patiently positioned Charlie's feet.

Charlie's eyes brightened hopefully. *Attractive and plays golf,* he thought. Could he be that lucky?

"You do?"

"Ah ha. To tell you the truth, it's a very frustrating game. I really get upset when the windmill thingy hits my ball and shoots it back to me."

"Um, that's not real golf."

"Oh. It's not?"

"No."

She actually looked hurt for a moment. Charlie was about to apologize when she threw him a 'gotcha' look.

"I'll tell you what, Best Man. If you give me your undivided attention, there just might be enough time for you to get in nine holes before sunset."

"I'm not a very good dancer," Charlie confessed, as he checked his watch. Maybe he might get in nine holes at that.

"No problem there. I am a very good teacher. If I can't teach you the Macarena in thirty minutes, I'll hang up my dance shoes."

"Well, I wouldn't want that on my conscience, teacher."

"Glad to hear that. Shall we begin?"

Charlie managed to get through the next thirty minutes while only stepping on her foot one time. However, he had to admit, other than that one misstep, he rather enjoyed the class. She felt wonderful in his arms. She fit like a glove, as they say. She wore no perfume but her hair had a sweet trace of fresh strawberries. It was a bewitching scent a man would not mind waking up to every morning. When the music ended, he stepped back reluctantly.

"Sorry about your foot, teacher."

Her frown reminded him of the time he mowed the back yard and his father shook his head and told him to do it again.

"We're going to have to have a few more practice sessions, Best Man. I can't have you going to the reception and having you tell people you learned your moves from me. My reputation could get ruined."

Faith's serious tone sounded as if she meant every word, but the twinkle in her eyes and whimsical smile promised it would not be all that bad.

"I would hate for that to happen, teacher."

Unfortunately for Charlie, despite the hard dedication of his dance instructor, he actually got worse over the next two weeks. She became increasingly frustrated with his lack of improvement. Even the worst of her students always showed some progress; and she taught kids as young as eight.

"Maybe you're too distracted by golf scores?"

"Well, something is distracting me," he confessed.

Of course, she had become the distraction. She knew it, but she was a complete professional. She left it up to him to make the first move. After all, the man leads.

"Well, what should we do about that, Best Man?"

Charlie grinned.

Faith knew his name after their first lesson, but she kept calling him Best Man, and so he continued to call her teacher. Their odd formalities had slowly given birth to an underlying sexual tension they both felt but never openly acknowledged.

"The wedding is this Saturday."

"I know. I'm invited."

"Yeah, that's right," Charlie said.

They stared at each other very awkwardly as Sinatra's 'The Way You Look Tonight' played. The truth was he really wanted to do more than dance with her. Actually, a lot more. Moreover, he suspected she felt the same. However, he was reluctant to take the plunge. His life was contentedly stable now. He was well established at the university and his golf game was just good enough to give him delusions that he could break par and go semi-pro. The last thing he wanted was something serious, and he suspected Faith was a serious type woman. He really did not think he was ready for that.

"We still have a couple more days," he said.

She smiled like an angler finally getting a strong nibble on their line.

"Sure it won't interrupt your golf?"

"Probably."

"Should we risk that?" she asked whimsically.

"I wouldn't want your reputation to suffer if I were to break the bridesmaid's foot."

"Well, I do appreciate that. Shall we give it another go?"

Charlie never did trip over his own feet at the reception because he twisted his ankle the day before when he stepped in a gopher hole on the eighth fairway. He ended up limping about in an ankle brace during the wedding and reception.

When Faith saw that brace, she immediately suspected he might be shamming. However, when the groom confirmed the story, she said she would forgive him if he bought her dinner sometime. Charlie was unable to follow her logic on the matter. Thinking fast he offered to buy her dinner at Mike's hamburger stand across the street from her dance studio. He secretly hoped she would accuse him of being a cheap date and get off the hook.

"Great," she told him happily. "I eat there all the time. They even named a burger after me."

"Really?" he replied doubtfully.

"Really. Double patty with pulled pork, mango, and grilled onions."

Charlie's features registered a face only a sour lemon could spawn. It triggered an eyebrow snap from Faith.

"Sounds horrible. What is it called?"

"The Going on Faith Burger, what else?" she replied proudly. "You'll love it."

"I doubt it."

"Oh, no, please don't tell me you're one of those vegans?"

"Would that be a deal killer?"

Her face split into one of genuine revulsion that almost made him laugh.

"Hell ya it would."

"Well, you don't need to worry, teacher, I'm a carnivore through and through."

"Great. The last guy I took to Mike's ordered a salad. A

salad! Can you believe that? I like a salad as much as anyone, but please. I said good-bye right then and there, and walked away. I have to eat there."

"Brutal. You're tough."

"I figured after ten lessons you would know that. Are strong women a turn off for you?"

"I generally prefer them to be soft and squishy and know their way around a kitchen," he said seriously.

"Neanderthal," she shot back. Then she seemed to soften. "It's nice to know you're not all extinct. I was beginning to wonder."

"Well, we are on the Endangered Species List, but there's still a few of us left."

"I'm glad to hear it. There might be hope for you yet, Charlie."

He smiled at the very first mention of his name.

"I aim to please, Faith."

She reacted with a head tilt to his first real smile.

"Wow, you have nice teeth when you smile. You might want to do that more often," she suggested. "Just a little inside baseball advice, but women love a man with a great smile."

"Is that a fact?"

"Yes, it is."

Eighteen months later, they were married, and this time he did not hurt his ankle playing golf. By then he was a better golfer and a worse dancer. He still did not like the Going on Faith Burger, but she still loved him anyway.

Charlie found himself smiling as he recalled those wonderful times that seemed so long ago now. Sensing a pair of eyes on him, he looked up from his chair. His eyes focused on the student in the front row of his class staring at him curiously. Charlie wiped the smile from his face. He stood up, walked around, and leaned against his desk. He crossed his arms restlessly. His eyes darted up to the wall clock. It was five minutes to twelve. Back to business.

"Five minutes, everyone."

Taut faces snapped up and checked the clock. The collection of faces dropped back down to their tests. The ripple of frustrated murmurs seemed to match their urgent scribbling. Here and there, heads tilted left or right. One could sense eyeballs straining to focus on fellow classmates papers. Some of those eyes turned up to their professor at the front. His grim expression somehow seemed directed to each set of eyeballs. Their heads dropped down. Hands and minds raced against the clock in game show fashion to complete their final exam.

Professor Charlie Walker shifted his lean, five foot eleven inch frame against the desk. He was as antsy as his students. However, his nervous twitches had nothing to do with the exam. Dressed in casual slacks and polo shirt, he still twisted irritably against the sweat accumulating under his arms and back. His keen brown eyes drifted yet again to the wall clock, fixated on the minute hand. Two more minutes, just one hundred and twenty seconds, and he could leave. As a kid, he remembered how many times in class he stared at the minute hand, trying to will it forward, so class would end, and he could leave school to go out and play. However, the business he had lined up for today was going to be anything but play.

Sensing movement at the back of the room, Charlie snapped back into teacher mode. He spotted the surreptitious elbow thrust from one student into another. Even with their heads down, the movement of lips was easy to spot.

"Hmmm," he said with just enough emphasis to get their attention.

Charlie's eyes drifted across the now half-empty classroom. The other half had completed the final over the last half hour and dashed out. He was anxious to join them. He looked down to his vibrating cell phone. He checked the text message and gave it an inadvertent nod.

"All right, time's up everyone," he announced.

There was a last rush of writing as others slow-walked their tests to the front. One by one, they dropped them on Charlie's desk. He caught several anxious looks as they met his eyes.

"Congratulations on surviving ancient Roman history," he said with a smile. "Remember, it's not the right or wrong answers that matter. It's the size of my grading curve."

A ripple of relieved laughter eased that post-test tension many experience when right answers suddenly pop into students' heads.

"I'll be in my office for the next hour. Enjoy your summer," Walker said as he collected the pile of tests.

His eyes danced over the top one. Instead of groaning internally as he often did with the task of grading fifty papers, he felt relief. His teaching assistant was going to get the fun job of plowing through them. While many professors burdened their TAs with the job, Professor Walker felt a twinge of guilt over it. However, he just did not have the time to decipher the chicken scratches that partly resembled English, but looked more like ancient hieroglyphics from some ancient, undiscovered civilization.

He stuffed the tests into his battered leather bag and followed the last student out. A warm breeze greeted him as he exited Turner Building. The sun was shining brightly on this early June day. It was warmer than normal for this time of the year, but he actually felt sharp jabs of clammy coolness that dug right down to his bones. As he walked briskly to his office on the other side of the campus, he ignored the clamor of students hurrying to their next test, or perhaps going home after a grueling school year. He ducked an errant frisbee that flashed by his head. He barely acknowledged the student's apology as his thoughts drifted to matters that were more important.

Upon reaching the admin building, he nodded to fellow professors. A few spoke to him, but all he could manage were polite nods. Usually he would stop and have brief chats with them about the long semester having mercifully ended, or lamenting on another failed semester in educating the future leaders of the world. However, he had no time for such friendly interchanges.

Charlie ducked into his office and shut the door. He set his leather bag in the remaining sliver of space on his crowded desk. He dropped into his creaky leather chair. Checking his watch, he saw he had a few minutes before he could make those important errands. The irritable clamminess he had been feeling had finally subsided; at least for the time being. Now he felt nervous anticipation in his chest as if his racing heart was under great stress. He pulled open his desk drawer and poured himself a shot of Jim Beam. The smoky liquid curling down his throat did its job. He put the bottle back.

As he rocked back and forth in his chair, his eyes scanned the walls of his spare twelve-foot-by-twelve-foot office. Almost every square inch of space was wallpapered with maps, diagrams, and charts of ancient Judea. The largest was an incredibly detailed map of Jerusalem around the year 26 CE. The diagrams tacked around the map were hand drawn sketches of the interior of the city. Some were hand fashioned by him, and still others he had collected over the years. He knew their nooks and crannies like he knew the layout of his own home. In fact, he knew them so well he believed he could navigate the actual places blindfolded if necessary.

Reaching for his leather bag, he pulled out the tests and absent-mindedly started to review them. He sighed again at the scratches that passed for English, or a poor facsimile of English. In the era of texting, the simple act of writing coherent, legible sentences had nearly forced him to become a philologist. He did not envy Beverly's task in deciphering them. Nevertheless, such is the burden of being a TA. Still, he had been pleasantly surprised that he had such a large class wanting to learn about ancient Roman history. He knew there were many easier classes taught by professors who were more than happy to phone in their lessons. Maybe not all was lost with this present generation. Then his mind reeled by a particularly indecipherable answer to the last essay question.

"Sorry I'm late, Professor. I've been running late all morning."

Charlie looked up to Beverly who had just entered the office.

Beverly was a bright, enthusiastic 26-year-old teaching assistant. She was dressed in jeans and a long sleeve shirt. Her tilted Yankee baseball cap hid most of her auburn hair.

"Hi, Beverly. How's your week looking?" Charlie asked.

She shrugged, her eyes gazing at the walls.

"Nothing special. I'm not going back home til July. Do you need me for something?"

Walker scooped up the fifty tests and hoisted then in the air. His smile was not warm and inviting, but more like a warning. She came around the desk and accepted the gift.

Beverly examined the tests cautiously then looked back to her professor. She enjoyed working with Professor Walker more than the other faculty members. For one, he treated her as an equal. Most of the other professors were stuffy old birds who were well mannered but incredibly reluctant to engage with her out of fear something they spout might be misinterpreted.

"I have to go away tomorrow and I'm not sure when I'll be back. Do you think you can grade these for me? If not, I can get Professor Larkin."

Beverly now scrutinized the tests a little more closely. Her chest heaved up. Her mouth compressed into a thin horizontal line. Then it morphed into a sort of twisting pucker. This was going to be a challenge.

She finally shrugged.

"Sure. I can handle it; if you trust me," she replied.

"I would not have asked you if I didn't, Beverly," he said with relief.

She flipped through a few more. Charlie could tell she was not relishing this task. He was suddenly rueful dumping this on her. It was not her job. It was his job. Moreover, Professor Larkin did owe him a few favors.

Beverly sighed and nodded. She threw the tests under her arm and directed an inquisitive stare at him.

"Is everything all right, Professor Walker?" she asked.

Charlie nodded.

Of course, he could not explain the real reason for dropping this burden on her. She probably would not have believed him in any case.

"I'm sure you'll do a great job. I know you'll be fair."

"I'll start right away. Have you looked at them?" she asked with a raised eyebrow.

"Oh, yeah," Charlie said with a turn of his head that jerked a small laugh from her.

"Sure you still want to be a teacher?"

"I'll let you know after I plow through these tests," she mused.

"If you need any help, go to Professor Larkin. He owes me a few favors," he advised. "And thanks again. I'll make it up to you."

She nodded and walked out.

Charlie sighed with relief knowing his last responsibility as a professor was done. Now he could devote all his energy to the seemingly impossible task before him. He rocked back and forth and shut his eyes.

Ever since he got that surprising text from his brother-in-law at seven a.m., his thoughts roiled like a tiny ship in a tempest. He had managed to slip out of bed without waking Faith. He slipped outside to get a grip on his emotions. His plan had to be moved up a week. His greatest foe, time, had struck once again. Seven whole days lost. It had to be tomorrow or never. To confirm the text, he immediately called Ben Miles. He was at the lab as expected.

"I figured you'd call right away," Ben said.

His voice was carefully guarded and low, as if he might be in a room with other people and did not want to be heard.

"What happened?"

There were a few seconds of silence. When Ben replied, Charlie could tell from the more relaxed tone that he had shifted to another room for privacy.

"Gregori and Banbridge have been ordered to fly to

Washington. They take off in a few hours. You know what that probably means for us," Ben explained.

Charlie paced back and forth. Carefree birds were singing. Agile squirrels were dashing up and down the large elm tree that dominated his back yard. Darting hummingbirds battled for sugar water from the nearby feeder. For a moment, he almost envied their simple lives. Eat, sleep, sex. It did not get simpler than that. However, he had no time for such trivial reflections. His whole world had just turned over.

"Charlie? You there?" "Yeah. I'm here."

Charlie felt a pair of eyes on him. He turned and saw Faith peeking out from the blinds in their bedroom. Her face formed a question. Charlie smiled, and nodded, signaling everything was okay. Her face disappeared, the blinds swinging back into place.

"Okay, I guess we go tomorrow then."

Charlie's voice was matter of fact but inside his stomach was doing backflips. Could they get it all ready by tomorrow? There was no choice. They had to. Somehow, some way, they had to get it all ready.

There was a long pause before Ben replied. He sounded dubious. Knowing his strong opposition to his plan, Charlie was not surprised.

"Are you sure?"

"Do we have a choice?"

"Yeah," Ben replied, whispering again. "Don't do this. Shit. Maybe it's a sign, Charlie. You're a big believer in signs, aren't you?"

Charlie ignored the dig.

"Operation Hail Mary is on, Ben. Can you be ready?" he said.

Ben growled non-committal.

"Well?" Charlie pushed back, not about to let Ben take the easy way out. "Can you be ready by tomorrow or not?"

"Yeah, I think so. I'll talk to Sidesh when I get a chance."

"You mean you haven't told him yet?"

"No. I was going to tell him next week."

"Great," Charlie snapped.

"Take it easy. I'll have to call you back."

The phone went dead.

Charlie grabbed a patio seat and leaned back. His mind wrestled with all the things he now had to do to be ready for their trip tomorrow. It was going to be a hectic twenty-four hours. Maybe that could be a good thing. He would be so fixated on getting ready that he would have no time to rethink the viability of his plan.

Charlie contacted Oscar and Dwayne. Naturally, both were sound asleep and more than a little irritated with such an early call. They became even more so when he told them they needed to provide the gear he had contracted for by this afternoon. They both assumed they had another week to get it all together. When Charlie promised to double their fees, they became much more agreeable. They assured him everything he asked for would be available after three.

Charlie checked his watch. It was nearly 7:30. There was so much to do and barely enough time to get it all done. The last, and most important act, would be telling Faith about the trip. Originally, he planned to explain it over the course of a week, subtly preparing her for what he had in mind. Now that plan was out the door. He was just going to have to drop the 'bomb' on her tonight. He prayed it would not unravel his long weeks of planning. Maybe this might be better. She would have less time to think about it. But for now that would have to wait.

Faith appeared behind the sliding glass doors in the kitchen. She was holding up a cup of steaming coffee. Charlie nodded and walked back inside.

Charlie's buzzing phone jerked him back to the present. He leaned forward in his leather chair and picked up the cell phone. It was a simple text message.

Charlie. Order is ready for pick up. Oscar.

Charlie nodded, biting his lower lip. He prayed Oscar did the job he promised. He would have no time to get alterations.

Once again, Charlie's attention focused on the diagram of ancient Jerusalem on the wall. Doubts on its accuracy rippled through him. He finally pushed the creeping reservations away. He told himself he had done the best job he could. It had to be right. Of course, if everything worked as planned, he would know soon enough.

"Let it go," he said out loud.

Charlie jerked to his feet. He could not sit anymore. Too screwed up with energy he grabbed his leather bag and left the office. His walk to the nearby university theater was more of a jerky sprint. He suddenly realized he must look more like a criminal leaving the scene of a crime than a well-respected history professor. He regained control of his stride and settled down to a more measured gait.

The Davison Theater was one of those new architectural nightmares of twisted metal and glass. Everything was weird with angles and curves that suggested something out of a Freudian fever dream. Students squatted lazily on the steps leading to the front entrance. Most had their faces glued to their cell phones. One couple, off to one side, was smoking weed and making out shamelessly. The sweet odor wafted into Charlie's nostrils. The scene brought forth a couple memories of a drama student he dated briefly his third year at USC. She was fun, wild, and willing. When you were in college, those were the best sorts of girls to date.

Hurrying up the stairs, Charlie pushed open the doors and crossed the lobby. The noonday sun cast distorted geometric shadows across the checkered pattern of black and white linoleum. He reached the double doors leading into the theater and carefully pushed them open. He stopped and looked down to the stage below. A rehearsal of Shakespeare's Julius Caesar was underway. He grinned with surprise. Dead white playwrights were not really in fashion these days. However, Professor Oscar Fernandez was indifferent to present day fads. When several students complained about his choice, he listened very patiently and then told them they could resign from the class. Of course, such was Oscar's reputation that no one took him up on the offer.

Charlie spotted him on the stage directing several of his student actors. From the way his face was buried in his hand, he surmised it was not going too well.

"All right, let's try that again, Alec," he said.

Charlie started down the center aisle to the stage as he watched the rehearsal. Oscar waved his hands and stepped forward. The students stopped and turned to their irritated professor.

"Okay, that's not working. Jason you need to enter faster and take center stage. You are Julius Caesar. You are ruler of the Roman Empire. You're not entering a Seven-Eleven to buy a Big Gulp."

When several of the student actors spotted Charlie approaching the stage, Oscar turned around.

"Sorry to interrupt, Oscar," Charlie said.

"Okay, give me a couple minutes everyone," he said.

Oscar grabbed a wrapped package sitting at his feet and stepped off the stage. Oscar was barely five eight but with his aquiline features and jet-black hair, he reminded one of a matinee idol from old Hollywood. Of course, the actresses adored him. The rumor was he liked being adored.

"Here you go," he said, offering him the package.

Charlie accepted the lengthy cardboard box. It was much larger and heavier than he had expected. White string bound the box tightly. He set it down by his feet.

"Is everything in there?" Charlie asked.

"Yeah. Everything you asked for."

Oscar stared at Charlie. His upturned face had many questions.

"You kind of caught me by surprise this morning. I thought I had another week to get all that ready. So it's kind of a rush job. I had the wardrobe department work their asses off all morning to get it done. I hope it's what you want."

"Knowing you, Oscar, I'm sure it will all be perfect."

Charlie produced an envelope from his leather bag. He handed it over. Oscar never bothered to open it. He merely glanced at the envelope, folded it, and shoved it into his back pocket.

"Thanks, Oscar. I really do appreciate you getting this all done so quickly."

"So, what are you really going to do with those outfits? Are you planning on starting your own theater group?" he asked, grinning.

"No, nothing like that," Charlie simply replied.

He decided to change the subject. He looked past Oscar.

"So, how's your play coming?"

Oscar glanced back to his actors huddled on stage working their lines. His tired shrug spoke volumes.

"One of the actors suggested we should have a woman play Julius Caesar and a man play Calphurnia. He said it would be sui generis. Sui generis."

"Interesting idea," Charlie said, barely able to suppress a grin.

"Yeah, that's one word for it."

"What did you say?"

"I agreed it would be sui generis. But then I suggested having a bunch of men stab a woman on stage might not be received well by the audience."

Charlie laughed.

"First performance is next Thursday you know. You'll be here, right?"

"I hope so," Charlie replied. He meant it. It would mean he had succeeded. "Thanks again. I'll see you next week."

Charlie grabbed the package and walked back up the aisle. Oscar watched him leave. He shrugged and returned to the stage.

"Now Alec, let's hold back a little on the dramatic pauses," Oscar requested.

"It's the way Brando played Marc Antony in the movie," Alec said.

"Alec, you are not Brando."

***

The staccato roar of the machine shop greeted Charlie as he entered the cavernous basement of the Wright Building of Design. The odor of freshly cut wood and burnt metal drifted lazily in the air. Every drill press, sander, lathe, and worktable was surrounded by students working on prototypes, newly-fangled bicycle designs, and other 'things' he could not recognize. In the right booth, another group was carefully sculpting a half scale model of a bullet-shaped car. They scrapped off thick chunks of clay or slapped some back on. Opposite them, another group was assembling oddly-shaped solar panels.

Charlie's phone vibrated in his pocket. He checked it. Faith wanted him to pick up a bottle of wine for dinner. He groaned. As if he did not enough things to do, he had to hit the liquor store. He texted a quick OK. As he looked back up, he ducked instinctively as a drone, the size and shape of a large dragonfly, flew right up to his face. It hovered there, buzzing, with the flapping neon wings flashing blue and green in a mesmerizing, pleasing blur. It spun about and shot back to the young woman working the remote control.

Looking off to the shop manager's office, Charlie spotted Dwayne O'Connor waving to him. Charlie nodded back and navigated his way across the busy shop. He entered the office and shut the door. The racket of the shop dropped off just enough to allow a conversation without having to raise one's voice.

"Good afternoon, Chuck," Dwayne said.

The burly, bald man of fifty rocked back in his large, rocking chair. An open beer sat in a makeshift cup holder. Dwayne was casually clad in stone-washed jean overalls and a Grateful Dead t-shirt doused with yellow sawdust and shimmering metal shavings.

The huge metal desk sprouted stacks of manuals and books. Charlie focused his attention on the gunmetal green box resting on the center of the desk.

Charlie pointed to the box.

"Is that it?"

Dwayne nodded, stealing a pull on the beer can. His narrow eyes locked on Charlie. Calloused hands rested heavily the metal box as if he were not sure he wanted to surrender it. A key protruded from the lock.

"It's the best I could do on short notice. Fortunately, most of the work was done already. I just needed to complete the last set," he said.

When Charlie raised his eyebrows, Dwayne finally lifted his hands off the box and sat back. He gulped the rest of his beer and flung the crushed can into the nearby trash bin.

Charlie pulled the box to the edge of the desk, turned the key, and flipped up the lid. He probed the contents very carefully. He held up several of the coins close to the bare fluorescent bulb dangling from the ceiling.

"Here," Dwayne said, offering a magnifying glass. "They're damn good if I don't say so myself. The reference material you provided helped a great deal."

Charlie took the glass and scrutinized one of the gold coins. He ran his fingers over the stamped pattern. He whistled, nodding with approval. He returned the coins to the box, shut the lid, and locked it. He reached into his leather bag and offered the envelope to Dwayne.

Dwayne hesitated, staring hard at the envelope almost as if it might blow up in his face. Charlie finally set it on the desk.

"It's probably a tad late to bring this up but I hope you're not planning on doing something, illegal, with those, are you? Counterfeiting for example?" he asked.

His tone was wary while his eyes darted past Charlie to see if anyone was watching them.

Charlie hefted the steel box. The dull clink of metal on metal resounded. The box was heavy. If Dwayne was having second thoughts, he could be in serious trouble. Charlie had no time to get another set of coins struck. It would likely stop him from going forward with his plan.

"You know me better than that, Dwayne," Charlie promised. "I'm not going to be breaking any current laws."

Dwayne jabbed a finger at the metal box.

"But you refuse to tell me why you need those."

"I wish I could. All I can tell you is it's not for anything nefarious. Dwayne, you're just going to have to believe me."

Dwayne studied Charlie's face for a long moment. Finally, he grabbed the envelope and opened it. He took out the certified check for forty thousand dollars. He whistled.

"It better be important for this kind of money."

"It is. Thanks again," Charlie said. "I really have to run."

Charlie turned to leave. Dwayne stuffed the check into the center drawer. He rose from his chair and walked out with him.

"How's Faith by the way?"

"Well as can be expected," Charlie replied.

"Brenda and I pray for her every night."

Dwayne escorted him to the exit.

"Thanks. We really appreciate it."

"We should all get together for dinner next week," Dwayne suggested.

"I'd like that. I'll call you," Charlie said.

"Great. Have a good weekend."

"You too."

Charlie shook Dwayne's hand and walked out.

Chapter II

Ben checked his watch as he followed Anton Gregori and Larry Banbridge to the Cyngus Labs parking lot. The exhaustive meeting had gone on longer than Ben had expected. He had come to realize, through painful experience, working on government projects was not the panacea others had promised him. Sure, the funding was unlimited, but so was dealing with government bureaucrats who were obsessed with mountains of paperwork and incomprehensible, oppressive regulations.

"What time is your meeting with the Secretary tomorrow?" Ben asked as casually as possible.

"It's set for two in the afternoon. But I won't be shocked if he pushes it to later in the day. He's not a stickler for schedules," Anton Gregori complained irritably.

"Sounds like you're not looking forward to this."

Anton snorted as he searched his pocket for the keys to his Range Rover. He finally ripped them out and opened the door.

"I hate politics more than I hate dentist appointments. And the Secretary is not the sharpest blade in the drawer."

"The guy's an idiot," Larry added. "Damn, he's an idiot's idea of an idiot."

"He's going to have a million questions about the project and we'll have to hold his hand through each and every one of them. Hey, why don't you come along Ben? You know how to deal with these perfumed princes. I'm afraid he'll spew out something stupid and I'll damage his precious ego."

Ben laughed, shaking his head.

"Nope. Two's company, three's a crowd. Besides I have plans for the weekend."

"Really? Going somewhere?" Larry asked.

"I have a little jaunt planned."

"With who?" Anton inquired with a raised brow.

"Is it with Inga in accounting? It's Inga, isn't it? Damn. I knew she had a thing for you," Larry revealed.

"That's news to me," Ben replied, acting genuinely surprised. "No. It's with my sister and her husband."

That silenced them. They knew all about his sister's situation. The two nodded sympathetically.

"Oh. Well, say hi to Faith for me," Anton said.

"Yeah, same here," Larry added.

"I'll do that. Have a safe trip."

He watched the two get into their respective vehicles and drive off. There were only a few cars left in the lot. One belonged to him. The second was Sidesh's prized corvette. The last two belonged to the security guards. The rest of the staff had already been cut loose for the long weekend.

He watched until the vehicles were well out of sight before hurrying back inside the main building. He passed the security guard huddled behind the large lobby desk. He barely acknowledged Ben as he returned to the magazine he was reading. Ben stepped into the elevator and pushed the button for the sub-basement.

A rush of icy air swirled into the elevator when the doors slid opened. He hurried up the long corridor, passing locked offices and labs. His footsteps echoed dully on the linoleum floor. He hesitated at the double doors, peering through one of the small windows. He spotted Sidesh hunched over the main computer workstation. There could be no further delay now. He had to make his pitch and make it good. He knew he was taking a big gamble appealing to his friend and co-worker, but without him, the plan would become even more complicated. When he analyzed the possible outcomes, he calculated there was a ninety percent chance Sidesh would refuse to help. In fact, there was a better than even chance he would report Ben's crazy plan to their superiors. If Sidesh did, Ben would not only lose his job but also his security clearance, and with it, his career. No firm would hire an engineer, no matter how talented, who had been branded a security risk by the government. But there was nothing else to do but go forward and hope for the best.

Ben pushed open the swinging lab doors and entered the spacious chamber. Sidesh glanced at him and then returned to typing on his keypad.

"Did they finally leave?" he asked.

"Yeah, it's just the two of us."

"I'll get the wine. You light the candles," Sidesh joked.

Ben moved through the main Cyngus lab. He paused briefly by something large and spherical under a black tarp. After staring at it for a spell, he stepped over and around the minefield of snaking cables and metal cabinets. He took the chair next to Sidesh and watched him.

Doctor Ben Miles was thirty-five years old with short, dirty blonde hair that nearly matched his sallow complexion. Working incredibly long hours in underground labs meant he was prone to sunburn, the result being cheerful, Santa Claus cheeks. A millimeter or two over five ten, he was surprisingly thin considering the poor diet of fast food take out he had become accustomed to that last few years.

"What do you think the DOD is going to do when they hear what Anton and Larry have to tell them?" Sidesh asked.

Sidesh Kumar was a 30-year-old engineer. Although he really preferred the term 'rocket scientist.' According to him, women seemed to swoon whenever he told them he designed giant rockets. Like Ben, Sidesh was wearing a loose fitting white lab coat over jeans and a sweater.

"You know what they're going to do. We've talked about it enough."

Ben jabbed a thumb toward the covered object in the far corner. Sidesh followed the thumb and set his eyes on the hidden object.

"They'll bury that with their flying saucers, alien bodies, and God knows what else."

Sidesh managed an agreeable laugh and shrugged.

"So be it. We can finally get back to work on the engine. That's why they hired us in the first place. Damn, I'm hungry. Are you? Why don't we check out that Thai place by the mini mall?"

Not getting a reply, Sidesh turned to him.

"No Thai? Please not Subway again," he pleaded. "I've got a hankering for some Thai food. Hankering. That's a word right? I saw it a movie the other night. Besides, the waitress at the Thai place thinks rockets are cool. Wait until she sees the rocket in my pocket."

Sidesh laughed uproariously and shrugged when Ben did not respond in kind. He then considered Ben's blank expression. He spun a quarter turn in his seat and faced Ben.

"Is something wrong?"

Ben stroked his chin thoughtfully, inching his chair up closer to Sidesh. He leaned forward, setting his elbows on his knees.

"Sidesh, there's something I need to talk to you about," Ben explained in a suddenly somber tone.

Sidesh's face registered concern.

"Shit, you're firing me. It was just a joke. I don't have a rocket in my pocket. While I do but I don't talk to women like that. You know me, Ben. It's just guy talk. We can still do that right?"

"No Sid, you're not being fired. But I'd forget the rocket in my pocket talk."

Sidesh sighed, relieved.

"Great. Am I getting a raise then?"

"No."

Now he frowned, his eyes narrowed appreciably.

"Sid, I need your help with something important."

Sidesh just nodded non-committal-like.

Ben's voice dropped almost to a whisper. *Who knows*, he thought to himself, *the walls might have ears*. Ben suspected the NSA were interested in the research they were doing there. They were being monitored constantly. In fact, every six months they compel everyone to endure lie detector tests. It was all very taxing.

Working for the government always came with a price.

"Okay. Here's the tale," he finally said.

***

Charlie parked the Ford Explorer directly across the street from Faith's Dance Studio. The front of the studio was all glass so passersby could peer inside. Charlie checked his watch. It was nearly four p.m. *The class should be finishing up*, he thought. He decided to wait until everyone had left before going inside. Parents were already assembling by the front entrance or peeking through the glass to watch their daughter's lesson. Several were taking snapshots or video with their cell phones.

The enthusiastic eight- to ten-year-old girls listened intently to Faith as she ran them through their final dance routines for the day. All ten girls wore identical sky blue short-sleeve tutus and ballet slippers.

"Okay, one more time," Faith said patiently.

One by one, the young girls completed the dance moves they had been practicing for the last hour. Faith nodded with approval after each one.

"Very good. Better. Higher with your hands. That's right. Excellent, Carol. Tilt your head more, Hannah," she told them in a carefully measured tone.

Satisfied, she called them all together. She went down on one knee until she was at their eye level. The exhausted girls were still bursting with energy, jostling elbows, giggling with excitement.

"Okay, I saw a great deal of improvement from everyone. I'm sure that's because you've all been practicing at home like I told you to do, right?"

She raised an eyebrow that generated more tittering from the girls. A few blushed. Others looked away awkwardly.

"That's what I thought. If you really want to improve, you have to invest the time. Practice may not make perfect, but it helps."

Faith glanced toward the window facing the street. She

smiled and waved at the many familiar faces pressed against the glass. A few waved back. The young girls turned and waved to their parents. Faith turned back to her students.

"Okay, that's it for the day. I'm very proud on how hard you've all worked. Good job. Come on, I'll walk you out."

She led the way to the exit. Several of the girls flashed some of their dance moves as they followed her. She opened the door for them and the girls rushed over to their parents.

As always, Faith greeted the parents one by one. She took a moment to speak with several but most were in a hurry to leave. For some of them, Faith served more as a temporary babysitter than a dance teacher. But others seemed to be genuinely invested in their daughters learning to dance. As the last one drove off, Faith experienced the inevitable let down after finishing a class. She loved teaching. It did not matter if it was one or a dozen, young or old, she always felt a thrill passing her enthusiasm for dance to others.

When she reached for the door, a needle-like pain struck her left shoulder. She recoiled as her trapezius muscle clenched. Faith leaned into the door, trying to breathe through the spasm. Then carefully reaching back with her right hand, she massaged the rigid cramp. The dense muscle resisted her pressing fingers. She pushed even harder until finally, mercifully, it released. When the pain passed she walked back inside.

Charlie grimaced watching Faith's sudden attack. He clenched the wheel with both hands. He was just about to hurry over when she seemed to recover and go back inside. He gathered himself and got out of the vehicle. He dodged a couple of passing cars and entered the studio.

Faith heard the door open and close. She turned around half expecting it to be one of her students who had forgotten something. Then she saw who it was.

"You're late," she said rather thinly.

Charlie shrugged, "Sorry. My wife asked me to pick up a bottle of wine for dinner."

She frowned, unsympathetic.

"Oh, I tried to warn you about her. Wives are nothing but trouble."

They walked toward each other. Faith was wearing black tights and a purple tank top. A yellow scrunchy bound her long hair. Her wide-set brown eyes possessed a sort of twinkle as if she could break into a smile at any moment. But she was not smiling now. She appeared quite serious.

"Yeah, I know. But she makes the best damned apple walnut pancakes," he explained.

Her head tilt was like a sympathetic shrug.

"Does she?"

Charlie nodded.

He watched her walk toward him. He searched for some hint of weakness or fatigue in her stride. She seemed to sense him studying her movements. Her challenging look seemed to say: Don't look at me like that, I'm fine.

They met in the middle of the dance floor. There was scarcely an inch separating them. Her hair still had that enticing strawberry scent. She leaned forward, pressing her bosom against his chest. He was about to wrap his arms around her when she took his hands in her own.

His parting lips began to form a question. She knew the question immediately. She shook her head and briefly placed her finger against his mouth.

"Ready for your next lesson?" she asked, raising her eyebrows.

There was no hint of slurred speech today. Her voice was firm but still had that soft, almost musical tone.

"Yes," Charlie replied.

He knew he should have said no. Dancing was becoming increasingly difficult for her. In fact, he knew she only really danced with him now. She did not want people to know about her condition. It never looks good when a dance teacher trips over her own feet.

Besides, he could never say no to her.

She turned her head toward her Amazon Alexa on a nearby shelf and spoke very carefully.

"Alexa, play Bolero."

The music started to play almost instantly.

Charlie took Faith's left hand into his, while his other hand snaked around her waist. Her left hand came over his shoulder, pressing firmly into his back.

As the music kicked in, Charlie slid left slowly, then quickly moved forward before sliding right. He repeated the steps several times.

"Ready for the crossover breaks?" she asked.

"You're the teacher."

"I think you're ready."

Charlie started awkwardly. With his mind on something far more important, remembering Bolero dance steps was not exactly a priority for him. But he did not want to disappoint her. *Slow, quick, quick, slow*, he told himself as his muscle memory came alive. He caught an approving smile as she enfolded back into his arms. Slowly, he found himself feeling the rhythm of the music. He savored the warm sensation of her body grazing against his own. Just as the music climaxed, Faith seemed to lose her balance for an instant. But he never let go of her. She regained her composure almost immediately.

"You're really improving," she said quickly, as if nothing had happened.

"Am I?" he asked. "Well, it's only taken forever."

"I know. I've never had a student with your lack of enthusiasm," she said.

"Well, as you know, golf is more my game," he replied. "But it helps some when you have a crush on your teacher."

Charlie brushed his fingers across her flushed cheek. His face was serious now. As his mouth began to open, she placed her finger over it again.

"I'm fine. My foot slipped. Honest."

She spoke in a clipped, efficient manner as if she had practiced the words beforehand.

Charlie decided to accept her obvious lie. Now was not really the time anyway. She rested her head against his shoulder as they crossed the dance floor to the back of the studio. They settled on a small wooden bench. She leaned against him.

"How was your last class?"

"It was good. The students seemed genuinely interested in dead white guys walking around in togas. Maybe there is hope for the future. By the way, your brother is coming over tonight."

Faith showed surprise.

"Ben?"

"Do you have another brother?"

"Smart guy. Why is he coming over?"

"To see you, of course. He's not coming to see me," he joked.

Faith pondered that for a moment and forced a smile. She was exhausted after four arduous lessons. Earlier in the day she nearly tripped twice teaching the ten o'clock class. Both times, she was just able to catch herself from falling. She was actually hoping for a quiet weekend with Charlie. Now with Ben coming over, she was going to have to force herself to put on a brave front.

"Great. We need to make a stop before we go home. Give me a couple minutes to change."

"Take your time."

Charlie carefully watched her stand up, his eyes searching for the slightest tremor in her limbs. He saw none. But she had become an expert at hiding them from him for the most part. She darted into her office for a quick change of clothes.

Charlie paced across the dance floor. He stopped and stared at his reflection in the long wall of mirrors. He found himself wondering for the first time if he would ever see this place again. The possibility startled him. He always assumed they would be coming back, but there was no way to know for sure. A million and one things could go wrong. He actually started on a list of those things and finally stopped at one hundred and three. He ripped it up and buried the list in the trash. Whatever the risks, and there were so many, this was the only option now. The only thing to do now was to go forward and hope for the best.

"So what's with the long face, professor?"

Charlie turned to Faith. She was wearing a knee-length skirt and blouse. He held out his hand to her. She gripped it tight. He pulled her tight into his arms and kissed her for a long time. She gasped after their lips parted.

"Wow. A guy only kisses his wife like that if he's really horny, or he did something naughty and doesn't want to tell her."

They headed out of the studio, hand-in-hand.

"Well, which one is it?" she asked.

"Oh, I'll tell you later."

"Oh, oh, now I'm worried," she said.

"Don't be. Everything is fine," he assured her.

She squinted at him as they exited the studio. His hand seemed unnaturally tight in hers. His eyes avoided hers as they crossed the street. He opened the door to the Explorer and helped her inside.

"You know, I can still manage to get into and out of cars, honey," she assured him.

"I know you can. I just want to show you that chivalry is not dead."

He closed the door. He leaned through the window and watched as she pulled the bottle of wine from the paper bag. She read the label and tilted her head. She smiled happily.

"Excellent choice. I have to say you sure know how to pick out a great bottle of wine."

"Before I met you I didn't know the difference between a Merlot and a Zinfandel."

"That's true. I trained you well, grasshopper. But then again darling, before I met you I didn't know the difference between a birdie and a bogey."

He kissed her through the open window. He circled around, got behind the wheel, started the motor, and drove off.

***

"I'm not helping," Sidesh said simply, almost matter-of-factly.

He tossed the empty Orange Crush soda can into the recycling bin. There was a sort of finality at the way the can rattled inside the bin.

Well, that was a waste of thirty minutes, Ben thought. He sighed wearily. Sidesh's blunt response did not surprise him. He would be risking more than his career by helping him. Although there were no laws prohibiting what Ben was planning, he had no doubt the Department of Defense could be very creative when their people went off the reservation. Sidesh would likely be kicked out of the country after a few years in jail.

Ben placed the palm of his hand over his nose and rubbed it thoughtfully. Then he raised both hands up, palms facing his friend.

"You're not going to get caught, Sidesh," he promised.

"You're right, I won't. Because I'm not doing this. And neither should you."

"Sid, I know how crazy this must sound to you. It sounded crazy to me when my brother-in-law told me his idea. But it's my sister's life. I have to do this. Believe me, if there was another option, I wouldn't be asking for your help. I know what I'm asking of you."

Sidesh just shook his head, his face contorted into a mish mash of disbelief and bemusement. He finally laughed.

"This is insane, Ben. You realize that don't you? Damn, they haven't even invented the word for how insane this is," he exclaimed.

"You don't think I know that?" Ben replied, his right finger twirling around the side of his head. "Even now I know how bonkers this must sound. It does to me. Hell, it would to anyone. But I've made my decision."

Sidesh stared at Ben. His face scrunched up with astonishment and a question.

"This isn't like you, Ben. You're probably the least religious guy I know. You no more believe in God than Santa Claus. So where is all of this even coming from?"

Ben rocked back in his chair. Sidesh was right. He did not believe, not even a little bit. But here he was asking his friend to risk prison on what he would call a delusional fantasy if someone had approached him with this plan.

"Does it matter?" Ben countered.

"Of course it matters. You are planning to risk your life on this crazy scheme. I want to know why you're really doing this. I think I deserve to know considering what you're asking of me."

Ben stared at Sidesh. He then got up and walked across the room to the covered object. He pointed at it. His eyes brightened. His voice resonated with almost feverish excitement.

"Sid, ever since I was a kid, this is what I believed in. This. Science. Something I could touch and feel with my own hands. Numbers that added up to a solution. Mysteries that always had an answer based on reason; based on scientific truth. Not a bunch of mumbo jumbo magic. But don't you see this thing we've created might give us the answer for that now? I will have the opportunity of going back and getting the answer that has confounded men for thousands of years. Is there truth in faith? Or is it just a lot of malarkey?"

"I thought you were going back to help your sister," Sidesh said, raising an eyebrow.

"I am. If there is any truth in faith, it's back there. And back there is going to be the only answer for her. There isn't one here. You know that."

Sidesh nodded.

Ben came back and sat down. He took a deep breath.

"Look, I'm going forward with or without you. It will just be a lot of easier if you're here watching our backsides."

Sidesh rotated jerkily left and right in his chair. His eyes locked on the tarp-covered object. His grim expression flashed the final inner argument playing out in his mind. He then looked back to Ben.

"Suppose you don't come back? Then what? The DOD will come down on me like a ton of bricks."

"It's simple, Sid. You erase the drives and the security footage. They'll never know a thing. All they'll have will be a mystery. You'll be totally in the clear," he promised.

Sidesh grimaced again and turned away. His shoulders heaved up and down several times. Ben stared at his back, holding his breath. While it was true he did not really need Sidesh to pull this off, he would feel a lot better knowing he had his back.

"Would you like a soft drink with your sandwich, Miss?" he mumbled to himself.

"What did you say?" Ben asked.

Sidesh turned to Ben with resignation.

"I was just practicing when I'm back in New Delhi taking orders at McDonalds."

Ben exhaled with relief, and then grabbed Sidesh's shoulder.

"Thank you, Sid. Let's get to work."

"Hey, I'm starving. What about lunch?"

"I'll order from Subway."

CHAPTER III

Faith shifted in the front pew facing the Statue of the Virgin Mary looking down upon her from the massive apse. Finding a more comfortable spot, she clasped her hands tightly together and finished praying. After crossing herself, she looked up and gazed upon the face that looked down upon her. After so many visits, Faith felt she knew every inch of the statue by now. Her eyes followed the lovely folds of her long tunic and the intricate ways it clung to her slim figure. She admired how the lengthy veil draped about her head and fell over the shoulders. However, she was always drawn to that kind, gentle face that looked down upon her. The heavy-lidded eyes seemed to be watching over her. It was during these all too brief moments that Faith believed there might be hope for her.

Faith had been making this pilgrimage at least once a week for the last year and a half. It began the day she received her diagnosis. She shivered involuntarily as that dark memory enveloped her fading body. She had been anticipating bad news all through her many tests. But when she saw the physician's grim mask when he entered the examining room, her heart seemed to seize up. When he uttered his dire prognosis, her body recoiled as if someone had gut punched her. If it were not for Charlie's arm around her waist, she probably would have hit the floor.

The doctor gave Faith and Charlie a moment to recover from the bleak news. Then in a soft but firm voice, he methodically informed them of what to expect as her disease progressed. It was almost as if he was discussing new wallpaper patterns instead of a death sentence. Faith, dazed, overwhelmed, only caught bits and pieces of what awaited her. Paralyzed muscles. Muscle deformation. Frequent tripping and falling. Difficulty in swallowing. Uncontrolled laughing and crying. Compromised breathing. Respiratory failure. It seemed to go on forever. He never mentioned the word "death." But there was no need to.

Faith's eyes watered until his stoic face became a wraithlike blur. She continually wiped her eyes with a dwindling pack of tissues. She never spoke. She just numbly nodded her head as if it were on a spring. After it was mercifully over, he set up another appointment to discuss treatments he warned could only slow down the disease's progress. Then he delivered the ubiquitous statement all doctors roll out after uttering their hopeless diagnosis.

"New cures are being discovered every day. I don't want you to lose hope."

It was a long walk out of the hospital and back to their car. She moved robotically, head stiff, eyes staring straight ahead. She had heard and read of out of the body experiences, when people claimed they could watch themselves doing something, as if they were spying on themselves. Now she understood it all too well.

She managed to hold it together until Charlie got her to the car. The moment her hand touched the door handle she fell apart. Tears exploded from her face as she buried her face into his shoulder for what seemed forever. Charlie did not say a word as she sobbed. He knew there was nothing he could say that would not have sounded trite at that moment. Finally, she felt vitality course back into her limbs as if she had drawn strength from his body. She pulled partly away from Charlie, her leaking eyes now red. She wiped the tears away, taking several heaving breaths. She looked past Charlie, not focusing on anything in particular. Then her eyes closed, opened, and scanned the parking lot. She turned and focused on Charlie. His face was still mostly a misty blur.

"I'm okay," she whimpered.

He did not say anything. But he knew she was anything but okay, so he still held on to her just in case.

"Really, I'm okay," she repeated.

She gripped his arms and stepped back as if to show him she was not going to topple over like an old elm. She searched her purse for a tissue. Then she realized she had gone through all of them in the doctor's office.

"Give me your handkerchief."

He dug into his pocket and gave it to her. Faith wiped the lingering tearstains from her cheeks. Her eyes finally focused on Charlie.

"That's better. See," she said, half-assuringly.

She then noticed his face was stained with tears. She wiped his cheeks. She then handed the handkerchief back.

"Take it. I think you need it more than I do," she said.

They just stood there as a cold rain began falling. A gang of black clouds had rolled in, blocking out the sun. They both looked up at the sky, feeling the icy stings on their long faces.

"Let's get in the car before we catch pneumonia," Faith said.

He turned to open the door for her. She raised her hands in protest, flashing a rare frown.

"I said I was fine."

She got in. Charlie settled behind the wheel. He started the car, switching on the wipers. A boom of thunder rattled the windshield. The rapid pitter-patter of rain pounded the roof. They sat there, not knowing what the next step was for them. An hour earlier, it was just the two of them. Now another presence had suddenly invaded their happy lives. Of course, they could not see the malevolent entity waiting to strike, but they felt it hanging over them all the same.

"You want to go home?" he finally asked.

Faith shook her head. She reflected for a few moments, staring straight out. Charlie watched her as the reflection of rain running down the windshield played against her pallid face.

"Not yet. Charlie, take me to Saint Borromeo's."

He looked at her with surprise for a moment. She managed a thin smile. Then he nodded and pulled out.

They drove to the church in silence. Charlie stole quick glances at her as he drove. Faith would point out to the rain-swept windshield for him to keep his eyes on the road.

"Honey, please keep your eyes on the road. I'm not ready to

go back to the hospital."

When they reached the church, Charlie pulled out the collapsible umbrella from the back seat. He popped it open and came around to Faith's side. The two hurried through the rain and dashed inside.

They hesitated at the back of the near-empty church, both feeling they did not belong there. Water dripped off the umbrella and onto the polished floor. A few parishioners, deep in prayer, were scattered in various pews. Faith watched them and wondered on what, or for whom, they might be praying. She felt a sudden kinship with these strangers. On the right, a young woman was lighting a candle. Faith's eyes gazed over the church before focusing on the statue of the Virgin Mary located in the superbly-carved apse. She started forward across the nave at a slow, respectful pace. Charlie watched her and then followed. Their footsteps echoed off the vaulted ceiling thirty feet above them.

Saint Borromeo's reflected an earthy, Spanish colonial-style architecture. Brightly lit from above by a half dozen ornate lanterns, and from the intricately-designed stained glass windows on either side, the church had a graceful majesty that today's churches of hygienic steel and glass clearly lacked. You could feel man's hope for salvation in the serene reliefs and sublime hand-carved sculptures.

"Give me a moment," she told Charlie as she walked alone to the altar.

Faith genuflected before the steps leading to the altar. She stared left at the statue of the Virgin Mary. She stepped back and slid into the first pew, knelt down, and prayed for the first time in many years. Surprisingly, it did not seem strange to her now. She felt a warm inner peace embrace her that brought back distant memories when she would attend church as a child with her mother. Like many people, she just stopped going at some point. She felt guilty at first, but that soon passed. She was way too busy living her life to devote one hour a week to prayer. It was not that she stopped believing. It had just become too much of an inconvenience. But in an instant, that wonderful, happy world she had been taking for granted had turned upside down. She was now staring at a grim future that terrified her.

"I know I've been away for a while. I hope it's not too late for me," she whispered to the statue looking down upon her.

Charlie sat down several pews back and watched her. He never felt more helpless than at that moment. So he also started to pray. At first, he felt silly and a little hypocritical wanting 'God's' help now when he needed it most. He imagined God asking where he had been hiding all these years. But as he stared up at the large crucifix above the altar, the guilty sensation passed and he started to pour out his heart, and even his soul, for help.

"Never had much use for church growing up."

Charlie looked back over his shoulder. Ben was sitting behind him, his arm lazily hanging over the back of the pew. His eyes skeptically gazed about the church. His crooked smirk revealed his disdain for anything religious. It vanished when he caught Charlie's facial rebuke. He then sat up, trying to be a little more respectful.

"How is she doing?" Ben asked.

Charlie looked back to Faith. Her head was tilted forward, pressing into her clenched hands. His head shrug conveyed the sad reality.

"Not great. But she's holding it all together somehow. Mostly for my benefit."

"Yeah, that's my sister. Always trying to be super woman. You come here a lot now don't you?"

Charlie nodded solemnly, "Ever since we found out."

"Why?"

Ben almost spat the word.

"You know why. Because it's all we have left now."

"A miracle?" Ben said.

"Yes, Ben. A miracle," Charlie replied.

Ben turned his gaze to the crucified Christ statue. The idea of someone being nailed to a cross freaked him out as a child. How barbaric and bizarre to do that to someone. Religion could make people crazy and do all manner of crazy things. He finally looked back to Charlie.

Charlie seemed to sense Ben's thought and gave him a grim smile.

"What?" Ben asked.

"There are a lot of non-religious people who do bad things," Charlie said. "History is chock full of them."

"You should know, professor."

"Is everything ready for tomorrow?"

Ben nodded, but not with a great deal of confidence.

"As ready as we can be. Sid promised he'll help."

"Will he?"

"Yeah. He'll help. Are you ready?"

Charlie's head rocked up and down. He read the stoic skepticism in Ben's long face. This was the moment to test Ben's resolve on his plan.

"You don't have to go you know," Charlie said casually. "Only Faith and I have to go. In fact, you might get in the way. The more people who go multiply the possibilities of something going wrong. Isn't that part of chaos theory?"

Ben seemed startled by him. He knew Charlie did not want him coming along. He was not sure why, but it was not over concern for him. The fact is they were never that close. That is, until Faith received her grim prognosis eighteen months ago. From that moment forward, they seemed to forget prior conflicts, if only for her sake.

"I love my sister as much as you do, Charlie," he said. "I'm going. All the way. Besides, you may actually end up needing me. Had you thought about that?"

"So you still want to go even though you don't believe,"

Charlie chastised.

"Ben Miles in a church," Faith said softly. "Now I've seen everything. You know, this might be one of the signs of the apocalypse."

Ben and Charlie had not seen Faith walk up to them. She seemed pleasantly surprised seeing her atheistic, science is everything, brother sitting in a church.

"Sit down. Don't worry, I won't burst into flames," he said softly.

Ben slid over as Faith sat next to him. He hooked his arm around her, drawing her close. She seemed to be in good spirits but that was probably just for show. She stared at him with a curious little tilt of her head.

"Did you something naughty, Ben?" she asked.

Ben traded a look with Charlie. His response was tinged with reticence.

"No. At least, not yet."

"So did the DOD finally give you a holiday?" she asked.

"Not exactly. They closed the lab for a couple days," he revealed.

"That's wonderful. So you're spending the whole weekend with us."

It was not a question, or request. Her tone suggested he did not have any option in the matter. Soon enough she would know all about their true weekend plans.

Ben nodded to her and glanced at Charlie.

"Well, that's the idea."

Originally, she thought Ben coming over for the whole weekend was a horrible idea. Now she felt genuinely overjoyed by the prospect. She had not seen much of him the last few months. Her face warmed. She leaned into her brother. Then she looked him over a little more clinically, giving his arm a squeeze.

"Hmm, you look skinny. Do they even feed you?"

Ben shrugged.

"Occasionally they throw us a bag of peanuts. So where do you want to go for dinner? There's this great steak joint I've heard about," he said.

She shook her head adamantly.

"Home. I feel like cooking tonight."

When Ben made a motion of protest, she shook her head again. The last thing Ben wanted was her tiring herself out making dinner.

"Nope. I'm cooking. But my two boys have to do the dishes."

"Deal," Ben agreed. "It'll be nice not to have a microwave meal for once."

"If you had married Kelly you could have all the home cooked meals you wanted," she reminded him.

When he started to object, she cut him off.

"Yeah, I know, you're married to your work. Yada, yada, yada. I'm sorry. I won't bring it up again. Shall we go?"

They got up. Faith and Charlie made the sign of the cross and headed back up the nave holding hands. Ben took a last skeptical gaze at the vast cathedral thinking of all the wasted money building it. His eyes then locked on the crucified Jesus again. He appeared ready to say something to it. Then he thought better of it and walked out.

CHAPTER IV

Ben drained his wine glass and set it down. He groaned with contentment. It was the best meal he had eaten in a long time. Faith grilled the thick steak to perfection. The grilled veggies were equally delicious. He turned to his sister who seemed genuinely happy at how the evening had gone. Then he wondered how long that serenity would last when they sprung their plan on her. All through dinner, he traded furtive looks with Charlie when she was not paying attention. He felt a twinge of guilt at their subterfuge. He was not sure how Charlie felt.

Ben pushed his chair away from the patio table. He sighed as he gazed about their spacious, yet intimate backyard. The flames crackling in the wood fire pit nearby sounded like a gentle rain. The large elm tree in the middle of the yard swayed gently in the early evening breeze as a harvest moon played peek-a-boo between the undulating branches. Divergent scents from Faith's flower garden and the still-smoking barbecue grill battled for supremacy. Under different circumstances, he would be a happy man right now.

"More wine?" she asked, holding up the half-empty bottle. Her hand trembled when she lifted it up. Her other hand quickly balanced it.

He waved off the offer. The wine was excellent, but he was teetering on the edge of intoxication. He wanted to stay in complete control of his faculties now knowing what the rest of the evening was going to bring.

She offered Charlie another glass and he shook his head. She poured herself a half glass. The neck of the bottle banged into the glass until Charlie steadied it. She opened another page of the scrapbook she had started from the first day she met Charlie. Her hand twitched nervously as she revealed a crushed rose preserved in a plastic bag. Under the thorny stem was an unsigned note.

"Hey, remember this?"

Charlie frowned, remembering it all too well.

"First flower he ever gave me. He left it at the dance studio. Except he forgot to sign the note," she said, laughing.

Ben grinned and nodded, showing polite interest. He threw Charlie a raised eyebrow-like signal. He gave a short nod back to him that seemed to say, "I'll get to it."

Faith turned more pages. She beamed at the large photo of Charlie and Faith, standing cheek to cheek on their wedding day. Charlie had a ridiculous grin of a guy who looked as if he had just won a million dollars.

"Wow, would you look at that adorable face," she said.

"You are that," Ben said to her.

"Not me, silly rabbit," she retorted.

She turned her head at Charlie.

"That good looking guy over there."

Charlie stared at the photo, trying to recapture the feeling of that day. His mind just could not make the leap that far back now. But he had to make an effort for her sake.

"Well, I knew I had just won the lottery," he finally said, knowing she would appreciate the comment.

Faith smiled wide, having no trouble remembering every moment of that wonderful day. As she sighed, a warm tingle ran up her spine. Then she saw the pained expression on Charlie's face. Her smile upturned into a frown.

"Don't start, mister," she warned. "We're having a wonderful time. Don't spoil it."

Charlie nodded with remorse. He started gathering the dishes to take them to the kitchen.

"I'll start with these," he said. "You bore your brother with more pictures."

"He's not bored."

She looked to Ben who was wearing a bad imitation of a cheerful smile.

"Am I boring you, Ben?"

"No, not at all."

"Good. I don't think you ever saw this one," she said.

Charlie walked back inside. He set the dirty dishes in the sink and started scrubbing them down. He listened to Faith going into detailed descriptions of each picture in the Charlie & Faith Love Story. He knew Ben would listen politely all the while being completely disinterested.

"Hey Charlie, I didn't know you skied," Ben yelled from outside.

Charlie grimaced. Why did she keep that picture from their ski trip? With his legs wrapped around a tree, and his head lathered with snow, he looked like a complete fool.

"You call that skiing?" Charlie replied.

"Why did you tell me you could ski?" she asked, knowing the answer.

Charlie let the dishes soak. He wiped his hands with a dish towel and returned to the yard. Ben and Faith rocked in the canopy swing, the scrapbook straddling their laps.

"Well, I was trying to impress you," he said.

He poured himself a half glass of wine to steady his nerves. If anything, he had become more apprehensive. He was never much of a wine drinker.

"You damn near impressed yourself around that tree," Faith giggled.

"The things men do to get laid," Charlie said.

"You didn't have to worry that much. I was raring to go by then," she said, smiling at him.

Charlie threw a serious look to Ben. He nodded. He took the scrapbook from Faith and set it down on the small iron table. He carefully took her hands in his own.

"Hey, let's put 'this is your life' on hold for a minute, sis. We have to talk," Ben explained.

Faith turned from Ben to Charlie, and then back to her brother. She stiffened, her contented mood turning sour.

"Talk about what, Ben?" she said matter-of-factly. "That I'm dying? No. Not tonight. Please, Ben. I've finally made my peace with it. Can't we just have a nice evening for once?"

"Faith, we have a plan," Charlie blurted out.

"A plan? A plan for what?" she asked.

"To save your life," he told her.

He sat down in the lawn chair opposite the swing. He leaned forward. All day he had rehearsed this conversation in his mind. Charlie knew what he wanted to say. Now he prayed he could get through it.

Faith had a blank expression. Then she flashed a little anger. She crossed her arms almost petulantly.

"We've been through this. We've talked to every doctor, specialist, and quack there is. There's no cure for ALS. How many people have we've gone to, Charlie? Twenty? Thirty? It's done. Please, no more. Not tonight."

Charlie's head rocked as if on a hinge.

"You're right, Faith. We've been to every medical specialist we could find. Science can't help you now. But there is someone who can."

She started, arching her back as if someone pricked her spine with a stick. Her tone became flinty, almost combative.

"Who, who can help me, Charlie?"

"Ben, this is where you might want to step in."

Ben set his hand on her knee and rubbed it. She turned to him now.

"Yeah. Sure. Okay. Faith for the past few years I've been working with a team of engineers and physicists trying to build a new type of engine for NASA; one that we hope could propel a space craft as close as possible to the speed of light," Ben said calmly.

"Yeah, you told me about that. Sounds very exciting. Did you do it?" she asked.

"No, no, not yet. But we had a breakthrough several months ago. I won't go into the details of it. You wouldn't understand it anyway," he explained. "Hell, we're still trying to wrap our heads around it. But it does work. At least our early testing shows it works."

She shrugged, "Wha-what works?"

Ben hesitated, glancing to Charlie to pick up the argument. He just jerked his head for Ben to keep going.

Ben sighed.

"Time displacement. Time travel."

Faith's eyes popped big. Her face registered a look of disbelief. Then she flashed an almost cheeky grin.

"Time travel? Are you serious?"

Ben nodded.

"So you're saying you can travel *back to the future*?" she said, raising an eyebrow.

"Yes. We can."

"Really? I was joking. My God, that's incredible. But, but what does all that have to do with me?" she asked.

Charlie leaned forward a little. He was finally feeling a more confident now. He took a deep breath.

"When Ben spilled the beans to me a month ago, by accident _"

"I was pretty hammered."

"-anyway, when he told me I immediately thought of *someone* who could save you."

Faith searched Charlie's face hoping the answer might be etched across his forehead. Then she flashed annoyance.

"Okay, how much wine did you two drink tonight?"

"Not nearly enough," Ben replied.

He leaned back into the softness of the swing. He checked his phone. 9:20 p.m. Less than twelve hours to go.

"Faith, Ben thinks we can do it," Charlie said.

"What are you two talking about? Do it? Do what?"

"Well, we've never actually tested going back two thousand years," Ben added.

Charlie delivered a glare that forced an inelegant shrug from Ben. This was no time to throw around potential problems. Convincing Faith was going to be tough enough without him being negative.

Faith seemed very bewildered at this point. She stiffened. When she spoke to Ben, her speech unexpectedly began slurring until she regained her composure.

"Okay, this is ri-ri-ridiculous. Ri-Right? Is this a joke, Ben?"

Ben reacted to her skepticism. His voice turned edgy.

"A joke? Faith, what did you use to say about me when we were growing up?"

Faith thought about it and then she remembered. She chuckled with embarrassment.

"Oh yeah. Men are from Mars. Women are from Venus. And you're from Vulcan."

She put her arm around him, flashing genuine sorrow.

"I'm sorry, Ben. I was like twelve when I said that."

"I don't joke about what I do," he said coldly.

Now it finally registered with Faith that they were dead serious. She stood up and paced across the patio. Their eyes followed her as her mind wrestled with what they had told her. She stopped and stared down at them. Her incredulous face finally seemed to register understanding of where this was all going.

"Two thousand years. Two thousand years," she repeated to herself.

Charlie nodded for her to keep going with her train of thought.

"What are you suggesting?"

"I think you know, Faith," Charlie said simply.

She stared down at the patio tiles. Finally, she shook her head with disbelief as it all dawned on her.

"Oh my God. I don't believe this. This is ridiculous."

She directed her attention to Charlie.

"Let me see if I have this all straight. You want us to travel back...two thousand years into the past and find...Jesus...and then ask him to heal me. Right? That's what you're suggesting, isn't it?" she said.

Her voice was strangely dispassionate considering the words that came from her quivering lips. She tilted her head at Charlie and then at Ben, raising her right eyebrow until it looked like it might touch her hairline.

"Well? Am I right?"

Ben nodded to her, his mouth forming a tight grin.

"Ah, yeah, yeah, that's about it in a nutshell, sis. I really couldn't have put it better myself."

Faith looked back to Charlie. He just nodded to her. Her hands flew up. Then she touched her forehead and ran her hand down her face. She shook her head and laughed.

"Okay, maybe I'm the one who had too much to drink tonight."

"We're serious Faith," Charlie finally said.

"As serious as we can be," Ben added.

Charlie watched her close. He was not sure how she was going to react when they dropped their plan on her. In his mind, he ran through any number of scenarios. Shock. Probably. Surprise. Of course. Disbelief. Naturally. But she seemed almost bewildered by their mad idea.

Faith placed her hands on her hips and thrust her upper body forward. Her head nodded as if she was accepting this was the real deal, that they were completely serious. Then she laughed.

"Okay funny men, just to humor the both of you, when are we going to do all this time traveling?"

"Tomorrow morning," Charlie said, simply.

"Tomorrow morning!"

The word burst out of her like an expletive.

"You can't be serious? We're going tomorrow?"

"Yeah. In less than twelve hours," Charlie said.

"It has to be tomorrow, Faith," Ben explained patiently. "The suits are all in Washington explaining what we've discovered. The staff is on leave. Once the DOD gets wind of what we've created, they'll take over the program. Or they'll bury it so deep it'll never be seen again. We have to go tomorrow or we don't go."

She held her pose for a long moment, directing an admonishing glare a mother might deliver to a naughty child. When they did not say anything, she turned away and stared into the fire pit. The red-yellow glow danced over her form.

Ben shrugged at Charlie. He then pointed at him to go to her. Charlie shook his head.

Finally, she spun around with a look of incredulity, her right forefinger wagging at them.

"This...is crazy. You know that, don't you? Charlie, it's...*crazy*."

Charlie bobbed his head in complete agreement. He clasped his hands together as if he were begging her.

"You don't think we know that, Faith? But sometimes *crazy* is the only option," he said.

Despite the warmth of the fire, her body trembled. It was not from her illness. She shook her head defiantly and moved closer to the fire, her back to them.

Ben took a deep breath and sighed.

"Hey, I think she's sold, Charlie."

Charlie ignored the sarcasm and walked over to her.

Faith stared blankly at the sea of stars twinkling brightly through scattered clouds. Off to the right there was a much brighter star. Maybe it was Mars or Venus. The stinging breeze pushed the heat of the fire aside and triggered goose bumps over her arms. She rubbed her arms vigorously when she felt Charlie come up behind her. She leaned back into his chest as his arms encircled her.

"Charlie...this isn't real, is it? It's not real," she whispered.

"Faith, this is as real as it gets. We've been praying for a miracle for eighteen months. Well, this is it."

"No, not this. This is impossible."

"No, it's hope. I guess it all comes down to this. Do you trust me, Faith? Completely trust me?"

Her head nudged up and down.

"Then you need to trust me now. I know we can do this. I've planned it all out."

Faith turned around and looked up at his face. Even in his arms she felt cold. His hands rubbed her back. Her legs suddenly seemed heavy. Her mind reeled, as if she had been sedated. This was all just too much for her to digest.

She heard Ben walking up. She pulled free from Charlie and approached her brother. He was sipping his glass of wine. He seemed perfectly calm as if he had just suggested they go to Hawaii for vacation.

"Ben, ju-just how dangerous is this thing we're going to do?"

"Faith-," Charlie started to say.

Faith raised a finger silencing Charlie. She looked back to her brother. Ben looked to Charlie for help.

"Don't look at Charlie. Look at me," she commanded.

Ben looked to Faith. He was not going to sugar coat what they were planning to do tomorrow. She had a right to know all the risks. It was her life that was at stake.

"It's dangerous," Ben said, cutting Charlie off.

He ignored his brother-in-law's glare. He placed his hands on her shoulders. He felt her body shivering. He realized that dropping all of this on her like this had been wrong. But it was not as if they had a choice. Circumstances had forced their hand.

"But I'm confident we can get you to where you need to be. We've done tests and we've succeeded in going back. So, there should be no problem there. That you can believe, even if you don't believe, in the rest of it."

All Faith heard was the word *dangerous*. The rest passed right over her. She shook her head vehemently. She pulled away from Ben, pointing at him while directing her stare at Charlie.

"Did you hear him, Charlie? It's dangerous. You of all people know what life was like back then. No. No. We're not doing this. We're not. You could both get hurt. Or worse."

"We're ready to take that chance," Charlie insisted.

Ben rolled his shoulder in an unenthusiastic shrug.

Faith redirected her wagging finger at Charlie, raising her voice; something she rarely did.

"We're not doing this! Do you hear me?!" she yelled. "It's...it's..."

"...crazy," Ben added.

Charlie stepped up to her and grabbed her hands. He stared into her eyes that glowed bright from the reflecting flames.

"Faith, if I were the one dying, would you take this chance for me?" He did not wait for a response because he knew what she would say. "There just isn't any other choice now. If there were, we would not even think about doing this. So we're going. That's final."

Faith was about to protest again but stopped herself. She knew from the determined look on his face she was wasting her breath. She might have been able to fight Charlie, but not the both of them. They had overwhelmed her.

Charlie glanced over to Ben.

"You still don't have to go."

Ben drained the wine glass. He desperately wanted another glass, but he knew he would pay a heavy price in the morning. He set the glass down and walked over to Faith and put his arm around her.

"You'll have a much better chance getting there and getting back if I go. Besides, I haven't worn a toga since my frat days."

"Ben," Faith said.

He rubbed her arm, giving her his best reassuring smile.

"I'm going. I wouldn't miss it for the world."

"Is Sidesh really on board?" Charlie asked.

"Totally. He's very excited to help," Ben lied.

He saw Faith's inquiring glance.

"I have to have someone minding the store while we're away.

It's all good. He's completely trustworthy."

"What time do you want us there?" Charlie asked.

"Eight. Try not to be late," he replied, checking the time on his cell phone. "I should be going. I'd like to grab a few hours' sleep before going to the lab."

A rush of conflicting emotions suddenly struck Faith. It was as if a dam had burst. She embraced her brother, squeezing him tight.

"I don't know what to say. I don't even know what to feel," she mumbled.

"Hey, everything is going to be okay, sis," he whispered in her ear.

They walked Ben to the front door.

"See you in the morning," Charlie said.

Ben nodded. He got in his car and drove away.

Charlie and Faith returned to the kitchen. They never spoke as they washed the dishes, shoving them into the dishwasher. Doing the dishes now seemed incredibly absurd considering what they planned to do in just a few hours.

"I'll finish up here," he told her. "Why don't you get ready for bed. Ben's right. We'll both need a good night's rest for tomorrow."

She stared at him. She wanted to say something. However, nothing came to her. The three glasses of wine she drank did not help matters.

"Go on. I'll be along in a few minutes."

She nodded dully and walked off.

Charlie finished tidying up. He then spent a couple minutes looking over the scrapbook. When he reached the end, he wondered if any new pages would be added to their life. He returned it to the shelf and walked to the bedroom.

When he looked in, Faith was already in bed under the covers. The bedside lamp cast a warm orange glow over her distraught features. Her forlorn eyes gazed up at him. Her hand came up and reached out for him. He came over to the bed and sat on the edge. His fingers intertwined with hers. She squeezed his hand tight and pulled him on top of her.

***

As hard as she tried, sleep proved so elusive that Faith finally accepted the half sleeping pill Charlie offered. She hated taking any sort of drug to help her sleep. It usually took the rest of the next day to get over its debilitating effects. However, even with the sedative, she found herself fading in and out of a kind of trippy drunkenness, until finally, mercifully, that first sliver of dawn leaked through the vertical blinds. With her arms tight about her pillow, she stared at the thin lines of sun light streaking across the carpet, coming up the side of the bed, and caressing her arm. Charlie's head was resting across her back. She could tell from his breathing he was awake as well. They had not spoken a word since Charlie gave her the pill.

"Are you awake?"

"Yes," he replied softly.

"I didn't dream all that from last night, did I? We are really going to do this, aren't we?" she asked.

He laid a soft kiss on the small of her back.

"Yes, we are. Don't be afraid."

"But I am. I'm terrified. Aren't you?"

He thought a moment. He knew he should be afraid. Instead, he felt great anticipation. All of the hectic planning and preparation from the last month had given him confidence that this could work. However, he could sense her apprehension by the stiffness of her body.

Faith turned around and looked down at him. His head rested on her belly now. She ran her fingers through his hair, softly stroking his head.

"Charlie..."

"We're going," he said firmly. "And we're going to find him."

She sighed deeply. A surge of doubt struck her.

"What...what if we actually make it there and he's not...even if we can find him, how can you be sure he can help me?"

Charlie kissed his way slowly up her body. He pushed her long hair away until his lips brushed against her ear. He kissed it while stroking her head.

"Because I believe he can," he told her.

Faith looked at him for a moment and then gazed at the ceiling fan turning lazily. It still had that irritating squeak. Why had they never fixed it? She looked back to him.

"I didn't slip yesterday," she confessed.

He hovered over her until their noses touched. His lips caressed hers as he spoke.

"I know. You never slip," he said, kissing her softly.

"Hold me," she said, fervently.

Charlie embraced her tightly, her breasts pressed into his chest. Her hands dug into his back. She felt a nauseous wave of guilt wash over her.

"I... I try to fight it, Charlie," she gasped. "Sometimes I beat it, but every day it gets stronger. I'm-I'm sorry."

She kissed him hard and pulled him even tighter into her body.

CHAPTER V

The first minutes of their drive to Cyngus Labs started in an awkward silence. Charlie stuck to the slow lane hovering around the minimum speed limit. Early morning commuters were not reticent in smacking their horns when they shot by them. Charlie ignored their protests. The last thing he wanted was to get into an accident today of all days.

Faith glanced at the speedometer. The corners of her mouth curled up at his unusually conservative driving.

"So today of all days you finally decide to obey the speed limit."

His eyes darted to the speedometer. Fifty-four miles per hour. He shrugged irritably and pushed it to fifty-five.

"Is that better?"

"I wasn't criticizing, darling."

"Sorry."

"Tell me what's going to happen when we get there," she asked.

Faith still did not completely believe what they had told her last night. Time travel? The whole idea was silly. They must be planning something else. What it could be she had no clue. She shifted in her seat and glanced at the world passing by.

"Ben will tell you everything when we get to the lab. He can explain the process far better than I can."

"But he told you how it works, didn't he?"

"Yeah, he told me."

"Does it involve a DeLorean sports car by any chance?"

He stole a glance at her. She flashed a teasing smirk.

"No. There's no DeLorean sports car. It's a machine. He'll show it to you."

"You haven't seen it, have you?"

"Of course not. I don't have top security clearance for the

lab."

"Then how are we getting in today?"

"Ben told you last night. No one is going to be there but him and this other guy, Sidesh. Don't worry. We got it all figured out."

"Worry? We're going on a trip two thousand years in the past to find Jesus. Why would any of that worry me? It'll be like a trip to Starbucks."

"You still don't believe any of this, do you?"

Faith shook her head.

"I thought about it all last night and this morning. You two have planned something for me. I don't know what. But it can't be what you said last night."

"Well you're going to find out soon enough we're not joking. Until then it might help if I passed along a few words in the language spoken back then. The original plan was to tell you all this today and go next weekend. Over the next week I was going to give you some language and history lessons."

"They didn't speak any English back then?"

"No. English wouldn't be spoken until the fifth century CE. Back then the people there generally spoke either Aramaic or Latin."

"Jesus spoke Aramaic?"

"That's right."

Faith nodded.

"So, for example, 'Praise God' in Aramaic would be, 'Yishtabach Shemo'. 'Yishtabach Shemo.'"

He looked at her to try it.

"Yishtabach Shemo. Yishtabach Shemo."

"Good. Now hello and goodbye is basically the same thing. 'Sh'lam.'"

"Sh'lam. Sh'lam."

"Very good."

"How do you say, 'I love you' in Aramaic?"

Charlie pulled off the highway and stopped at the red light. He glanced at her. She smiled warmly at him.

"Well, it depends. If you say it to a man, it's 'Rikhmith-akh'. If to a woman it's, 'Rikhmith-eykh'."

"Oh," she said.

She leaned over toward him. He turned and met her soft lips for a brief kiss.

"Rikmith-akh, Charlie." She pointed ahead. "The lights changed."

Faith saw the Cyngus building as they rolled up the long, curved driveway. Tall pine trees, in close formation, lined both sides. The sleek building was a one-story structure of black steel and glass that reflected the early morning sun. The sweeping roof was concave shaped, almost resembling a sinister smile. The place could pass for any run-of-the-mill corporate office building. The only differences were the three huge satellite dishes on the curved roof. They were all pointed in different directions. They looked like something from one of those big budget sci-fi films.

Charlie stopped at the gate. The disinterested security guard leaned out of his one-man booth. Charlie told the bored man who he was while flashing his driver's license. The guard barely glanced at the ID. He checked his clipboard and waved them through.

"This is the first time you've seen the place, isn't it?" Charlie said as he rolled into the parking lot. Only three vehicles were parked in a lot that could easily accommodate fifty.

Faith nodded pensively. She suddenly felt queasy as if struck by a bout of airsickness. She was glad she had eaten a small breakfast of coffee and toast. She did not think she could keep anything down that morning the way her stomach was doing cartwheels.

Charlie parked alongside Ben's SUV. He turned off the motor and glanced at Faith. He could sense her guts were turning over something fierce now. Her bare arms had sprouted a forest of goose pimples. Truth be told, he was fighting the same intestinal contortions. But he would never tell her that. This was man-up time. It certainly was not the moment to show hesitation, or even the slightest sliver of doubt about their plan.

"Charlie, what about all that stuff you see in all those books and movies about going back in time and maybe changing the future? You know, someone steps on a butterfly, and the dinosaurs rule the world, or something?"

"What about it?" he asked.

When Charlie broached his idea to Ben, the two of them hashed over the classic paradox of time travel. Suppose you go back and accidentally kill your great grandfather. Would you ever be born? But if you were never born, how could you go back to kill your grandfather in the first place? They never came up with a satisfactory answer for the obvious reason no one had ever gone back in time.

"Well, as far as we know," Ben said cryptically.

"Couldn't we mess up the present if we go back?" she asked. She looked tensely at Charlie.

"I thought you didn't believe any of this time travel talk."

"Yeah, that's true. But humor me anyway."

"Ben and I talked about that possibility," Charlie said.

"And?"

"And we think if we're really careful we'll be fine. We're not going back to assassinate Hitler, or make a killing in the stock market. We're not going back to change the past. We're going back to change the present," he explained.

It was not a perfect answer, but it was the only one that made sense. Of course, there was always the unexpected. However, that did not bear thinking about. They would just have to be careful.

"But couldn't we -," she started to say when Charlie grabbed her hand.

"We're going to be fine, Faith," he promised.

She just nodded. She should have known Charlie and Ben had discussed this.

"Ready?" he asked.

She did not respond. She just sat there fiddling with her

hands. Inside she was shaking like a child going to her first dentist appointment.

"What's wrong?"

"Why me, Charlie?"

"What do you mean?"

Charlie twisted over and looked at her. She just kept rubbing her hands nervously. Her voice was hushed.

"Why should I have this chance when there are so many other people who need a miracle? What makes me so special?"

"Because you're special to me. And you are to Ben. There are people in this country getting cancer treatments that are not available to someone in Chad or Tibet or some other country. That's not fair, but that doesn't mean that person doesn't deserve to get help. This is no different if you think about it."

"You know that's not true."

Charlie gently turned her face toward his.

"This is my truth. I love you. Ben loves you. And we are going to do everything we can to save you. That's all that should matter now. Okay?"

Faith finally nodded.

"Good. It's time."

They got out of the car. Charlie opened the back and grabbed the two packages he had picked up the day before. She pointed at them as they walked toward the front entrance.

"What are those?"

"Oh, just a few things we'll need for our trip," he said vaguely.

Ben was waiting for them in the lobby. He did not say a word. He just hugged his sister, and nodded to Charlie. He escorted them to the elevator. He ran his security card over the reader and down they went.

"Everything ready?" Charlie asked.

"We're as ready as we'll ever be," he said.

The elevator doors slid open. A long corridor opened up

before them. As they strode down it, their footsteps echoed dully. Faith fought the sudden urge to turn and flee. Ben seemed to sense her trepidation. He tightened his grip on her hand and winked at her. It did not make her feel any better. As crazy as it sounded, she thought she knew what a condemned man felt on his way to meet his maker. However, in her case, she was hopefully walking to her salvation.

Ben pushed open the swinging doors. They slowly entered the huge lab. Faith shivered abruptly as if entering a deep freeze. Ben put his arm around her and warmed her up.

"We have to keep things a little chilly down here in the Bat Cave. That's what we call it. Our equipment comes before human comfort," Ben explained.

She stared in amazement at the machinery that filled the massive chamber. The room seemed to vibrate with unrestrained power. She suddenly felt very small and insignificant. Turning left, she saw the lone figure in the room. Seeing them, Sidesh got up from the computer console and walked over.

"Sidesh, say hi to Faith and Charlie."

He nodded politely and shook their hands. His inquiring eyes locked on Faith for an uncomfortable moment. *So she is the one,* they seemed to say.

"Nice to meet you," he said, forcing a smile.

Faith suddenly realized there was a white rat sitting on Sidesh's shoulder. The curious animal wiggled its nose at them, its whiskers quivering.

"Oh, sorry," Sidesh said.

He set the rat on the console. The animal shot over to a small dish and started devouring part of Sidesh's breakfast burrito.

"Hey, not yours!" Sidesh said.

The rat ignored him and kept eating.

There was a moment of conspiratorial silence in the room as the four looked at each other. Faith finally broke the silence.

"I-I want to thank you for helping me," Faith said.

"I'm happy to help," Sidesh said.

Looking into her helpless eyes pushed away any doubt Sidesh had about going through with this. He had a sister of his own back in India. He knew there was nothing he would not do for her.

Sidesh turned to Ben, and then switched back to being the cold, detached scientist.

"Final computations are done. Should we send the Eight-ball?"

"Yeah, let's do it," he said. "No point in dilly-dallying now."

"Eight-ball?" Faith asked.

Sidesh pointed all the way across the room to the large black sphere in the corner. The tarp that covered it the day before had been tossed off to the side.

"That's our ride," Ben said.

Charlie and Faith looked back at the menacing black sphere that had a band of illumination across its equator.

"Eight-ball is a lot better name than Time Displacement Vehicular System."

Ben waved them over to the console where four chairs were waiting.

"Come on," he said.

Sidesh grabbed the chair that sat in front of the workstation. His fingers danced over the large keypad that had more keys than any that Charlie or Faith had ever seen. He initiated a program and the center screen that measured five feet across came alive with multi-colored graphic user interfaces. A tremendous surge of power filled the room. The floor vibrated under their feet.

"I'll give you the reader's digest version of what's going to happen," Ben explained. "First we send the Eight-ball, with no passengers, to the time and place we've programmed into the system."

Faith's head turned over thoughtfully.

"But, Ben, if it goes back here how does it end up thousands of miles away in Israel?"

"Great question," Sidesh said, glancing back over his shoulder for a moment.

"Yeah, that is a great question actually," Ben agreed.

Ben grabbed two balls off the desk. One was a tennis ball, the other a golf ball. He held the smaller one away from the larger one.

"One of the many rules in time travel is that time changes space."

He pointed to the golf ball.

"As you know, the Earth rotates on its axis once a day even as it revolves around the sun once every three hundred and sixty five days."

Faith nodded as Ben moved the golf ball, the Earth, around the yellow tennis ball, representing the sun.

"So, for example, let's say we go back a week. The Eight-ball would not appear here, but actually somewhere where the Earth was a week ago, okay?"

Faith nodded again.

"And that would be bad," Ben said.

"That would be really bad," Sidesh added.

"Now, fortunately, time is non-linear. It appears to have many paths, with rivers, or creeks. We've learned that these time tributaries, for lack of a better word, can be mapped and navigated," Ben said.

"Like black holes," Sidesh added.

"Black holes?" Faith inquired.

"A black hole is a collapsed star. There are theories that if you could travel through one and survive, a highly unlikely proposition, you could end up in another part of the universe, maybe even another time. Some scientists speculate that might be the fastest way to travel across the galaxy someday. But we're not dealing with black holes, so we're safe."

Before proceeding further, he waited to see if Faith understood him. It appeared she did. Of course, he already explained all this to Charlie several weeks ago. However, he could see explaining all this was having a calming effect on her.

"Now Charlie has given me the when and where we need to be to find you know who."

He raised a dubious eyebrow. That triggered a reaction from Charlie that said, *not now, Ben*. He rolled his shoulders.

"Anyway, I started programming the computer a month ago to do just that."

Faith flashed amazement. She turned to Charlie.

"My God, you were planning this that long ago?"

Ben pointed a finger at Faith and nodded.

"That was the exact face I made when Charlie told me his idea. Only I threw in a few four letter words."

"More than a few I'll bet," she said, still staring at Charlie.

She was floored that Charlie had been planning this for weeks, and she was utterly clueless as to what he was up to. Like many wives, she thought there was no secret her husband could keep from her for long. What else was she in the dark about? Faith's hand twitched suddenly. Charlie grabbed it and gave a gentle squeeze.

"Why the test if the computer has it all figured out?" Charlie asked.

"Well, we think the computer has it right," Ben said. "There's that old saying, measure twice, cut once."

"Plus, there's always the chance the Eight-ball could materialize inside a mountain," Sidesh interjected casually.

Then he caught Ben's admonishing stare.

"But that's not very likely. Maybe, one chance in four."

"Ben..." Faith muttered, her nervousness shooting up several notches.

"He's exaggerating, Faith," Ben assured her. "We'll be fine."

"Probably," Sidesh mumbled under his breath.

"Go ahead, Sid," Ben said.

Sidesh entered the launch code and pressed the execute button.

There was an immediate surge of power. The overhead lights dimmed briefly. Computer screens lit up. A deep, bone-rattling vibration rattled the computer console. A pen spun off the desk before Ben could catch it. Faith grabbed Charlie's hand. The rat shot off into his little box, burying itself in torn newspapers.

All eyes turned to the Eight-ball. An effect like Saint Elmo's fire engulfed it, and crackling tendrils of white lightning shot around the circumference. Slowly the Eight-ball lifted off the platform. A painful, musical whine that a demonic organ might generate stung their ears as the great sphere shimmered, turning wavy, as if made of rubber. Then, with a sharp pop, it was gone.

"Wait for it," Sidesh muttered.

Charlie and Faith stared incredulously at each other. Then from the empty spot where the sphere had disappeared, a flash of blinding light created an ethereal whiteout effect for a few mind-numbing seconds. Faith crushed Charlie's hand when everything went white. They shook their heads, blinking rapidly until their clouded vision cleared.

"You two okay?" Ben asked. "Sorry about that. I guess I should have warned you. When it leaves it creates something like an energy wake."

"Thanks, Ben," Charlie said.

"Okay, any second now," Sidesh said as he watched his monitor.

The blinding flash of light created the whiteout effect again. When they rubbed their eyes clear, they saw the Eight-ball was back on the platform. It bled an icy mist as if it were cooling down. No one said anything for a few seconds.

"Did it work?" Charlie finally asked.

Sidesh pointed excitedly to the big monitor.

"Oh, it worked all right."

They looked at the screen.

"Say hello to 33 CE, or there about," Ben said.

On the screen, a slightly distorted video rotating three

hundred and sixty degrees revealed a great valley near dusk. Several crude-looking houses came into view. The panning camera slowly revealed a walled city bathed in purple light in the distance.

"Oh my God," Faith muttered, spellbound. "Is this real?"

"As real as it gets," Ben replied. "That is Jerusalem two thousand years ago, give or take."

Faith looked at Charlie. The amazing sight blew them away. For the first time Faith started to believe what they were about to do was real.

"Look," she said, pointing to the screen.

"Hey, looks like we have a visitor," Sidesh said.

On the screen, a young boy, silhouetted by the setting sun, approached the Eight-ball's camera. He was clad in dirty rags. He took several steps closer, his eyes as big as silver dollars. Suddenly he spun around and raced behind the closest house. The rotating camera then revealed a nearby hill pitted with caves.

"That's what we want," Ben said, pointing to the caves. "That should work perfectly."

Sidesh nodded in agreement. "Yeah, that should do fine."

Ben checked another video, from the camera mounted on top of the Eight-ball. This video was a scan of the stars above.

"How can you be sure it's the right time and the right place?" Charlie asked.

Ben had already explained all that to Charlie weeks ago, but he was really asking him for the benefit of Faith.

"Oh that's easy. We got a star fix. The Eight-ball has a camera on top that takes images of the stars," Sidesh explained. "That's why the test was for nighttime."

"The position of the stars will give us the date. You see, every day the sky changes. The position of the stars, the planets, galaxies, everything, because the universe is constantly expanding. So by getting a shot of the stars then, and comparing it to today, we can get an approximate date," Ben added.

"How accurate will it be?" Faith asked.

Ben pointed to the screen.

Software was quickly calculating the stars positions in the sky to the passage of time. Across the screen, a date flashed—March 33 CE - Error Margin 1.4%.

"This is probably as close as we're going to get," Ben said. "The further we go back, the margin of error increases. But we're definitely in the right neighborhood and very close on the date; if Charlie's information is right."

Ben looked at Charlie with flash of doubt.

"It's right," Charlie assured him.

"And what about coming back, Ben?" Faith asked.

"Oh, that's the easy part," Sidesh said as his fingers raced across the keyboard, reprogramming the software for the real trip.

"He's right," Ben said. "The Eight-ball is programmed to come back right here at the very moment we left, plus one or two seconds."

Then Ben hesitated.

"What?" Charlie asked.

"There is one kicker, however. We have to come back no later than twenty-five hours after we arrive. That's how long the Eight-ball has sufficient stored power to bring us home," Ben said.

Ben held up a pair of palm-sized devices about the size of a cell phone. The LCD screens on both read 'twenty-five hours.' He handed one to Charlie.

"This one's for you."

"And if we're not back aboard in twenty-five hours it won't work?" Faith asked.

"No. The Eight-ball is on autopilot. We can return at any time up to twenty-five hours. But at twenty-five hours precisely it is programmed to return regardless of whether we're aboard or not," Ben explained.

"Meaning we'd be left in the past," Faith said.

"Yep," Ben said simply. "Probably forever."

Charlie frowned, biting his lower lip. He stared the device.

Twenty-five hours? He did not anticipate such a small window of time. Would twenty-five hours be enough? It was going to have to be.

"Ben, have you ever sent a person back in time?" Faith asked.

Ben and Sidesh traded looks.

"A person? No. We haven't gotten that far yet," Ben said.

"We did send Art back, though," Sidesh added.

"Art?" Faith asked.

Sidesh picked up his rat. He stroked its fur.

"Say hello to the first time traveling rat in history."

Faith reached out and ran her fingers over it furry back. Normally she would be terrified of getting this close to a rat. But not today. There were far bigger things to be terrified about.

"And he came back okay?" Charlie asked.

"Other than a bad case of the munchies he was fine," Sidesh said.

He placed the animal back in its box.

Ben looked at Charlie and his sister. Part of him hoped that one, or both, might change their minds about all this. But Charlie looked as determined as ever. He could not get a sense of his sister's state of mind. She appeared overwhelmed by it all.

"So, are we still on?"

"Yes. All the way," Charlie said firmly. He had not heard anything to dissuade him from going through with the plan.

"Faith?" Ben said.

Faith felt the three pairs of eyes fixed on her. She thought about saying no. However, she could see from the determined expression on Charlie's face that there was no going back now. So she surrendered to the inevitable.

"Okay, then. Come on, let's get suited up before I come to my senses," Ben said.

He looked to Sidesh. He jabbed his thumb at the monitor, indicating the frozen video of the caves.

"Sid, we've kicked the tires long enough. Punch a ticket for that cave."

Sidesh looked doubtfully. "Are you sure?"

"Yes, damn it. We're going. Just get on with it."

Sidesh just shook his head and went to work reprogramming the Eight-ball for the real deal.

CHAPTER VI

Ben led them back down the hallway they passed through
earlier and guided them into a side room. Recently converted from a
large storage area, it now served as a fitness center for the hard
working staff. The main section was jammed with all manner of
exercise gear, including state-of-the-art stationary bikes, treadmills
and free weight sets, all purchased courtesy of the U.S. taxpayers.
They worked their way through the maze of equipment and entered
the adjoining locker room.

Charlie set the boxes on one of the long benches facing one
row of lockers. He pulled the string on the larger of the two and
peeled back the lid. He handed Faith and Ben their new clothes. Ben
held up the coarse brown tunic and the blue and white striped linen
robe. The tunic resembled a poncho-style undergarment with a V cut
for the head and two slits for the arms. The robe, or mantle, would
go over the tunic. There was also a belt, or girdle, made of faux
leather, that would secure the tunic. He smirked with derision at his
new wardrobe.

"Do we have to really wear this get up?"

"Yes, of course."

"Can I at least keep my briefs?"

"No. Here are your sandals," Charlie said, handing them
over. "If you need any help let me know."

"I'm a big boy. I think I can manage."

Ben threw his clothes and sandals under his arm. He
vanished behind the next row of lockers.

Charlie turned to Faith. She was holding her ankle length
tunic against her body. She looked to Charlie. Whatever doubts she
possessed were over now. This was really happening. She started to
shake her head.

"Charlie, I don't think -."

"Oh yes, you can," he said, embracing her. Her body
shivered in his arms. He stroked her back until the shakes subsided.

"Want me to help you?"

"No. I'm okay. Just give me a minute."

She took her new clothes and went behind another row of lockers to change.

Alone now, Charlie undressed and placed his clothes in an unused locker. He ignored his own wardrobe for the moment and opened the metal box. He pulled out the thick money belt and buckled it tight about his waist. It was heavier than he expected. He checked the assortment of gold and silver coins in the various pockets. The fabricated coinage amounted to a small fortune. When he originally thought up his plan, he considered getting fake coins minted but then thought better of it. Why take the chance. It was only money after all.

Out of the same metal box, he pulled out the shoulder holster. He struggled to slip it on. He had never worn one before. He examined the nine millimeter Glock. He popped the magazine. He knew it was loaded having thoroughly cleaned it a few days earlier. He slid the magazine back into the well. He balanced the weapon in his hand. It had been years since he had fired a weapon. Although he hoped he would not need it, he was not going to take any chances; the risks of bringing a modern firearm into the distant past be damned. He slid the weapon into the holster and secured it.

Upon hearing Ben talking around the corner, he quickly grabbed his own wardrobe. He pulled his brown tunic over his head and pushed his arms through the slits. After making sure it hid the money belt and gun, he secured it with the girdle. He then slipped on his mantle. His mantle was a shabby blue-gray color also made of linen. Unlike Ben's, it was rather drab, which he liked. He knew it would not draw undo attention. He checked himself in the locker door mirror. The tunic felt cool against his sticky body. He realized he was sweating profusely, even in the cold interior of the lab. For almost a month, he had been planning this desperate undertaking and now the reality of it was hitting him full bore.

Ben stared into his own locker door mirror. It had only taken a couple minutes to undress and pull on his new threads. He found it difficult to believe people wore clothes like these. Remembering the toilet would not be invented until the sixteenth century, he realized going to the bathroom must have been a challenge back then. Toilet paper would not arrive until the mid-nineteenth century.

"What the hell am I doing?" he mumbled at his reflection. "How did I ever let Charlie talk me into this?"

Ben then rebuked himself. He was the one who leaked the great time displacement discovery to Charlie over far too many beers one night at a nearby pub as they talked about Faith's illness. But that was no excuse. General Wellman, their boss, had warned them not to discuss the project with anyone outside the lab, even among themselves. Early the next morning, Charlie called him up out of brutal hangover and revealed his madcap plan. Ben tried to get him to go sleep it off but Charlie refused to listen to him. With his dull head still ringing, Charlie laid out his insane plan in detail. At first, Ben only half listened, but when he realized Charlie was serious he sat up in his bed. Then after he was done talking, Ben hung up and refused to answer the phone. Within an hour Charlie was pounding on his door. Three hours and two pots of coffee later Ben found himself saying he would look into the feasibility of Charlie's brainstorm. When Ben came back two days later and told him in theory it was possible, that was all Charlie had to hear. Ben tried to explain he would be risking his career, and maybe even jail time, if he went along with this. But Charlie had his own ace in the hole. In the present, there was no hope for Faith. Maybe she had another two years. Probably less. Going back was her one and only chance. So, Ben reluctantly agreed, all the while hoping something would happen to foul up their plan.

In the weeks that followed, Charlie and Ben worked in secret, either at Charlie's university office, or at a local bar. They left Faith completely in the dark. There was no point in telling her their plan if some insurmountable problem arose. Ben had to admit Charlie came up with answers for every challenge, and there were many. He even gave detailed lectures on what life was like during the time of Jesus. The lectures covered culture, politics, food, clothing, money, and even language. It was too much to digest in so short a time, but it gave Ben a little more confidence that maybe this could all work out—that is, except for one little thing.

"I don't believe in this, Charlie," he said on the first meeting in Charlie's university office. The walls were already plastered with maps and charts of ancient Jerusalem.

"Believe in what?" Charlie asked, knowing the answer.

"Miracles," he said simply.

"The Gospels say Jesus performed them, Ben. Turned water into wine. Produced food to feed hundreds from one basket. Healed lepers," Charlie countered.

"They're just stories, Charlie."

Ben did not want to denigrate Charlie and Faith's beliefs. However, he was a man of science. You can't turn water into wine by the wave of the hand. You can't raise the dead with a prayer. Nor can you return from the dead.

"Where science ends, faith begins, Ben. There are plenty of medical miracles today where a person with a fatal illness, a confirmed illness, is healed with no medical explanation."

"That doesn't mean one doesn't exist," Ben retorted.

"I understand your skepticism, Ben. You're a scientist. You deal with accepted scientific truths. You want physical proof of any scientific claim. Evidence. But didn't Einstein say God doesn't play dice with the universe? See? Even Einstein believed there's a supreme being."

"Oh, you just had to bring out the big guns, didn't you?" Charlie smiled.

"Even if that were true, and there's no evidence to prove it's true, that doesn't mean He can perform miracles."

"How much do we know about the Universe, Ben? Do we possess one percent of all that is knowable? One thousandth of one percent? Hell, we don't even know what we don't know."

Ben nodded, "Agreed. But miracles?"

"But what is a miracle? It's a belief that something is possible that reason, or logic, says is impossible. I believe this is possible. Even if it is a one in a million chance, I have to take it. It's all I have now."

Ben glanced warily at the walls blanketed with maps.

"Okay. I'll go," he finally agreed.

But now staring before the mirror in his tunic, robe, and sandals, it all started looking absurd, if not outright insane, again. He stood up and posed in the mirror. He walked around and joined Charlie.

"Ramses, let my people go!" Ben exclaimed in a bad Charlton Heston impersonation.

Charlie stared at Ben. He did look slightly ridiculous in his period costume.

"Damn," Ben muttered when he saw Charlie's grim smile.

"You're off about thirteen hundred years," Charlie said.

Ben stared, shifting and turning, trying to get a feel for his new threads. The clothes felt as if they might slide off at any moment. That could be a little embarrassing. Worse than that, the sandals were too tight. The leather straps were already digging in-between his toes.

"Having second thoughts?" Charlie said.

"About the clothes? Yes. About going? No," Ben said.

He was not very convincing. He fiddled with the sandals again, shifting the leather straps. It did not help.

"Hey, I know we hashed this out before, but the language barrier ."

"We're good," Charlie assured him. "I speak enough Latin and Aramaic to get us by."

"But we don't," Faith said as she joined them.

Charlie and Ben stared at her. Her long, flowing camel-brown tunic and bright yellow stola clung to her natural curves. Her long hair flowed freely over her shoulders. Her new wardrobe seemed to suit her.

"You actually look beautiful, sis," Ben said.

"Do I?"

She seemed genuinely surprised. When she checked herself in the locker door mirror, she decided she rather liked the outfit.

"He's right. You do," Charlie said. "Don't worry about the language. I'll say you are both from the Far East. Jerusalem was a mecca for travelers from all over."

Charlie's words seem to reassure Faith, but Ben was not so easily convinced. They were going to be completely reliant on him. Charlie extended his hands out. Ben and Faith grabbed them.

"So, are we ready?" he asked.

They both nodded. It was the moment of truth.

"Let's go."

Sidesh did a double take when the trio returned. Whatever slim hopes he had that they would change their mind vanished at that moment. He joined them by the Eight-ball.

Faith watched Sidesh crack open the hatch. The reflective black sphere was about eight feet in diameter. At the base were four stubby legs. There were no windows nor portholes. She bent down and peered inside. The claustrophobic, pristine interior was all white. A trio of curved seats, also white, faced inward toward a center column. Small LCD screens and buttons protruded from the cylindrical column.

Ben stepped in first and took the far seat facing the controls. He settled in and buckled up using the over-the-shoulder strap. It was going to be a tight fit for three grown adults to fit inside the sphere.

"Faith, take that seat," Ben said, pointing to the one on the right.

Faith seemed to hesitate at the opening, her hands white knuckling the frame like a skydiver afraid to jump out of the open doorway. Charlie placed his hands over hers and gently pried her fingers open. He helped her inside. She had to bend all the way over to get into the seat. Her flowing clothes made moving about awkward. She finally managed to sit down. The bare metal seat was cold and uncomfortable.

"Buckle up," Ben said.

Faith reached to either side struggling to find the seat belt. She fumbled with the strap, her shaking fingers almost dropping the buckle. Ben reached over and did it for her.

"Thanks," she said sheepishly. "Do we really need it?"

"We shouldn't. The trip is over too fast. But it never hurts to play it safe," Ben said.

Charlie took the last seat by the hatch. He buckled up with no trouble. The sight of three people sitting in this high tech chamber while wearing ancient garb brought a twisted smile to Sidesh.

"Bizarre. Totally bizarre," he muttered. "Are we all set?"

Ben gave a thumbs-up.

"Good luck. See you in two minutes," he said.

Sidesh carefully swung the hatch shut. Ben secured it by pressing the LCD screen. He then pressed a couple other buttons and pulled on a headset.

"What did he mean, see you in two minutes?" Faith asked.

"Well, for him it will be two minutes. The Eight-ball is programmed to come back here two minutes from now. But we'll still have our twenty-five hours in the past."

Faith still did not follow what Ben was saying. She rolled her shoulders at Charlie.

"Okay, let's launch this bird," Ben said into his headset.

Sidesh was back on the console. He initiated the program. Again, the tremendous surge of power shook the room. The lab throbbed as electric tendrils crawled crazily over and around the Eight-ball.

"Welcome aboard Time Travel Express Ventures. Please keep your arms and legs inside the vehicle at all times, and please enjoy your trip," he mumbled.

If Sidesh had turned slightly right toward the bank of security monitors, he would have seen a trio of figures approaching the front entrance to the building. However, he was too busy monitoring the launch sequence.

Inside the Eight-ball they could feel the buildup of power more than hear it. The tingling sensations of thousands of ants crawling over their skin made them squirm and twist.

"Wha-what's going on?" Faith squealed.

"It's okay. It'll pass," Ben promised.

He had no idea if it would pass. Only the rat knew how this felt and the furry creature could not tell them.

But the tingling sensation did not stop. It intensified, becoming painful, as if those ants had small teeth and were nibbling on their flesh. They turned and twisted in their seats. They scratched at their arms and legs. Then everything inside the sphere turned to taffy, stretching out to infinity. Faith stared as Charlie and Ben raced away from her, their bodies elongating, expanding wildly, like some comic book superhero. Charlie's head seemed to blow up, the top of his head inflating while his shrinking chin dropped almost to his waist. When she looked down at her hand, she screamed when she saw her fingers turning elastic, getting longer and fatter.

Then mercifully, everything whited out.

Faith felt as if she were a ball being tossed about in a silvery ocean. Her head felt lightheaded as if she were punch drunk. All was still pearly white. She blindly clasped her hands together, feeling them. They were normal again. They no longer felt bloated or distorted. She probed through the white fog, groping toward where Charlie should be.

"Charlie?" she whispered.

When she heard no reply, she started to panic. When something grabbed her groping hand, she yelped.

"It's okay. It's me," Charlie said. "Are you okay?"

"I-I-I don't know."

"Ben? Are you here?"

"Of course. Where else would I be?" he replied in the whiteness.

Suddenly the interior lit up and the white fog cleared. The three looked at each other. Then they examined their own bodies to make sure they were not missing anything. They were not.

"You two okay?" Ben gasped.

"Yeah."

"I think so," Faith said, breathless.

She suddenly felt drained as if she had no strength. She was about to say something to Charlie when the ominous sensation passed.

"Where are we?" Charlie asked.

Ben was already checking the instruments. He seemed satisfied with what he saw.

"Right where we wanted to be," he said, still catching his breath. "Should we go out and say hello to the first century?"

Ben unbuckled his harness. He triggered the handheld device. The hatch gasped open to reveal pitch blackness. Charlie leaned out the opening and took a cautious breath. The chilled air was damp, but fresh.

Charlie helped Faith out of her harness. He carefully guided her out of the Eight-ball. She had to lift her long tunic to avoid tripping over the rim.

"It's okay. I've got you," he said.

"I'm fine."

Ben came out last. The only light was that generated by the interior of the Eight-ball.

"Why is it so dark?" she asked.

Ben slid out a pen flashlight from a hidden pocket in his robe. Charlie had thought of everything it seemed. Or so Ben hoped. He shined the flashlight around. The narrow beam revealed the walls of a cave. It was appeared to be an abandoned mine. Twisted lumber buttressed the walls and roof. A few scattered tin cups and other trash littered the ground. Looking ahead, he then spotted an oblong shape of light about fifty yards up the tunnel.

"I had Sidesh program the Eight-ball to arrive in here. No point in advertising ourselves," he said.

Ben turned back to the Eight-ball. He triggered his device and the hatch closed. He slid the device carefully back into its hidden pocket. Their two devices were the only way to gain access to the sphere.

"Shall we?"

Ben led the way up the tunnel. Charlie and Faith stumbled over rocks as they followed him toward the expanding pool of light. They passed more rusting tools and discarded baskets. Ben switched off the flashlight when they reached the opening. He hid it inside the hidden pocket in his tunic. They peered out cautiously.

The ground fell away gradually, revealing a great valley. Off to the right, about fifty yards away, was a stone well. Beyond the well were several rundown homes made of mud and brick. Farther off, a road snaked all the way down to the great walled city about four miles in distance. Figures appeared to be moving in and out one of the large gates of the city. Squawking birds wheeled overhead in a bright sunny sky.

They shook their heads in wonderment. Faith pressed her body against Charlie. She was shaking with excitement. He took her hand and squeezed it.

"Oh my God," Faith gasped.

"Damn, you did it, Ben," Charlie said, amazed.

"Sure. Of course I did it."

They stepped completely out of the mine and into the sunlight. The sun's rays warmed them in contrast to the coolness of the tunnel. Their sandals pushed into the loose earth as they walked forward.

"Is that Jerusalem?" Faith asked in wonder.

"Yes, I think so," Charlie said.

He was sure it was. It looked exactly as he had expected from the many historical documents he had studied over the years.

"It doesn't look very big," Ben said.

"It's less than one square mile in size," Charlie said.

They stopped near the stone well. Charlie looked down into it. He dropped a loose stone. After several seconds, there was a faint splash. Looking left at the scattered homes, they saw no sign of people. However, heard the grunts of pigs and the squawking of chickens. They approached the closest hovel. It was a simple one-story structure about the size of a two-car garage. The walls appeared to be constructed of mud and stone. The roof appeared to be made of sycamore wood beams covered with brushwood and bound together with mud. Raggedy curtains hung from several windows. A three-foot high stone fence surrounded the back where several chickens strutted about, pecking at bits of grain.

Suddenly an object fell from the sky and rolled to their feet. Ben picked up the wood ball. Deep bites scarred its oblong surface. They looked up when a mangy dog raced up to them. It started barking at them, digging its claws into the earth. A moment later, a boy hurried toward them from behind the home. He skidded to a stop when he saw the three strangers. The boy appeared to be ten, or maybe twelve. He had short black hair and a sunburned, open face. He was missing the lower part of his left ear. He wore a short, dirty tunic, and shabby, worn down sandals.

They stared at him for a long moment. The boy scrutinized them with suspicion. There seemed to be something off about them. He was not sure what, but he knew they were not from around there. Then he saw his ball in Ben's hand.

Ben tossed the ball back. The boy caught it. He continued to stare. The dog had stopped barking and stayed by his side.

"Well, you're up Charlie," Ben said simply.

Charlie nodded and stepped forward. The boy took one-step back, and the antsy dog became agitated again.

"Hello...can you understand me?" Charlie said in Aramaic.

He was relieved when the boy nodded cautiously.

"Great. My name is Charles. This is my wife, Faith. This is

Ben. What's your name?"

The boy spun around and raced back to the house.

"Argos! Argos!" he yelled.

The mangy dog barked once and scurried after the boy.

Faith grabbed Charlie's arm.

"What did you say to him?"

"I asked him his name. I think."

"Well, we're off to a great start," Ben said.

The three stood there for a minute, looking over their surroundings. The sloping hill that overlooked Jerusalem beyond was lush green with many trees. Beyond the road, farther down in the valley, small farms and pastures were visible. It all appeared very idyllic.

"It's much greener than I expected," Faith remarked.

"Two thousand years of bloody conflicts can do a lot of damage to the environment," Charlie said.

Charlie stepped toward the home where the frightened young boy had dashed into with his dog. The cracked walls were a dirty mustard and clearly in need of repair. Faith and Ben followed him around to the front where they found a closed, dilapidated door. Just before they reached it, a woman came out. She wore a raggedy coffee-colored robe that partly hid her features, but her movement suggested she was young. From behind the hood, she considered them cautiously as if she wished to hide her identity.

"Good day," Charlie said in Aramaic.

She did not move or speak for several moments. She seemed ready to bolt back into her home if the need arose. The boy and the dog peered out from behind her. The dog barked. The boy silenced the dog with several sharp commands.

"Charlie, I think she's frightened," Faith said.

Faith stepped closer. She smiled pleasantly.

"Hello," she said, remembering the greeting Charlie gave in Aramaic.

Faith glanced back to Charlie. He nodded that she spoke

properly.

The woman smiled guardedly. She still seemed ready to retreat inside if necessary.

"Charlie, tell her we're travelers from far away," Faith said.

"Yeah."

Charlie smiled, motioning cautiously with his hands.

"We've traveled a great distance on our way to Jerusalem," Charlie explained. He pointed to the distant citadel. "Is that Jerusalem?"

The woman nodded. She took a tentative step toward them.

"Keep going, Charlie. Ask her about you-know-who," Ben said. He checked the device surreptitiously. Twenty-four hours and forty-five minutes remained.

"We've come to see the Nazarene. The man they call Jesus. Do you know this man?" he asked.

The woman shook her head. But Charlie sensed she had knowledge of him by the way she reacted at the mention of his name.

"Great," Ben said.

"It might help if we told her our names, Charlie," Faith suggested.

Charlie nodded. He introduced Faith, Ben, and himself. He then indicated that he wanted to know her name.

She hesitated, glancing at the boy and the dog. The boy was clearly her son.

"My name is Miriam," she finally replied.

The boy ventured out and tugged on Miriam's tunic. She leaned down and he whispered something to her. She thought for a moment, and then turned to the trio.

"This is my son, Daniel. Would you like to come inside and refresh yourselves?"

"Thank you. We would," Charlie said.

Faith repeated what Charlie said.

Charlie and Faith followed her inside.

Ben glanced around. Several people had gathered at the well, and were drawing water from it. He stared down to the white city beyond. He flashed an incredulous look.

"Damn. We did it. We really, really did it," he muttered.

He went inside.

CHAPTER VII

The interior of the home struck Faith and Ben as being very shabby. Charlie was less critical, knowing this was a typical home for Judeans during this time. Divided into two rooms and separated by a curtained door, the place resembled a modern day cabin rather than a home. A raggedy beige and gray curtain hid the inner room that was likely the sleeping quarters. There was no flooring, just simple bare earth stamped down. Only the wealthy could afford paved floors. However, the floor appeared to have been brushed recently. A wood table and several bare wood chairs sat on one side. Opposite that, a loom hung from two vertical poles buried in the earth. Miriam probably earned a modest living weaving clothes. Three crude wood shelves protruded out from the mud and stone wall. The shelves held some earthen pots and dishes. Although there was an oil lantern on the table, the place depended on the sun for light. Wood crossbeams formed the main support for the roof. A mixture of brushwood and mud covered the beams. Charlie suspected the roof leaked badly during heavy rains. A thick wood crossbeam lay near the door. It was likely used to secure the door at night.

Daniel poured wine from a small jar into some metal cups. He handed them to their guests. They thanked him. He smiled kindly and offered a chair to Faith. She thanked him again and sat down.

Miriam, while trying to be friendly, was still guarded. However, once inside she lowered the hood of her garment. She had a lovely, olive-skinned face with sad, almond-shaped blue eyes. Her flowing black hair was chaotic as if it had not been washed recently. Seeing Ben's appreciative smile, she absently rearranged her hair with her hands.

Charlie reached into his tunic and set two silver Denarius coins on the table. They were exact copies of the coins of the day. The head of Tiberius Caesar, the current emperor, was stamped on the front of them.

Miriam stepped to the table. She picked up the coins and offered them back to Charlie.

"I cannot accept this," she said.

While her voice had a gentle quality to it, there was also firmness. Charlie refused to take them back. She finally nodded politely and hid them in her robe.

Daniel watched Ben sip the wine.

"Thank you, Daniel," he said.

Daniel proudly held up his wood ball. Ben examined the handcrafted ball. He held it up.

"Did you make this?" he asked in English, pointing at the ball.

Daniel smiled and nodded.

"Very nice."

Ben sipped some more wine. It was a bit on the sour side but he drank it anyway, if only to be polite. He turned to Charlie.

"Charlie, ask her if she knows someone who can help us find Jesus."

"Should we ask her what year it is?" Faith said.

"Better not. She might think we're crazy if we ask her that," Ben said.

"We need to find the Nazarene, Miriam. He's also called Jesus. He's a carpenter and a preacher. Have you heard of him?"

She finally nodded.

"Do you know where we might find him?" Charlie asked.

She thought about it, and then shook her head. Charlie sensed she was telling the truth. He thought for a moment. The idea of walking down to Jerusalem and blindly asking every stranger if they knew Jesus would not seem to be a good use of their limited time. It also might draw too much attention to themselves.

"Is there someone in Jerusalem who can help us find him?"

She thought a moment. It was obvious she knew of him, but seemed reluctant to volunteer any information. Faith leaned forward toward her.

"Please, we need to find him," Faith implored.

Miriam looked at Faith. The two women considered each other, as if sizing each other up. After some reflection, she turned back to Charlie.

"I know a man who might be able to help you," she said. "His name is Nicodemus."

The name triggered an immediate reaction from Charlie. He was familiar with Nicodemus, if it was the same man. He nodded eagerly.

"Yes. Nicodemus. Where can we find him?" he asked.

She hesitated. Miriam appeared fearful all of a sudden as if she had revealed a secret. She pressed her lips together, crossing her arms.

"Please. It's vitally important that we speak to him," Charlie said.

"You might find him in the temple. I'm told he is there every day," she revealed.

The dull clip-clop of approaching horses interrupted their conversation. Ben, standing by the narrow window, peered through the tattered curtain. What he saw startled him. He waved to Charlie.

"Charlie! Over here!"

Charlie hurried to the window that faced the distant dirt road leading to Jerusalem. He spotted them bursting out of a swirling dust cloud. A patrol of Roman cavalry numbering some ten men on lean horses was hastening down the road. Bright red capes flew in the breeze. Their leather cuirasses and metal helmets shone bright in the noonday sun. Short swords dangled menacingly from their belts. Alert, sunburned faces, caked in dust, gazed in all directions.

"Roman cavalry," Charlie said.

"Romans," Ben mumbled.

Ben suddenly felt very uneasy watching the patrol gallop down the road. He felt as if he were in enemy territory, hiding from the bad guys. He drifted away from the window.

The leader of the patrol, Tribune Gaius Macro, searched

right and left as they passed petrified people scattering out of their path. A square red patch covered his right eye. The other eye carefully checked every woman he passed. He ripped back on the reins violently bringing his horse to heel. He pointed to a hooded woman.

"Come here, woman!"

The frightened woman stood frozen. She looked right and left at her companions who quickly drifted away from her as if she were contagious. She stood alone, shaking under Macro's dark gaze.

"I said come here!"

Macro's guttural command sent a chill through the young woman. She cautiously stepped over to his horse.

"Show your face, woman!"

The woman again looked back to her fellow travelers who were of no help. Her hand shook as she pulled her hood away, revealing her face to Macro.

Macro growled with animalistic frustration. He dug his sandaled feet into the flank of his steed and road on. The terrified woman dashed out of the way, narrowly avoiding the galloping horses. She stumbled back to her companions.

Miriam had joined Charlie and Ben by the window and watched the scene unfold down the road. Her face twisted instantly into a mask of white terror. She stepped back, almost tripping over Argus, who yelped.

"Daniel!" she said.

Daniel flung himself into her arms. Miriam seized him roughly. Miriam struggled to breath. Her eyes clamped shut as she mumbled incoherently under her breath.

Faith rose up and hurried over to Charlie. She looked out as the cavalry patrol continued on to Jerusalem. There was something about them that fired fear right down into her bone marrow. Faith instinctively dropped back into the shadows, joining Ben. Charlie watched the patrol until they were lost in their horses' dust. He traded guarded looks with Ben and Faith.

Faith turned to Miriam and saw the sheer panic in her face. She looked close to fainting.

"They're terrified, Charlie."

"Well, like most of the people during this time, Jews hated the Romans," Charlie said. "They ruled their empire with an iron fist."

"That's not hate, Charlie. It's fear," Faith said.

Ben looked to Miriam and Daniel. He raised his palms in an attempt to calm them.

"They're gone. It's okay now."

Faith stepped over to Miriam and Daniel. Miriam seemed ready to pass out. She shook like a dangling leaf battered by a strong wind.

"It's safe now. They've ridden off."

Slowly, she stopped shaking. Her hectic breathing eased. However, she still clung to her son.

Ben held up the device to Charlie. He saw the time.

"We really need to go if we're going to find him."

Charlie nodded, "Yeah. We'll just have to be careful and avoid the Romans."

"Will they be a problem?" Ben asked.

"Well-," Charlie started to say.

The heavy thud followed by Miriam's gasp spun Charlie and Ben around. Faith was sprawled on the dirt floor, her limbs shaking. They dropped down to her. Charlie turned her over and stared at her face. She had passed out.

"Faith! Faith!"

He brushed the dirt off her face. He lifted her body and cradled her head. Beads of sweat dotted her cheeks. Her eyes fluttered open and tried to focus on his face. Her head then went limp, falling over.

"Hold on. I've got you."

"Water. Quickly, Daniel," Miriam said to her boy.

Her frantic terror from just a moment ago was forgotten in

the face of this new crisis. She dropped down next to Faith.

Daniel grabbed a bucket of water and handed it to Miriam. She dunked a rag into the water and applied the compress to Faith's face.

"Bring her inside here," Miriam said, pointing to the inner room behind the curtain.

Charlie scooped up her limp body and carried her into the next chamber. The room was a third of the size of the other room, and was their sleeping quarters. On the floor were two emaciated mattresses of straw covered by wool blankets. There were no windows. He set her gently down on one of them.

Charlie felt her forehead. She was not running a fever. Miriam slid in alongside him and placed the wet compress back on her forehead. Faith's chest heaved in sudden spasms.

"What is it?" Ben asked.

Charlie looked up to Ben, flashing alarm.

"I don't know. She's never had an attack like this before."

Ben dropped to one knee and grabbed his sister's trembling hand. His eyebrows came together gloomily. He directed a frown to Charlie.

"What? What is it?" Charlie asked.

Ben did not respond. He appeared reluctant to speculate his worry. Charlie jerked his head back and the two left the room. Ben had his arms across his chest, his eyes directed to the dirt floor. Charlie grabbed his arm.

"Talk to me, Ben. Do you know something?"

Ben looked up. His head bobbed as he marshaled his thoughts.

"I wonder if the time displacement did something to her."

"Did something?"

"Didn't you feel it?"

"You mean the tingling and itching sensation? Yeah, I felt it. So?"

Ben paced anxiously about the room. His mind wrestled with

some of the concerns the team had about time displacement. The concerns were theoretical since they had only done a few tests. Ben stopped and stared at Charlie.

"Charlie, we came back over two thousand years. The trip might have aged us, or affected us, more than I originally thought it would. More than a few seconds. Weeks. Maybe months. I don't know. Maybe more."

"You mean her disease could be further advanced now?"

Ben nodded, almost guiltily.

"But I don't feel different. My hair is no longer, is it? My fingernails haven't grown," he said, holding up his hands.

"That's true," Ben admitted.

Charlie sensed Ben was not being completely truthful.

"You suspected something like this might happen though, didn't you?"

Ben looked away. Charlie grabbed him and spun him around.

"Well?"

"Charlie, I told you from the beginning there were a lot of unknowns regarding this trip. We had only done some preliminary tests. We're in uncharted territory here. I don't know what to tell you. The trip back might have affected us in ways we don't know yet. I just don't know," he explained.

Charlie seemed ready to punch Ben, but he got a grip on his confused emotions. He peeked into the back room. Faith was still in bed suffering fits of trembling before relaxing. Miriam was tending to her, applying the compress. She looked back to Charlie. She flashed deep concern and then turned her attention back to Faith.

Charlie faced Ben.

"We need to get to Jerusalem."

Ben shook his head.

"Faith is no shape to travel, Charlie."

"How much time?"

Ben checked the device and held it up to Charlie.

"We should wait, Charlie. Maybe she'll come round with

some rest."

Charlie considered the idea and rejected it. Maybe she would not come round. Maybe she might die. He could not just sit there and hope. He had to act.

"No, Ben. We need to go. Now."

Ben finally nodded, suspecting he was right. But he did not want it to be his decision.

"We're going to need help. We can't go stumbling around Jerusalem asking strangers for help. You told me he has enemies. What if we talk to the wrong person?"

Daniel, who had been watching the two talk, got a sense of what they wanted to do. He tugged on Ben's robe. He motioned them toward the front door. They walked over, away from the other room. Daniel glanced furtively to the curtain separating the rooms.

"I will take you to Nicodemus," he whispered, guardedly. "For a price."

"Daniel says he'll help us. For money."

"Smart kid. I like him." Ben shrugged to Charlie. "Do we have a choice?"

Charlie produced another Denarius. Daniel bit the coin. He put it into his tunic. He jerked his head stealthily, and ducked outside. Ben followed the boy. Charlie returned to the back room.

Faith was awake, now but her face was deathly pale. Her limbs felt heavy as if weighted down by heavy chains. Her fluttering eyes blinked as she tried to focus on the people hovering over her. They wavered in her blurred vision.

"Charlie," she called weakly.

Charlie dropped down on one knee. He stroked her face. He was scared, but he pushed it way down.

"I'm here," he said. "Faith, we have to get to Jerusalem."

Faith motioned as if to rise, but her body had no strength. Her frustrated eyes darted down to her arms and legs as if she was making sure she still had them.

"I don't understand what's happening," she muttered in

confusion. "I can't-"

"Shhh. It's okay. Just rest."

Charlie looked to Miriam. He was about to ask a great deal of this woman he had only met an hour ago. But he had no choice now. The idea of carrying Faith all around Jerusalem in search of Jesus was impossible. Despite his extensive knowledge of Jesus' movements, he still knew he could be anywhere. Miriam sensed his dilemma.

"We must get to Jerusalem," he said.

She thought for a moment, glancing down at Faith. She looked back up to him.

"I will watch over her," she promised. "She will be safe with me."

"Thank you."

"Go. I'll be fine. Be, be careful," Faith gasped.

Charlie kissed her softly on her lips and then on her forehead. He squeezed her limp hand.

"I'll be back for you. I love you."

He turned to Miriam, and smiled gratefully.

"Thank you."

Charlie joined Ben and Daniel outside the hovel.

"Is she okay?" Ben asked.

"Let's get moving," Charlie said.

Daniel led the way to the road that would take them to the city. Argos came streaking after them. Daniel yelled at the dog, pointing back to their home. Argos finally turned about reluctantly and shuffled back.

The sun beat down on the three as they trudged the four miles down to Jerusalem. It was hot going, and the strange wardrobe Charlie and Ben were compelled to wear did not help matters. They sweated profusely in them. When they were only two miles away from the city, more Roman cavalry raced past them flinging up a choking cloud of dust. They turned up their loose tunics to cover their faces until it settled. The galloping legionnaires cursed and barked at everyone in their path. Panic-stricken people and carts scattered out of their path. Charlie and Ben could see the hatred in the eyes of the oppressed populace.

"Nice guys," Ben mumbled after several dry coughs.

They watched the people get back on the road and continue their pilgrimage to Jerusalem. Nearby, an old man struggled to get his donkey cart out of the ditch he was forced into when the cavalry patrol rode by. With both hands on the bridle he pulled to get the cantankerous animal back on the road. However, the stubborn animal resisted with whiny hee-haws. He even tried to cajole the animal out with earnest pleas.

"Come on now, Chloe. I don't have all day. Move."

Charlie nodded to Ben. They walked over to the gasping man.

"Greetings. Peace be upon you. Do you need some help?"

"Greetings. Peace be upon you," the old man said. He wore a white scraggily beard and had the bushiest eyebrows Charlie had ever seen. Although he was seventy or eighty, he appeared quite spry for his age.

The old man then considered the strangers' offer for a moment. Finally, he nodded, thanking them. In the back of the cart were several bleating lambs, still upset at being tossed into the ditch.

"Give me a hand, Ben. Why don't you get back in the cart?" Charlie suggested to the man.

The old man thanked them again and climbed back onto the cart. He grabbed the reins. Daniel watched as Charlie and Ben got in front of the mule and grabbed the bridle. They braced their feet and pulled as the old man flicked on the reins. After several irritated howls, the mule reluctantly scrambled out of the ditch, pulling the rickety cart out with it.

"Thank you," the old man said, very grateful for the assistance.

The old man looked down at the trio, and with a wave of his gnarled hand offered them a ride on the back of his cart.

Charlie thanked him. They settled on the back end of the cart. The old man barked a command to Chloe and they continued on to the city.

"What did you say to him?" Ben asked.

"Greetings. Peace be upon you," Charlie said in Aramaic.

Ben tried the phrase himself several times.

Charlie nodded, "Good. But you should have known that one already. I went over basic phrases weeks ago."

Ben shrugged guiltily.

"You didn't practice, did you?"

"No. I guess I never really thought we'd really go through with this insane plan of yours. Foreign languages were never my thing anyway."

Ben noticed the host of noisy animals being driven down the road. Their bleating and whining smote on his ears.

"What's with all the animals, Charlie?"

Charlie asked the old man a question. He nodded in reply, turning very sober. Ben saw it.

"What is it?

"It's Passover week. All these lambs and goats are to be ritualistically slaughtered at the Temple."

Ben looked back at the bleating lambs and felt a twinge of compassion for them. It was one thing to kill an animal for food, but to kill one for some religious ceremony seemed incredibly barbaric to him.

"Passover week. Is that good or bad for us?" Ben asked.

He then saw Charlie's face turn grim.

"What is it, Charlie?"

"It's good. It's okay," Charlie said warily.

"What is it? Tell me," Ben asked.

"If today is what I think it is, this is the day Jesus is betrayed and arrested," Charlie revealed.

Ben stared, trying to remember what that meant. All he could think of was what he had seen in those old films like *Ben Hur*. Once again, he felt a surge of guilt for not knowing more about this time period after all the material Charlie had provided him.

"But isn't that when he was crucified?"

"Yeah, that's right," Charlie said remotely. "But that won't happen until tomorrow."

Ben began to understand now. Now he showed concern.

"We came too late. Right? We're too late."

Charlie raised his hand in an attempt to pacify Ben. However, inside, his guts were turning over. If they could have just arrived twenty-four hours earlier they would have had the perfect opportunity to see the Nazarene on his last pilgrimage to the temple. According to some historical accounts, he healed a number of sick and lame people, including several lepers.

"Not necessarily. There's still time if we can find him before sundown. That's when he'll be arrested."

But Charlie did not sound confident. Ben could see him wrestling with his thoughts. Ben grunted, angry with himself.

"This is my fault," Ben said. "My computations were off."

"Take it easy, Ben. We can still do this. His arrest won't be for at least another six or seven hours."

"You're not sounding very confident."

"We'll be fine if we can find Nicodemus."

"Won't be easy," Ben said, still filled with doubts about what they were trying to do. Ben checked his device again. They still had plenty of time.

Daniel had listened to the two men speak in their strange tongue, trying to follow their conversation. He thought if he watched their lips he might be able to decipher their words. He finally gave up.

"So where do you think we'll find him?" Ben asked.

Charlie shrugged.

Ben was astonished.

"What does that mean? You're the historian. You're supposed to be the expert."

"I know."

Charlie half-turned to Ben who was almost falling off the edge of the cart. He gazed about the countryside. This was his first real chance to take in the wonder of it all. For any historian, this was the ultimate dream come true. Every question or belief he had ever had could be answered with absolute certitude now. A strange giddiness struck him. Ben sensed his excitement.

"This might be quite a moment for someone like you," Ben said.

Charlie nodded.

"Based on what you know, where should we find him?"

"Ben, the historical record is fragmentary. It's based mostly on biblical passages in the New Testament that won't be written for years. Decades even. There are no completely reliable hour-by-hour records on Jesus' movements. Historians have been debating this day for several thousand years," Charlie said helplessly.

Ben grunted, "So, we're winging it is what you're saying?"

Charlie nodded.

"Nicodemus knows Jesus. If he's the man I think he is; if it is him, he will even speak up for him when the Sanhedrin judges him. I think he'll help us."

"The who?"

Charlie stared at Ben, triggering a contrite look from his brother-in-law.

"Okay, I confess, I didn't read all the material you gave me. I was a little busy programming a two-thousand year time jump, and doing other stuff."

"Other stuff? Ben, the Sanhedrin is a court with complete authority on enforcing Jewish religious law. Even the Romans don't interfere with them."

"Why not?"

"Because the Romans learned the hard way not to. You can tax people, rule them with an iron fist, but when you mess with their religious beliefs, people get a little ornery. And the Jews can get very ornery if you mess with their faith."

"Good to know."

Ben turned from Charlie and looked back up the dirt road. The distant collection of small hovels was tiny and insignificant now, almost lost in the cloud of dust thrown up by all the carts.

"She'll be okay, Ben."

"I hope so."

Not so far behind the cart, a cluster of thirteen men were walking up the same road toward the city. Their tunics were made of wool but their cloaks were of fine linen. Their cloaks served the additional purpose of keeping them warm at night if no quarters were available. Their well-worn sandals had seen better days but still sufficed to protect them from the countless pebbles and rocks littering the dusty road. The leader of the group was a few inches taller than all but one and thus stood out among the group. His well-formed beard framed a handsome, but troubled face. These lean, vigorous men were young, ranging from their mid-twenties to early thirties.

One of the men quickened his step and walked alongside their leader. He sensed the unusual tension in his master's demeanor. He seemed reluctant to voice his concerns. However, he finally spoke up.

"You are strangely subdued this day, Master," Peter said.

Jesus had been reticent ever since the incident in the Temple. For all the time Peter and the others had followed him, he had displayed great serenity in the most tempestuous of moments. However, on that day he flashed a stunning anger that astounded his brave followers. Before they could even react, he was overturning tables covered with money. Coins exploded in all directions as he seized a whip and slashed left and right, sending terrified animals and the moneylenders fleeing. With mouths agape, they watched him throw open cages, allowing captive doves to escape. What amazed them even more was the shocking fact that no one stopped him. They all fell back, stunned, having never witnessed an event like this in the Temple, his harsh words branding them.

"How dare you turn my father's house into a market!"

The temple officials soon recovered from their confusion and confronted him. The Nazarene's followers stood by him as the officials challenged his outrageous conduct.

"I will destroy this temple and raise it up in three days," Jesus told them.

"Three days? It's taken over forty years to erect this temple, and you are going to raise it in only three days," they scoffed, thinking the man before them was insane.

He did not reply. He simply turned about and marched out of the temple followed by his disciples.

Peter searched his master's face as they continued up the road. His troubled face revealed a discreet smile.

"Are you well, Master?"

"A troubled mind gives way to deep reflection."

The master's steady voice traveled out for the others to hear. They drew closer to him.

"Will there be trouble in the city?" one of the others called out, his voice edged with uneasiness.

"Yes."

Peter looked ahead toward the gate. Known as the big fisherman, he was several inches taller than his master. He could easily see over the multitude streaming into the city.

"We should not go then. Why seek more conflict?"

Jesus turned to Peter. He then looked back at his other followers, his brown eyes fixing on one of them in particular.

"The path I am on cannot be altered. My road is set and I must follow it."

"Can we not alter our path? Can we not change our destiny?" Peter asked.

Peter showed concern now. He had never heard his master sounding so fatalistic.

"You can. I cannot," he answered.

He laid his hand on Peter's arm. He managed a smile, but Peter could sense it was only through great effort.

***

Faith felt strength slowly return to her limbs. The baffling weakness that had struck her down had not completely passed, however. It seemed to be close by, lurking, ready to strike again. She was able to lift both arms, and felt almost proud in the ability to make her muscles function again. She saw Miriam smiling down upon her. Looking down the length of her body, she saw she could wiggle her toes. It was amazing how wonderful it felt to move them.

"Rest now," Miriam said.

Despite the language barrier, Faith understood her. She shut her eyes.

Miriam pushed herself to her feet. Her knees ached from tending to the strange woman. As blood flowed back to her limbs, she spotted Argos sitting obediently in the corner. However, there was no sign of Daniel. Argos never left Daniel's side. She quietly walked into the main room to find it empty. She hurried out the door. Argos trailed after her.

Miriam shielded her eyes from the sun and searched for her boy. The distant road to Jerusalem was still choked with people.

"DANIEL! DANIEL!"

She searched behind the hovel thinking he might be feeding the chickens. Not finding him, she came back to the front, and scanned the road yet again. She now realized Daniel was with the two strangers. Her heart thumped hard in her chest at the idea of her boy traveling to Jerusalem. She was about to bolt after him, but restrained herself. She could not leave the woman behind after she had promised to look after her. She shut her eyes tight and prayed to God to watch over her child. Then she retreated inside.

CHAPTER VIII

Charlie and Ben twisted their heads toward the open gate when the shadow cast by the walls of Jerusalem fell over them. Charlie recognized it as the Essene Gate. This was just one of some half dozen gates the city possessed. Ben whistled at the massive wall protecting Jerusalem.

"Damn, that is one serious wall."

"It sure is. It goes completely around the city. Almost four miles. It was designed to withstand a siege," Charlie revealed. The walls looked to be at least twelve feet thick at the base and nearly thirty feet in height. It was a very impressive structure.

"I bet it did the job."

"Yeah, it did, until the year 70 CE."

Ben looked to Charlie, "What happened?"

"The people revolted against Rome. The Roman army besieged the city for five months before sacking it. They put tens of thousands to the sword—men, women, children—and enslaved the rest."

Ben shook his head, "Rome didn't fool around, did they?"

"No, they didn't. You can't build empires by being nice, Ben."

The two looked back up. Patrolling the ramparts were Roman soldiers watching people come and go.

"Why all the soldiers? Is it always like this?" Ben asked. It was not until this moment he wondered what would happen if they got into trouble. There was no one they could turn to for help. They were completely on their own. It sent a shiver up his spine.

Charlie called out to the old man and questioned him. He reacted with an angry screed while punching his free hand up at the soldiers above.

"Yeah, that's what I thought. Pontius Pilate, the governor, is visiting Jerusalem. Normally he resides in Caesarea Maratima on the coast. But whenever he travels he brings along his own special guard," Charlie explained.

"It's good to be king," Ben retorted.

The old man stopped the cart after entering the city. An official of some kind approached and they started to haggle about something. Ben grabbed Charlie's robe.

"Is there a problem, Charlie?"

Charlie listened in to their conversation.

"It's okay. It's a custom official collecting a tax. All merchandise being bought in or taken out of the city is taxed."

"You can't even escape the taxman two thousand years in the past. Ben Franklin was right. Only two things in life that are certain—death and taxes," Ben commented.

After the man paid the tax, they rolled into the city. The oppressive clamor of people and animals smote their ears. For Ben this was particularly annoying as he did not understand what anyone was saying.

The Roman soldiers just inside the gate paid no interest to the old man driving his cart into the city. But they did eye Charlie, Ben, and Daniel briefly. They must have looked out of place sitting in the man's cart. Daniel passed his hand over his face until they were safely past them.

The pleasant smell of grass and trees of the countryside was swapped out now for something quite unpleasant. The air inside the city was a hot stew of animal manure, cooked food, and sewage. It stung the nostrils of Charlie and Ben. Daniel did not seem affected by the rancid mix of odors.

"Shit. Smells like the city dump," Ben groaned.

"Yeah," Charlie agreed.

He shook off the stench and concentrated on the wondrous sights before him. From the records that did exist, they had just entered the Essene Gate leading into the Lower City. This was the poor section of the town. Here, narrow, poorly-paved roads littered with trash separated the many dilapidated two-story limestone homes. Boisterous women in upper floor windows carried on conversations with passersby below. Half-naked children ran about at play, seemingly ignorant of their abject poverty.

"Looks like a slum," Ben commented.

"It is a slum. It's called the Lower City. This is where the poor of Jerusalem reside."

"What's that over there?" Ben asked, pointing to the left.

"That's the Upper City."

The homes and buildings, directly opposite the Lower City, were clearly better constructed and maintained. Most had fine red-tiled roofs. The clean white walls reflected the bright sun. The well-paved road they rolled over divided the two sections very neatly.

"So that is where the better half live."

"That's right," Charlie agreed.

"The more things change, the more they stay the same."

Along the bustling road, aggressive merchants hawked produce or prepared food for Passover visitors. Others sold everything from pots and pans, to jewelry, and even fine woven garments. Farmers drove carts laden with fresh produce planning to sell them to local eateries.

Ben pointed toward a large, three story amphitheater-like building off to the left.

"That's just what it looks like, Ben. It's the city theater."

Charlie could barely contain his excitement. For a few moments, the fantastic sights pushed his worry for Faith from his mind.

"We've done it, Ben. We're really here."

Ben looked at him. There was something in his attitude that concerned him. Ben's eyes gazed at the mass of humanity choking the street. How could they find one man in all this?

"How many people live here?" Ben asked.

Charlie saw Ben's face and realized what he meant.

"It's hard to say. The estimates range up to eighty thousand during this time period."

"Eighty thousand?"

Ben was aghast.

"During Passover, the number could be three or four times that. Not everyone stayed in the city. Some stayed in nearby towns while others stayed in tent cities. You saw some of them when we entered the city."

"Damn. A needle in a haystack would be easier to find."

"Relax, Ben. I don't think it will be as hard as that."

The cart stopped. The old man looked back. He pointed left and said something to Charlie. Charlie nodded gratefully and the three dropped off the cart. The old man swung the cart about and took a side road into the Lower City.

"The man said the Temple is that way. See that structure ahead? That's it."

Ben looked where Charlie was pointing. A large, gleaming structure towered over every other building in the city.

The trio jostled their way through the bustling crowd. People from all over the Roman Empire and beyond jammed the road bisecting the city. Charlie spotted travelers from as far away as Gaul and India. Traders pulled snorting camels and whiny mules burdened with merchandise from as far as Egypt and Arabia over the road. Colorfully dressed slaves transported wealthy men and women in superbly carved litters. Sellers rushed alongside the litters cajoling the lounging figures to buy their fresh food.

Ben showed disgust as he commented on the slaves carrying the rich patrons through the streets.

"Slavery was the norm during this period, Ben. The sad reality is that for most of history slavery was very common the world over. The universal idea that all people should be free is a relatively new philosophy. In fact, it's only been around a few hundred years," Charlie explained.

"That doesn't make it right."

Charlie stopped and ran his eyes up the steep flight of stone steps leading into the great Temple of Jerusalem.

Ben looked around for Daniel who had taken off into the

crowd. He felt a surge of panic, feeling responsible for the kid. Then he spotted him hurrying away from a fruit seller. He handed Ben and Charlie an apple each.

"Thanks, Daniel."

Ben took a small bite. The apple was sweet and juicy. He quickly devoured it.

"Who knew time travel could make you so hungry."

Charlie nodded in agreement as he ripped into his apple.

Daniel indicated the great stairwell.

"Nicodemus," he said.

"Okay. Lead the way Daniel," Charlie said.

Daniel led them past a scrawny man arguing with a vegetable vendor. The buyer caught sight of the three figures. His narrow eyes focused on the boy in particular. He waved off the aggressive vendor, and on instinct followed the trio up the long flight of stone steps.

"Reconstruction of the temple by Herod started in 20 BCE," Charlie explained. "All of the work was done by the priests. It wasn't finished until 63 CE."

"Great. Will that be on the final?" Ben said. "Wait, that's eighty-three years."

"That's right."

"Damn. Why did you say CE? Isn't it AD?"

"It's basically the same. CE means Common Era. They use it now, I mean in two thousand years, to avoid referencing Christ. Look at those limestone blocks, Ben. They must be almost twenty feet in length. Imagine moving blocks like that without heavy machinery."

With the coming Passover, the traffic in and out of the Temple was overwhelming. As visitors passed each other, they would greet each other, some renewing old acquaintances. After an exhausting climb up the two steep flights of stairs, the trio entered the meeting hall. The great hall, supported by twenty-foot tall columns of limestone and marble, stretched out the length of a football field.

"This is the center of Jewish power in Judea, Ben."

"So this is where we'll find this Nicodemus guy?"

"Yeah. He's one of the priests."

Lucan pushed his way through the sea of people crowding the stairs, rushing to keep pace with the three. He did not want to lose them. If the boy was who he thought, he was going to be a wealthy man.

Charlie took the lead now. He was well acquainted with the layout of the Temple, or at least how present day historians believed it to be. They passed through the meeting hall, turned left, and entered the massive Court of the Gentiles. This area was actually a vast bazaar where still more vendors sold everything from souvenirs to food.

"This place is huge," Ben commented.

"It takes up almost a quarter of Jerusalem."

They crossed the court and stopped at a stone fence, or balustrade, about four feet high that encircled the massive center building. Beyond the handrail stood the Inner Precincts, the Great Temple of Jerusalem itself.

"We can't go any farther, Ben. But this is it. The Second Temple of Jerusalem. Non-Jews are forbidden from entering, or risk pain of death."

"Then we should wait here I'm guessing?"

Ben stared at the thousands of people scattered across the court. Any one of them could be Nicodemus.

"Well, now what do we do?" he asked.

Charlie turned to Daniel.

"Can you find Nicodemus?"

Daniel nodded. The boy hurried off, vanishing into the teeming throng.

Ben noticed they had become the center of attention. Some of them stared, and then whispered furtively to each other. He felt a surge of uneasiness. He leaned toward Charlie.

"Why are they staring at us?"

Charlie stared at Ben. He pointed to his hair.

"Probably our hair style."

Ben set his hand on the top of his head, tugging at his hair.

"Oh, right. I guess they don't have Floyd's Barbershops in the first century."

Charlie gazed at the Great Temple. Billowing smoke swirled up from the top of the structure, staining the blue sky above.

"Someone having a barbecue?" Ben kidded.

"You're not far off. The priests are making sacrifices inside."

Charlie overheard people discussing business or family affairs. He could not follow all of their discussions, but he picked up enough. He was gratified that the years he invested in learning Aramaic had actually paid off.

"Is it like you imagined?" Ben asked.

Charlie shook his head, overwhelmed. He took a deep breath and realized his heart was thumping in his chest. It was all too much for him to absorb. He finally voiced his true feelings.

"If I only had time to really explore-."

"Charlie, we don't. We only have this much time."

Ben carefully flashed the device to Charlie and quickly returned it under his robe.

"The place is huge though. You could fit ten football fields in here," Ben commented.

Ben then glanced back to the men staring at them.

"Are you sure we can be here, Charlie?"

"We're good. Anyone can be in the Court of Gentiles."

Charlie now pointed to the huge block-like structure that ascended from the center of the courtyard. It was an impressive building forty to fifty feet in height. The walls of variegated blocks of red, green, and blue marble flashed incandescent in the sunlight. He located multiple entrances leading into the Temple.

"The main building in the middle you're looking at is the Temple itself. Like I said, only Jews are permitted to enter. Even

Romans are not allowed inside."

Ben studied the imposing structure. It paled in comparison to the graceful beauty of Saint Peter's Basilica. Here everything had harsh ninety-degree angles. There were no elegant curves or intricate decorative motifs. He guessed the technology and materials for more spectacular architectural designs was yet to be discovered or invented. Ben was grateful they were forbidden from entering it. He did not know why, but there was something ominous about the building.

"In there are where the animal sacrifices are performed."

"Animal sacrifices?" Ben said.

Ben looked disgusted. He could never imagine animal sacrifices taking place in Saint Borromeo's.

"This is Passover week, Ben. It commemorates the biblical story in Exodus when God, or Pharaoh, depending on your beliefs, freed the Israelites from slavery in Egypt."

"It's been awhile, but I've seen the Ten Commandments," Ben said.

"Well, Passover literally means passed over. During the final plague, the killing of the first born, God passed over the protected houses of the Jews, sparing them."

"But why the animal sacrifices?"

"It constitutes one of the main parts of Passover week. Families were required to offer a sacrificial lamb or goat to the Temple. Their Torah mandates that they ritually slaughter an animal on Passover evening and then eat it on the first night of the holiday."

Charlie considered Ben's revulsion of the whole Passover celebration. As much as he would have liked, this did not seem the time to go into an in depth explanation of the ritual. He wished Ben had invested a little more time in reading all the material he had gathered in the weeks leading up to their trip.

"Ben, you'll be pleased to know that after the Roman army destroyed the Temple in 70 CE, the sacrificing of animals stopped."

"Hmmm, nice to know. So, is this where they keep the Ark

of the Covenant, Charlie? You know, the actual Ten Commandments given to Moses?"

Ben grinned, pointing at the Temple with an almost boyish enthusiasm.

"No. Sorry, Ben. The Ark vanished around 586 BCE when the Babylonian Empire conquered Israel. It has not been seen since."

Ben's eyes gazed over the great temple with a mix of dubiousness and helplessness. If anything, he was having more doubts about their plan now than when Charlie had first proposed it. Again, he dug the device from his robe and covertly flashed it to Charlie. Nineteen hours and twenty-four minutes remained.

"Charlie, not to be a doubting Thomas, but..."

"I know what you're going to say. I see it in your face. I've heard it in your voice from day one. But did you ever stop to think about all of the coincidences in this?"

Ben stared.

"Ben, what are the odds Faith is not only married to a history professor, but has a brother who stumbled on a way to travel back in time?"

Ben thought a moment and laughed.

"Are you suggesting this is part of some...plan?"

"You said it, not me."

"Okay, I'll leave that one alone. So, tell me what's happening right now? Or what do you think is happening?"

Charlie reflected a moment. He looked up at the sun, guessing the time of day.

"If the Gospels are accurate, then Judas Iscariot is before Caiaphas and the other priests. He's not here. He's meeting them in secret at Caiaphus' home."

"Caiaphus is the number one guy in Jerusalem, right? See, I read some of your homework."

"Very good. As far as Jewish rulers, yes. However, Pontius Pilate is the real power here. Jewish religious leaders don't have the power to convict and execute criminals. That power rests exclusively with Pilate; or Herod, if it occurs in his district."

"So, how is this all going down? The Judas thing."

"Judas is offering to betray Jesus and turn him over to them...if the price is right."

"Thirty pieces of silver," Ben said, almost spitting out the words.

Ben suddenly realized that most of his knowledge of the Bible came from old films. For some reason he felt rather embarrassed by that. History always bored him. From what he remembered in school, he spent most of his time in those types of classes doodling rocket ships and airplanes.

"That's right. In their coinage, it's about 120 denarii."

Ben nodded. The very idea of betraying a fellow human being turned his stomach.

"Is that a lot of money?"

"Oh, it's about four months wages in this time period."

Ben was appalled.

"That's it? Why would he betray his friend for such a miserable amount of money?"

"Well, it's cold calculation on his part. He believes Jesus' days are numbered anyway. He thinks if Jesus really is the Messiah, then he can save himself, and if not, why not profit from the inevitable. There are others who believe Judas wanted Jesus to declare himself king, and openly rebel against Rome. But he refused to do that."

"Great guy."

Charlie did not have a comment. He looked around the immense courtyard, still taking in the scene. While he was still feeling an overwhelming sense of excitement being there, his sixth sense was warning him that time was no longer on their side.

"How much time do we have until he's arrested?"

Charlie shrugged, looking back to Ben.

"Like I told you before, we don't have a moment-by-moment historical account of what happens on this day. We have what we believe is a general order of events, but not hour-by-hour. But we don't have a lot of time."

Charlie looked north toward the ominous building that towered over the Temple. Ben followed his hard gaze. He spotted several Roman soldiers patrolling the battlements.

"What's that building? Is that part of the Temple too?"

"No. It's the Antonio Fortress. It's where the Roman garrison, that guards the city, reside. They built it there so it would overlook the Temple. If any rebellion were to be hatched against Rome, they knew it would be hatched right here."

"How many troops are in there?"

"Oh, around five hundred. As a matter of fact, their death squad is having their big meal for tomorrow."

"Why? What happens tomorrow?"

"Three convicts are to be crucified outside the city walls."

Ben thinks a moment and realizes what he's alluding to.

"Jesus is one of them, right?"

"No. He hasn't been condemned yet. Three other convicts are to be crucified; Dismas, Gesmas and Barabbas."

Ben's face contorted, his body shuddering when he tried to imagine once again what it must be like to be nailed to a cross. He glanced at his hands visualizing thick nails driven through them.

Charlie noticed Ben's revulsion but made no comment. He knew a great deal about crucifixion. He even wrote a detailed account of the crucifixion procedure, right down to what type of tools and wood they used.

"Nailed to a cross. Damn. But why crucifixion? Why not just poison them? Or hang them? There must have been less barbaric ways of executing criminals."

"That was the whole point of crucifixion, Ben. Governments of the day believed crucifying someone would terrify the public into being more obedient. It could take days for people to die on the cross. Even after death they would often leave the body on the cross for weeks as it rotted away while birds feasted on them."

"Sick bastards," Ben mumbled.

He caught several individuals watching and listening intently to them. He sighed in relief when he realized they had no idea what their conversation was about.

***

Tribune Macro marched through the great dining hall of the fortress. Long wooden tables and benches ran the length of the chamber. Stinking oil lamps hung from blackened crossbeams cast syrupy yellow-orange light upon the hunkered men eating their main meal of the day. The soldiers flung boisterous curses and boasts at each other. There was always a certain hard gaiety during the last meal of the day as the men let off steam. They sporadically roared for more food and wine from slaves who dashed from table to table. Garrison duty was often dull and routine, even in an inhospitable and querulous province like Judea.

Macro stopped at the last isolated table that stood apart from all the others. A dozen burly soldiers, six to a side, stooped over their food, shoveled heaping spoonfuls of gruel into their mouths or ripped off chunks of bread. Unlike the others, these men received extra rations for tomorrow for they had a special duty to perform. Crucifying condemned men was tough, backbreaking duty, and for that, extra calories often came in handy. Only the hardest of legionnaires were chosen for this particularly nasty duty. It took a special brand of brutality to nail men to crosses, and these men took great satisfaction in their jobs.

The men nodded to Macro respectfully as he passed by, and then turned back to their food and sour wine.

Licinius, Macros's second in command, appeared at the far end of the hall. His piercing blue eyes probed through the gloomy lighting and then stopped. He strode down the center lane and stopped before Macro.

"We have found them, Tribune."

Macro's sullen mood suddenly brightened. His one dark eye

lit up. His scarred face split into a gnarled smile. He jerked his head. Licinius turned about. Macro followed him out of the hall.

One of the men at the table gave a crooked jeer, shoving an elbow into the man next to him.

"They say a woman took his eye," he snorted through his mug, some wine spilling onto the table.

"His slave I've heard," his partner added.

"That's not all she took," a third said.

That forced a nasty chorus of laughter from the others.

"More wine!" the lead legionnaire barked.

CHAPTER IX

After checking to see Faith resting comfortably, Miriam returned to her loom. She did the work almost mechanically, wanting to keep busy so she would not obsess about her son walking into the lion's den of Jerusalem. As she painstakingly wove threads over and under the mass of vertical threads held in place by small stone weights, she prayed no one would recognize him. She found some hope in the fact that the city was overflowing with visitors for Passover Week. After all, who could spot one small boy among the tens of thousands? However, that reasoning did not reassure her. It would only take one person to spot him. After missing a thread, she gave up her weaving and sat back. She stared at the mass of red and yellow threads until they all seemed to merge into a burned orange color. Her troubled mind drifted off.

"Stop it! Stop it! You're hurting him!"

She recoiled with every vicious whip strike on her son cowering in the corner. Miriam clawed at Macro, grabbing his arm snapping back as he wielded that heavy whip. Daniel cried out for him to stop. But the more he begged the harder Macro's arm came down on him.

"Silence boy!"

Crack! Crack!

Finally, something inside Miriam snapped. She turned dazedly, her eyes locking on a large pitcher of wine that Macro had been drinking all day. She brought the heavy object down on the back of his head. He grunted and collapsed to the paved floor of his small villa outside of Joppa.

Miriam called to Daniel who looked up in shock. Seeing Macro reeling on the ground he rushed into her arms. She squeezed him tight, promising him he would be all right, when a massive hand seized her ankle. She fought to pull away but Macro's overwhelming strength finally brought her down on top of him.

"You bitch!" he cursed.

A pool of blood spread across the floor. She did not know if the wine jar, or his head striking the pavement, triggered it. Nor did she care.

His hand snatched her by the hair, jerking her head back so harshly that she blacked out. When she finally regained consciousness, she realized Daniel was shaking her. He helped her to stand. She teetered weakly. She saw her ripped clothes. She pulled her robe over her bruised body.

"Daniel, are you all right?" she gasped, fighting the waves of nausea slamming her.

"Yes, momma," he replied fearfully.

Then, she heard the furious animal curses. She looked down to see Macro reeling on the floor in an expanding pool of blood. His left eye was covered in it. His robe was drenched in red.

"My god!" she exclaimed.

She turned to Daniel, her eyes running down his right arm to the dripping knife he held. It was Macro's knife. She looked back up into her boy's pale face.

"Daniel, what did you do?"

"He was hurting you momma. He was hurting you."

"Oh my God," Miriam repeated in panic.

She seized the dripping blade and flung it to the floor. The long blade rang dully on the paved stones, a splatter of blood spraying out in a fan-like pattern.

She stared back down at Macro. He was rolling about in agony. His bloodied hands shoved between his thighs. Waves of panic surged in Miriam as her shocked brain tried to think of what to do. Fortunately, they were alone in the house as the rest of the staff was at the market. However, they could not remain in the house now. To stay would be a death sentence for the both of them.

Miriam pulled Daniel back away from Macro who appeared to have passed out. She looked around in desperation, thinking about what to do. They only had one option.

"Daniel, get some clothes together. But only what you can

carry. We have to get as far away as possible. Hurry!"

Daniel, now crying, dashed off.

Miriam stared down at Macro. His great chest heaved up and down, his body curled up into a defenseless fetal position. Her eyes turned back to the blade on the floor. For a moment she contemplated picking up the blade and killing the Roman. She scooped up the blade and hovered it over him. Her mind raced with the possibility of inventing a story of a thief breaking in and killing him. However, what if they refused to believe her? She even considered telling the authorities she killed him to spare her boy. But maybe they would not believe her. And if they did, where would that leave Daniel? She was all he had in the world. She finally knew there was only one thing to do.

Run.

Run as far away as they could.

When Daniel returned, he was carrying a leather sack that bulged with his meager belongings. She grabbed his hand and hurried to her quarters. It was a mad dash as she snatched her few possessions and shoved them into the same sack. Hurrying out she realized they had no money. Slaves had little to no money. However, she knew a secret hiding place where Macro kept some money. She grabbed everything she could.

"Come Daniel!"

They raced out of the villa as if the whole Roman army was after them. But where to go? She did not want to risk escaping by sea directly to Greece. A mother and child traveling alone would raise questions. She decided her best chance was Jerusalem. It was only twenty-five miles away. It was also large enough that they could hide out there until she could make better plans. But then land travel for a woman and child was equally dangerous.

After leaving the villa, the two made straight for the local synagogue where Miriam spoke to a kindly priest she had become acquainted with over the last two years. After recounting her horrific story, he agreed to help them get out of Joppa immediately.

Fortunately, a band of traders was headed for Jerusalem that very day. The priest approached Uri, a trader he knew well, and asked him to take them on as indentured servants. He agreed, but it took most of the money Miriam possessed for him to accept the great risk he was taking. Upon their arrival in Jerusalem, he found them a place to hide outside the city, promising to help them get away when it was safer.

Miriam shook off the horrific memory from only a few months earlier. She berated herself for their current predicament. She knew she should have left Judea after their frantic escape. They could have run off to other provinces. However, with limited money, and no one brave enough to guide them, a woman and child would have stood little chance traveling to her birth home in Macedonia. The more she thought about it the more she realized even those far off places might not have guaranteed their safety. Roman justice reached across the known world. How could the two of them stand against the power of an empire? She became despondent, again burying her face in her hands as she wept. If by sacrificing her life she could save her son, she would do so in an instant, but Tribune Macro would never be satisfied by such an offer. *Why must there be so much cruelty in this life?* she asked herself yet again, and then remonstrated herself for thinking such silly thoughts. Life was cruel and unforgiving. This was her lot, and there was no escaping from it.

From just outside the home, a woman's voice called out to her. She got up and peered cautiously through the raggedy curtain. She saw her neighbor holding a basket. She appeared to be alone. Miriam wiped her face and crept out the front entrance.

"Greetings, Rachel."

"Greetings, Miriam. I have some fresh bread for you. And some fresh dates."

Rachel was a middle aged, heavy-set woman with cherub cheeks and a gentle nature. She peeled the cloth off the basket, revealing several small loaves. The aroma of fresh bread seemed heaven sent. It had been several days since she had seen fresh bread.

She was down to one small, stale loaf.

"Oh, thank you. The bread smells delicious."

Rachel peered over Miriam's shoulder, looking at her home.

"You have visitors today?"

Miriam shook her head quickly.

"No. Why do you ask?"

"Oh, Hannah said she saw some people with you."

"Just travelers on their way to Jerusalem for Passover. They were lost," Miriam said.

"Oh. There seems to be a lot more this year than last. It's incredible the city can hold so many. Is Uri back from Joppa?"

"No. He will not be back for another week."

Miriam was getting increasingly nervous about Uri being away. While he was not the most reliable of men, she felt safer when he was around. He enjoyed a very modest living importing Greek wine. Unfortunately, he had a tendency to drink too much of his stock. However, she knew she should not complain too much since he had helped her escape Macro's vengeance. He had also promised to help Miriam and Daniel get out of Judea to some friends he had in Armenia.

"Where's Daniel? I have not seen him today."

"He's around. He's probably playing with Argos."

Faith could overhear the murmuring of voices from the bed. With great effort, she managed to sit up. She fought off the dizziness and numbness. Pushing off the edge of the bed, she managed to stand. A wave of dizziness struck again and she nearly lost her balance. Her hand reached out and braced itself against the wall. She took several deep breaths until her head cleared. She pushed the curtain aside and crossed the main room. She peeked out the window. She saw the two women talking. However, even if she understood Aramaic, their voices were still too low to understand what they were discussing. The woman finally walked away. Miriam, now holding the basket, turned around. She looked surprised to see Faith on her feet.

"Are you feeling better?" she asked.

Faith understood her by the inflection of her voice. She nodded that she did feel better. Then a wave of dizziness struck her again. She retreated to the bed and sat down. Miriam hurried over to her. She set the basket on the mattress.

Miriam motioned for Faith to lie back down. Faith shook her head. She realized if she lay down again she might not be able to get up.

"They're not back, are they?" Faith asked as she pointed out, and then turned her palms up.

Miriam shook her head. She offered Faith some of the food in the basket. At first, she declined, but Miriam insisted. Faith nibbled on the bread. It was warm and fresh. It tasted good. She had some difficulty swallowing but she managed after some effort.

"Thank you."

Then she tore into the bread ravenously and forced more down her throat. Then she looked at Miriam sheepishly.

"Sorry. Who knew time travel could make you so hungry."

After she finished, Miriam motioned for her to lie back down. Faith smiled pleasantly and shook her head. She was starting to feel some her strength return. Maybe not enough to go far, but enough to move about. She clasped Miriam's hand.

"I'm okay. Thank you, Miriam, for everything you are doing."

Miriam of course could not understand her. However, it was amazing how a person's tone and a few simple hand gestures could convey meaning no matter the language.

"I wish we could understand each other," Faith complained.

She saw Argos sitting curled up in the corner, but not the boy. She then noticed her son was not around.

"Where's your son?"

Miriam shrugged.

"Daniel. Where's Daniel?"

Miriam flashed fear as she pointed away.

"Daniel has taken them to the city."

Faith saw the trepidation in her eyes.

"Daniel...Daniel is with them?"

Miriam nodded.

Faith pointed at her, "You are worried about him?"

Miriam nodded again.

Faith finally understood that Miriam was hiding from something, or someone. It was a fear only a woman would sense in another woman. A surge of guilt struck Faith. Their arrival had brought some peril to this mother and child. This was not how things were supposed to happen. It was only now she realized even in this small way they were changing events.

"I'm so sorry we've become a burden to you, Miriam."

Miriam sat down next to Faith. She took Faith's hand and squeezed it.

***

Lucan leaned forward against the balustrade overlooking the Temple below. He fidgeted nervously like a condemned man. He did not like being in the great Antonio Fortress. Many men had entered this ominous building never to see sunlight again. He knew he had nothing to fear for the moment, but that did not drive away those jittery twitches. In fact, he was confident the gods were about to bless him with great riches for the important information he possessed. That is if the Tribune acted quickly.

Named after Herod's patron Mark Antony, the menacing fortress stood in the most strategic spot in the city. Constructed on a hundred and fifty foot rock escarpment, it secured the northern part of Jerusalem. Just as important, it commanded a sweeping view of the temple below.

Although Lucan had never explored the fortress before, he knew it was not strictly military barracks for the Roman garrison. It also boasted many luxury apartments for higher ranked officers, including an extensive network of baths. The Roman occupiers did not deny themselves any pleasures.

The view down to the temple was quite extraordinary. He had a clear view of the thousands of people scurrying about like busy ants. The dulled clamor from them was more like the squabbling of mindless animals. His eyes probed for the three strangers. But there were far too many people to make them out. He hoped the boy would still be there.

The baleful thud of approaching footsteps and clanking metal spun Lucan around. At first, all he saw was the dark figure of a man marching toward him. He looked immense. Lucan stumbled back into the balustrade. He swallowed with apprehension. His mounting fear did not vanish when Tribune Macro stepped into sunlight. He did not even notice his second-in-command following on his heels. Licinius was a leaner figure with a hawk-like visage. His deep mahogany tan made his stark, cobalt blue eyes shine even more ominously.

Macro glared down at Lucan with such intensity that he seemed to shrink inside. He felt a sudden need to relieve himself. He clenched his intestines, trying to stiffen his spine.

"You've found the boy? Talk! Have you found him or not?"

Macro's gravelly voice stung his body like a hundred blades.

Lucan's speech deserted him under the penetrating gaze.

"Well? Speak fool!" Licinius demanded.

Lucan's head twitched more than nodded.

"I have, Tribune. He's down at the Temple with two strangers."

Lucan exhaled in relief after getting the words out. Macro looked over him and gazed down to the court. His one good eye fixed back on Lucan.

"How can you be sure it's the boy I seek?"

"He must be the one. He's a boy of ten. Dark hair and features. The lobe of his left ear is missing," Lucan explained, his finger flicking at his own ear.

That seemed to satisfy Macro.

"What strangers does he travel with?" he asked.

Lucan could only shrug.

"And the woman?" he asked with more interest.

Lucan shrugged again.

Macro did not look pleased. When he grabbed Lucan, the informant felt the sudden urge to defecate again. He shuddered as the immense hands shook him. But he held his composure.

"I want the woman too."

It was not a request. It was a command that suggested something ominous if disobeyed.

Lucan thought fast. He had always been a man who could think on his feet when the situation demanded it of him. If he could find the woman as well, his reward would double, perhaps even triple.

"The, the boy will lead me to her," he stuttered.

Macro released Lucan and nodded. Lucan's knees nearly buckled, but he steadied up. He wiped the sweat from his brow.

Macro turned to Licinius.

"Go with him. Follow the boy wherever he goes. Find Miriam. Don't come back without them," he commanded.

"Yes, Tribune."

Licinius saluted.

"Follow me, Jew."

Licinius wheeled about and marched off without waiting for Lucan. Macro glared at Lucan, triggering a skin crawling convulsion that caused another explosion of sweat from his pores.

Lucan lurched after Licinius. Then he stopped and looked back to the tribune who was glaring down to the temple again. He briefly thought of going back to collect the one-half of the reward, but then thought better of it. He did not yet have the boy, or the woman. Besides, Macro was not the kind of man to pay until he had both in his grasp. He raced after Licinius.

***

Ben watched Charlie converse with a small group of who looked to be merchants. They had been waiting patiently for over an hour with no sign of Daniel. His thoughts turned to how his sister was doing. He was more convinced than ever that going there was a huge mistake. The whole thing seemed hopeless. Even if they could find him among the many tens of thousands of people, could he really perform the miracle Faith needed? If he could, would he? Then he checked himself. He was almost half believing in what they were doing. The idea that a man could cure an incurable disease with a wave of his hand struck him as utterly ludicrous. But here he was.

Charlie thanked the merchants and walked back to Ben.

"Did you learn anything?"

"About Jesus? No," Charlie said.

"What were you talking about?"

"I was asking them about their business and their lives. They've traveled all the way from Gaul for Passover. It's taken them months."

Ben flashed his displeasure. They did not undertake this incredibly dangerous trip so Charlie could brush up on his historical knowledge. When Charlie had spoken excitedly about coming back, Ben began to have misgivings that maybe he had an ulterior motive, besides saving Faith, in coming here. For a man like Charlie, a trip like this was a dream come true. What history professor would not give everything for such an experience? Of course, Ben knew if they jumped a thousand years into the future, he would have been totally on board for that trip.

Charlie seemed to read Ben's mind. He had to confess there were moments when the very idea of making this incredible journey filled him with overwhelming excitement. Reflecting over the tumultuous weeks leading up to today he had slept very little. Even his class work had suffered. There were a thousand and one details, and it had been up to him alone to pull it all together. Of course, Ben had his own tasks to perform. Every day he expected Ben to call him and tell him the trip was off for some reason or another. When Faith caught him several times prepping for the trip, he had to lie, telling her he was working on a new book. That was the most difficult part. He had never lied to her, but he realized nothing was to be gained by revealing their plan prematurely. So many things could have gone wrong. Thinking back, he realized getting this far had been nothing less than a small miracle.

The bigger miracle was yet to come, he hoped.

Ben was still staring at Charlie with reproach.

"What else can we do while we wait?" Charlie said.

Ben was going to say something when he spotted Daniel pushing through the throng with an elderly man in tow. The elderly man bowed his head politely.

"Greetings. Peace be upon you," he said.

Charlie said the same to him.

"Your name is Nicodemus?"

"I am Nicodemus. And to whom am I speaking?"

He had a deep, baritone voice that commanded your attention. Nicodemus was a stocky man, barely five eight. He looked to be middle age but could have been older. People aged faster in this harsher existence. His hair was a shocking white, while his full beard was streaked with gray. He wore the long, flowing robe of a priest.

Charlie introduced himself, and then Ben. Ben could only nod politely, frustrated that he could not follow their conversation. Nicodemus considered them with something approaching suspicion.

"Daniel has told me you are looking for a man named Jesus."

His statement was uttered in a guarded tone.

Charlie and Ben sensed his wariness. They needed to be careful. If they did not handle this properly, they might lose their one and only chance of finding the Nazarene.

"Yes, we are. It's very important that we find him. Do you know where he is?"

Nicodemus was quiet for a moment. His eyes gave the two

strangers a more detailed appraisal. There was something odd about them. Charlie's accent was unfamiliar to him. And their look and manner made him wary. He was a man who thought himself a fine judge of others.

"Why do you wish to meet him?"

Charlie looked to Ben.

"He wants to know why we want to meet him."

Ben nodded.

"I think he knows where we can find him."

"Yeah," Ben agreed. "I think you need to tell him why we're here, Charlie."

Nicodemus listened to their strange language, but it was unfathomable to him. Although he spoke several languages, including Latin and Greek, as well as a smattering of other local tongues, he could not follow anything of their conversation.

Charlie looked back to the priest. He was confident the man was the Nicodemus mentioned in Josephus's history of the period.

"It's been told that he has the gift to heal the sick. Is this true?"

Nicodemus nodded his head in understanding. While still guarded he appeared to relax now.

"Yes, it's true. He has healed the sick and the lame. It's been said he has even raised the dead."

Charlie sighed with relief. He then told Ben what he had said.

Ben was still skeptical, but hearing this man confirming Jesus as a healer gave him a small burst of hope.

"Nicodemus, we have come a very long way to see him." He then repeated to Ben what he had told the priest.

"That's one way to put it," Ben said.

"Please help us," Charlie pleaded.

Charlie and Ben held their breath.

Nicodemus stood there, contemplating their request. He saw the forlorn desperation in their eyes. There were unsettling rumors being whispered in the temple about Jesus after the episode the previous day. He had now attracted many enemies because of it. Powerful enemies. Could these men be associated with them? Could it be a trap?

"The man you seek has many enemies who wish to do him harm. How do I know you can be trusted?"

Charlie glanced over to Ben.

"He thinks we might betray him."

"Well, convince him we won't, Charlie."

"What could I say to you to make you trust us?" Charlie asked.

Charlie thought for a moment. Without possibly altering future events, he struggled to provide Nicodemus proof of their peaceful intentions.

"You are right about Jesus having foes within the Sanhedrin. Caiaphus himself is leader of the movement. Others have joined with him to take action against the Nazarene. I cannot tell you more than that without betraying a trust."

"No, that can't be true," he replied, aghast. "I know they are upset after the incident in the temple, but they would not act against him. How do you know this?"

Charlie thought quickly. Obviously, he could not tell him how he knew what was happening. Even if he did, he would likely never believe it.

"I heard about it from someone in the Sanhedrin. I cannot name him."

Of course, the paradox that the man standing before him was a historical source for his information could not be revealed.

Nicodemus's guard seemed to rise. He eyed the two strangers with suspicion.

Daniel tugged at the elderly man's robe. Nicodemus leaned down and Daniel whispered in his ear. Neither Charlie nor Ben could hear him. Nicodemus straightened.

"Daniel assures me you can be trusted."

Nicodemus then leaned down again and whispered to the boy. Daniel nodded eagerly.

"Wait here. I will take you to a place where you can meet him."

"The Garden of Gethsemane?" Charlie said softly.

Nicodemus's eyes darted around to be sure no one could listen in to their conversation. While the many people around the court looked toward the strangers with more than general curiosity, none were within earshot.

"How do know that's where we can find him?"

"I've been told he frequents the Garden."

"Yes, that is true. If what you say is true, we must be very cautious."

"Thank you," Charlie said.

Ben repeated what Charlie said.

Nicodemus turned and walked back into the temple.

Ben tugged on Charlie's arm. They still had to get Faith and bring her to Jesus. They could not possibly bring him to her.

"Now what do we do?"

"Daniel should take one of us to get Faith," Charlie said. "It might be best if you go."

Charlie did not explain why he believed that was the best course of action.

Ben simply nodded his head. In this case, he had to trust that Charlie knew best on how to proceed.

"Okay, I'll go and get her."

"Okay. Good. We'll meet up at the Garden of Gethsemane."

Charlie was thinking about what kind of shape she was in now. Was she conscious? Could she even travel?

"The Garden of Gethsemane?" Ben asked.

"Daniel knows where it is. Right?"

Daniel nodded.

Ben could see the distress in Charlie's tense expression. The ticking clock was not their enemy now. It was history itself.

"Don't worry, Charlie. I'll bring her."

"Okay, okay. But she might not be well enough to travel."

Ben wrestled with the problem. Carrying her for miles was not really an option.

"I have it. I'll buy a cart. Or horses.

"Good. Buy horses. Can you ride?" Charlie asked.

Ben nodded.

Charlie looked down to Daniel. He set his hand on the boy's shoulder.

"We need horses. Do you know where to buy them?"

Daniel nodded eagerly. He pointed to himself.

"Yes, you can buy a horse for yourself."

He reached into his tunic and produced a handful of gold aureus coins. He handed them to Ben.

"Daniel, after you get the horses, take Ben back to your home to get my wife, and then bring them to the meeting place."

Daniel nodded eagerly.

Ben leaned into Charlie and embraced him. It was probably the first time they hugged since the day Charlie married Faith. He pulled free.

"Charlie, one more thing. Be careful what you do, or say. This history has already been written. Okay? Remember why we came here."

Charlie looked surprised at what Ben had said. It was as if he were reading his thoughts somehow. He finally nodded.

"Hurry," he said.

Ben and Daniel rushed off.

Charlie carefully used his robe to hide the device from prying eyes. There was still time for what they had to do. He returned the device back to the inner pocket. He folded his arms and waited patiently for Nicodemus's return.

Daniel led Ben out of the court. They hurried down the same steps they had climbed just an hour earlier. Ben nearly tripped over his own robe several times as he descended the steep stairs. He cursed under his breath at having to wear such ridiculously awkward clothing. Reaching the main street, Daniel took Ben by the hand and headed straight into the Lower City.

CHAPTER X

Concealed behind a busy produce stand, Lucan nodded toward Ben and Daniel who were plunging through the bustling throng of people. He had almost missed them as they left the temple. He did not see the other stranger, but he did not care about him. The boy was all who mattered to him.

Licinius signaled the four legionnaires standing back in the shadows. They followed the two, keeping their distance.

The stench of fresh sewage was greater in the Lower City than in the rest of Jerusalem. The foul odor of animals hung in the air with a fog-like consistency that assaulted the senses. At least it did to Ben. He was constantly side-stepping piles of manure as they snaked left and right between shoddily-constructed limestone homes. Washed clothes dangled from ropes strung between the structures. They jumped clear of running children. The place reminded Ben of poor third world neighborhoods in his time.

Ben hurried to keep up with the boy. As he pushed his way past and around people, he suddenly realized how dependent he was on Daniel. If they somehow became separated, he would be completely helpless. He was confident he could get out of the city as there were multiple gates. But could he find Miriam's home again? He shuddered at the possibility of being lost two thousand years in the past. He quickened his pace, keeping Daniel right at his side.

Licinius seized Lucan, spinning him around. He glared at him.

"Miriam could not be living in the city. She would have been discovered long ago."

Lucan shrank under the centurion's penetrating gaze. He jerked his hands defensively, struggling for a logical reply.

"She must be in hiding somewhere. Someone must be protecting her."

He did not sound confident. He wondered again if Macro would pay him for the boy alone if the woman could not be found.

"Move faster. We're going to lose them," Licinius threatened.

People scattered out of their way. It was unusual for Romans to enter that section of the city. When they reached an intersection, they stopped and ducked between two homes. Daniel and Ben had stopped before a horse merchant. The boy was apparently negotiating with the owner. The owner led the two into a corral where a half dozen mares were feeding.

Licinius turned to one of his men.

"Horses," he commanded.

The soldier nodded and raced off.

"I only sell the finest horses," the owner boasted. "We have all manner of horse here. They are bred for every task a person might need. I've even sold horses to the Romans; and they only purchase the finest."

To Ben, the owner, Joseph, reminded him of every oily car salesman he had ever dealt with in the present. *Things never change*, he thought. Joseph was good natured, but pushy. His friendly grin revealed crooked yellow teeth in need of a good orthodontist.

When Ben just looked at him blankly, Joseph turned to Daniel.

"He's a stranger," Daniel explained.

The merchant nodded.

He looked Ben over a little more carefully now. His clothes were new, if a bit odd. The material was unlike any he had encountered before. It was not wool, or even linen. His sandals were new as well, but the straps did not look like ordinary leather. *So what*, he thought. *If his money was good, he had no concern for his identity. In fact, him being a stranger, he could now sell the horses at a premium.*

Daniel looked at Ben and waved his hands at the horses.

"Oh, you want *me* to pick them out. Great."

Ben walked around the corral, dodging the occasional dung heap. He checked out each of the animals. The last thing he wanted to do was buy a lame horse. Remembering a particular summer on his uncle's farm, he tried to recall what he had been told on what constituted a good horse.

Ben checked the horses' gums. Three of them had deep red or purple gums instead of pink. He then checked their feet. The three with bad gums also had cracked feet. He shook his head at Joseph. The salesman frowned, realizing he was dealing with a man who knew something about horses. Ben finally narrowed it down to two horses. He pointed them out.

Joseph told them what he wanted for them.

"He wants a thousand sesterii for the horses," Daniel said.

Ben froze. He only understood a couple words, sesterii, and thousand. What the hell was a sesterii again? His mind raced back to the day Charlie gave a boring lecture on Roman money. It was one of the few times he remembered paying attention. Sesterii was the smallest Roman silver coin. Then came the quinarius. That was worth two sesterii. Then came the denarius, also silver. That was worth four sesterii. The last coin was the aureus. That was the main gold coin minted by the Romans. One aureus was worth one hundred sesterii. He looked at the eight aureus coins in his hand. Other than a couple silver denarius coins, he was short two hundred. When he looked up, he saw Daniel and the horse trader staring at him.

"Tell him I'll give him eight hundred for both. I also want saddles and rigging."

Ben counted out the money coin by coin so Daniel could see them. His eyes bulged bigger than the shiny gold coins shimmering in the sunlight.

Daniel passed on Ben's counteroffer. The merchant protested that the horses were worth more. Ben realized that salesmen are the same the world over, even two thousand years in the past.

Not having ten Aureus coins, Ben decided he had to play hardball. He threw up his hands, and started to put the money away.

"Let's go Daniel. We'll go find someone else to buy horses."

While Daniel could not understand what Ben had said, the

meaning was all too clear. The two started to walk away. They were just clearing the corral when the merchant had a change of heart.

"Wait!"

"Thank God," Ben muttered to himself.

There was no time to search Jerusalem for another horse dealer. Ben and Daniel turned around, but did not start back immediately. They just stood there waiting for the merchant to make up his mind.

"You take advantage of my good nature," the merchant said. "Eight hundred and fifty."

Ben looked down to Daniel. Daniel motioned with his fingers what the merchant wanted. The boy now took over negotiations. He shook his head and held up eight fingers.

Joseph grunted and finally assented. The merchant ordered one of his stable boys to prepare the horses while he provided a bill of sale. Ben signed his name and had the silly thought that maybe two thousand years from now someone might find the contract. The merchant shrugged at the oddly scribbled name. He eagerly pocketed the eight gold coins.

Licinius was growing irritable waiting for the soldier to return with the horses. Macro would be livid if the two got away. He would not just take his fury out on Lucan, but him as well. Being shipped off to some remote outpost in North Africa was not a fate he would visit on his worst enemy. He was about to move in and arrest the both of them rather than risk the two getting away when the soldier rejoined them.

"The horses are ready."

Licinius signaled for them to retreat out of sight as Ben and Daniel prepared to mount their steeds.

The first thing Ben noticed when he was about to mount up was the saddles did not have stirrups. How could he know they would not actually be invented for several hundred years?

The stable boy helped Daniel onto the smaller horse. He grabbed the reins and beamed with excitement. He was thrilled to own his own horse.

"It's been a while," Ben said to himself.

Ben tried to launch himself onto the horse and could not make it. The stable boy grinned mischievously at his awkward attempt. When he caught Ben's scowl, the smile dissolved. He hurried over and cupped his hands. Ben placed his left foot into the hands and pushed himself up. Somehow, he swung his right leg over the saddle. He nearly fell over the other side before the stable boy seized his arm. Daniel and the stable boy laughed.

"Thanks," Ben muttered.

He grabbed the reins. *Now what?* he thought. He tugged the reins one way and then the other. The irritated horse twisted its head back to him and snorted with derision. Ben then remembered one of the first rules of riding.

Let the horse know who the boss is.

"Okay, Daniel. Let's go," Ben said.

Daniel kicked his heels into his horse's flank and the animal took off at a slow trot. Ben did the same, digging his sandaled feet into the horse's side. Nothing. He then gave it a stronger kick and the horse jerked forward. Ben hung on for dear life as he nearly lost his balance again. The horse trotted after Daniel as Ben bounced up and down in the hard leather saddle. As he was about to pass Daniel when he pulled back on the reins, slowing the horse.

People scattered as the two rode by them. They did not see Licinius, Lucan, and the soldiers hiding in the deep shadows between two homes. They waited a spell, and mounted their steeds. They followed them at a distance.

Daniel was overjoyed at having his own horse. He proudly held his head high, his back stiff and straight. Ben wanted to go faster but he was not confident enough to push the animal. After passing out of the Lower City, they exited the Essene Gate. Then after clearing the city, they turned north.

***

Nicodemus led Charlie through a confusing network of dark passages deep under the temple. The murmur of priests praying echoed through long corridors lit by flickering torches. The sudden blow of a blade striking bone interrupted the terrified bleating of lambs. The sharp metallic odor of copper from the many slaughtered animals filled Charlie's nostrils until he thought he might gag. To fight the reflex, he tried breathing through his mouth.

"Are you feeling unwell?"

"I'm fine," Charlie lied.

"The smell of blood does have some getting used to," Nicodemus explained. "It even overwhelms me at times."

Several times priests appeared in the corridor. Not recognizing the strange man, Nicodemus quickly explained that Charlie was a visiting cleric from Cappadocia, a distant Roman province. Nicodemus pulled Charlie away after the exchange of a few pleasantries.

"You were right. There are whispers that the Nazarene is in great danger. Caiaphus himself seems to be behind it. What else do you know about the danger to him?"

He kept his voice low so only Charlie could understand him.

Charlie thought about Ben's warning and dismissed it. Events were about to spin out of control. He had checked his remote stealthily when Nicodemus walked ahead of him. There was still plenty of time to get back to the Eight-ball. The real enemy were the forces gathering to arrest Jesus in a matter of hours. The moment they arrest him, his one chance to save Faith would be lost. Probably forever.

"He will be betrayed by one very close to him, Nicodemus."

Nicodemus stopped suddenly. Charlie had to check himself from bumping into the priest. The flicker of a torch cast a deep yellow-orange glare over the man's distraught face. His beard became living fire. His wide-open eyes shone like two tiny suns.

"How do you know all this?"

"I just know. It has all been arranged."

Charlie's plain, understated tone gave the man pause.

"He must be warned."

"Nicodemus, he already knows."

Charlie's words confused Nicodemus. Finally, he turned and led Charlie back into the shadows.

"Come along then. We must hurry."

***

If anything, the stream of people entering Jerusalem had increased from earlier in the day. Daniel and Ben had slow-going fighting the flood of people and carts entering the city. After exiting the Essene Gate, Ben had planned to gallop back to the house to get Faith. But that was impossible. They could barely make headway. Ben cursed at them to move out of their way to no effect. The frustration in not being able to communicate with Daniel to find a faster route back to the house exasperated him. Time was becoming their enemy.

As they maneuvered their horses through the throng, Ben saw Daniel grinning from ear-to-ear at having his own horse. He wished he could share that excitement. The boy suddenly reared up and pointed ahead. Ben understood what he meant. The massive flow of people was beginning to thin now. Daniel snapped his feet into his horse's side. Ben followed suit. They jerked forward, picking up speed.

Licinius and his men were a good hundred meters behind the two. The man and boy still did not suspect they were being followed.

"Faster," Licinius barked, kicking his heels into the steed.

They hurried on after them.

CHAPTER XI

Miriam pressed the sponge against the back of her neck, releasing a river of water down her scarred back. The cool water triggered both pain and relief. Her mass of bruises had finally begun to heal after so many weeks of discomfort. However, she knew they would probably never disappear. Macro's frequent whippings had been too brutal, too precise, for them to heal completely. She dipped the sponge into the bucket and once more squeezed it against her back. She arched her back and sighed with relief.

"Oh my," Faith muttered.

Miriam spun around to see Faith framed in the doorway. Faith had a look of horror as she stared at the nasty welts scarring Miriam's bare back. Miriam quickly jerked her robe back up, hiding her wounds. The two women stared at each other awkwardly. Miriam flashed embarrassment and then shame as she secured the robe about her body.

Faith was aghast at the sight. She also felt guilty at her intrusion. She almost retreated into the back room but thought better of it.

"I'm sorry. I should not have-," she started to say.

Miriam recovered her composure and turned away. Faith stepped cautiously forward. She forgot her paralyzing weakness for a moment.

"My God, who did this to you, Miriam?"

While Miriam could not understand the words Faith had spoken, she understood the question.

Faith lifted Miriam's chin and looked at her. Miriam's haunted face was as tortured as her back. She now understood why Miriam had reacted with so much panic when the Roman soldiers rode by. She was hiding from them. Faith also realized that by coming here they had put her and Daniel in great danger.

"Who could do something like this to another person?" she said to herself.

Faith watched Miriam shuffle around the room, putting things away. They finally sat down at the table and stared at each other. Faith grimaced with frustration at their inability to communicate. From the look Miriam gave back, she shared her irritation.

Faith reached across the table and took her hand. She pointed to the wedding band on Miriam's finger.

"Do you have a husband, Miriam?"

Faith pointed to her own ring.

Miriam shook her head. However, Faith suspected she had been but he was no longer around. Dead possibly. Faith then noticed the remnants of rope burns on her wrists. Why had she not seen them before? She realized she had been too absorbed in her own problems to notice them.

"Are you in hiding, Miriam? Is someone after you?"

It was all making sense now. Miriam and her son were on the run, hiding from the Romans. Could they be escaped slaves? She knew slavery was a very common during this time. From what she had recalled from some of Charlie's lectures she had attended over the years, the Romans would enslave countless thousands after conquering their lands. However, she knew even non-Roman societies had slavery. Shockingly, families would even sell some of their children if times were hard enough. Staring into Miriam's melancholy eyes, she wished she knew her story.

Faith caressed her hand.

"I'm so sorry, Miriam. We never should have come here. It was wrong of us to put you and your boy in danger."

Her heart poured out to Miriam, wishing she could help her somehow. Maybe when Charlie and Ben returned they might be able to do something for them. It was the least they could do considering how much they had helped them.

The clatter of approaching horses jerked Miriam out of her chair as if someone had slapped her. They both looked to the window. The rapid clip clopping was getting nearer. Miriam stood frozen in place, her chest heaving. Faith got up and crept toward the window.

"No. Don't," Miriam gasped.

Faith waved that she would be careful. She eased up to the window and cautiously peered through the curtain. Through the crack she spotted the approaching horses. Then she recognized Ben and Daniel riding them. She snorted when she realized Charlie was not with them. She looked back to Miriam.

"It's Daniel and Ben."

Miriam rushed to the window just as the two guided their horses up to a stunted tree. They dismounted and tied the horses off. They hurried toward the house.

Miriam dashed out to her boy and grabbed him roughly as if she were about to slap him. Then she pulled him in and embraced him so tightly that he gasped.

"Daniel, what did I tell you about going to the city? It's too dangerous. You know they are looking for us."

When Ben saw Faith standing in the doorway, he was appalled. Her face was deathly pale. Her once shiny, coiled hair hung limply. Her body seemed shockingly frail.

Faith reacted to his shocked facial expression and wondered how awful she must appear to him. He hurried over and hugged her. She felt feeble in his arms, but at least she was back on her feet. It meant she could travel. When he parted, she grabbed his arm. Her fingers were clammy.

"Where's Charlie, Ben. Is he all right?"

"Yeah, he's fine, Faith. We found the man who will take us to Jesus. We're going to meet them," Ben said. For a moment, Ben realized he was beginning to believe this might work.

Faith's eyes brightened with hope. Ben felt strength return to her body.

"Are you sure?"

Ben nodded.

Miriam ignored Ben and Faith as she dragged Daniel back

inside the house.

"What were you thinking? What if someone had seen you? You promised me you would stay away from the city."

Daniel looked up, innocent and brash as day. Unlike his mother, he had the naive bravery that comes from being young.

"I wanted to help them, Momma. It's okay. No one saw us."

Ben and Faith followed them into the house.

Once safely inside, Miriam's pent up fury quickly melted into relief. He was home again. That was all the mattered now.

"We have to go now if we're going to see him. Are you strong enough to travel?" Ben asked.

Faith nodded, "I'm fine. Really."

Ben looked at her. How could she have changed so much in the span of a few hours? Clearly, the time displacement of two thousand years had accelerated her illness. Had it done something to him or Charlie? He did not feel different. At least not in any way he was consciously aware. Then he pushed it all aside. They could deal with that problem later.

"Then we should get going. The clock is ticking."

Ben flashed the device to her. Daniel and Miriam saw it too. The shiny blue-gray metal case, and blinking lights, stunned them. When Ben realized what he had done, he shoved the device back into his robe.

"Ben, there's something you need to know," Faith said softly, pointing to their benefactors.

Ben seemed not to hear her. He turned to Daniel.

"Will you take us to the meeting place?"

Ben pointed out the door to their horses.

Daniel nodded eagerly.

Miriam sensed what Ben wanted of her son. She asked Daniel a question.

"I have to take them to meet Nicodemus, Momma."

Miriam shook her head adamantly.

"No. You're not leaving here."

"I have to. They won't find him without me."

Miriam dragged her boy into the corner where they engaged in an intense argument.

"What is it, Ben?"

"Daniel has to guide us to the meeting place. I won't be able to find it. But I don't think she wants him to take us."

"She doesn't. Ben, I think she's on the run."

"On the run? What do you mean?"

"I think they may be escaped slaves. At least she is I think."

Ben looked back to the mother and son. Daniel was not backing down from his mother. He kept shaking his head and pointing at Ben and Faith. Everything depended on that boy now. The Garden of Gethsemane was all he knew. From what he recalled from Charlie's boring lectures, it was located near Jerusalem. They did not have time to go searching for it if Charlie was right about Jesus' impending arrest.

"Faith, I'll never find this place alone. We need him."

Miriam turned away from Daniel and strode over to them. She pointed to the doorway.

"You must go now. Please. Please go."

Even without Charlie's translation, they knew what she meant. Faith grabbed Ben's arm.

"She wants us to go, Ben."

"I know, I know. But we're so close, Faith. We could be there in an hour."

Daniel came over and grabbed her mother's robe.

"Momma, I have to help them. They'll never find it without me."

She shook her head adamantly, and stood between her son and the strangers.

"No. It's too dangerous Daniel. If they find you, you know what will happen."

Ben slapped his palms together in a prayer form.

"Please Miriam. He has to take us. I'll look after him. I

promise. Here. Take these."

He displayed several silver coins. Miriam's dark eyes considered the badly needed treasure. The money could feed them for a month. It might even be enough to get out of Judea.

"I'll bring him back. You have my word. I won't let anything happen to him."

She struggled to make a decision when there was the heavy clatter and neighing of approaching horses. All eyes shifted toward the doorway. Miriam scrambled to the window and shuddered at the sight of men dismounting from their horses.

"Oh, no! No! Oh God!"

Miriam went into a panic. She seized her son. Her startled eyes darted about the room. She backed into the corner, dragging her son along, her arms tight around his chest.

Licinius led his men toward the hovel. He signaled with a hand gesture and two of the soldiers darted around to cover the rear of the place. Licinius strode toward the front door.

Faith and Ben spun about when the door crashed open violently. Licinius' silhouetted form filled the opening, blocking out the light. His eyes gazed upon the four figures. He stepped inside, followed by Lucan, and the other two soldiers.

Faith never witnessed such terror in someone's face before. Miriam's eyes nearly bolted from their sockets. Her arms squeezed her son so tight into her body he fought to breathe. Argos hurried in front of Miriam and Daniel and growled fiercely.

Licinius' eyes examined each person carefully. He then focused his gaze on Miriam and Daniel, recognizing them. He pointed a crooked finger at them like a dagger.

"You're to come with me," Licinius stated.

Miriam recovered her senses and released Daniel. She stepped up to Licinius. With tears rolling down her cheeks she clasped her hands together tight, offering them up.

"Please, just take me. Let my son go. He's just a boy, Licinius."

Ben and Faith could only watch helplessly. While they could not decipher the words, they could understand what was happening. Ben wondered if they meant to take Faith and him as well.

Licinius was having none of this. His grating reply was harsh.

"No. Tribune Macro wants both of you."

"They've come for them, haven't they, Ben?"

"Yeah, I think so."

"We have to do something. Offer them money."

Ben stepped forward. He raised his hands when the two soldiers reached for their swords. He flashed the silver, he had offered to Miriam a minute before, to Licinius. Licinius looked at the bribe, and angrily slapped the silver away. The coins flew across the room.

Argos suddenly launched himself at Licinius, locking his powerful jaws on his bare arm. The centurion exploded, grabbing the dog with his free hand. He growled in pain, and with a tremendous effort flung the dog across the room. Argos launched himself again, but Licinius was ready now. He whipped his short sword free and with a single flash of metal killed the brave animal. A jet of blood shot across the ground.

Daniel cried out and threw himself at Licinius. He windmilled his fists impotently against the Roman's chest. Lucan reached over and grabbed the boy, tossing him to the ground. Miriam screamed and clawed at Licinius' face now. He caught one slashing nail across his cheek, but he quickly wrapped her up in his strong arms. He shoved her into the arms of one of his men.

Watching this inflamed Ben in a way that shocked him. Before he knew what he was doing, he threw a badly aimed punch at Lucan but only caught him in the side of his head. Lucan squealed like a stuck pig, covering his bruised ear. Before Ben could deliver a better-aimed blow, he felt the sharp tip of Licinius' bloody sword push into his chest. Gasping for air Ben realized the futility of fighting these highly trained soldiers. He stumbled back, raising his hands up meekly.

"All right. Take it easy, asshole. Just relax. We give up," he muttered.

Faith pressed into Ben's arms. All of a sudden, the little strength she had regained turned to water. This was all too much in her weakened condition.

"Ben, we have to do something."

Daniel was down at Argos' side crying. The dog was nearly cut in two. A river of blood had pooled under the brave animal. Daniel looked up at the Roman, his face a mask of black rage. He cursed his impoverished strength to avenge his beloved companion.

Licinius still had his dripping sword pointed at Ben.

"Who are you?"

Miriam interceded, standing between them.

"They are strangers in Judea, Licinius. They don't understand you. Please let them go. They have nothing to do with any of this."

Lucan gazed down greedily at the silver coins scattered across the ground. He dropped to his knees and scooped them up. He shoved them into his tunic. Then he saw Licinius staring at him expectedly. He reluctantly handed them over to the Roman. Looking down, Lucan was the first to realize Daniel was missing.

"The boy! He's gone!"

Licinius looked around the room.

The boy had vanished.

In the confusion, Daniel, bleary eyed and angry, had scrambled out of the house. He raced to his horse, untied the reins, and leaped into the saddle. He whipped the horse about, and took off down the road just as Licinius burst out of the hovel.

"AFTER HIM!"

Licinius flung the two soldiers, who had been watching the rear, toward their tied up horses.

"If he gets away I'll whip the hide off you! Go!"

The soldiers raced to their mounts and took out after the boy.

Licinius returned inside. He glared at the four of them.

Trickles of blood ran down his arm and cheek. He was tempted to kill all of them and inform Macro they resisted. But what would stop one of his own men, or Lucan, from telling Macro the truth? He slowly took control of his anger and then jabbed his sword at them.

"Take all of them," he commanded.

The two soldiers stepped forward. They grabbed Ben and Faith.

"Ben," Faith gasped.

Ben stepped forward. How could he make him understand they had nothing to with this situation? He hated the idea of these men taking Miriam and the boy, but he realized there was nothing he could do for them. They were in a hopeless situation.

"Please, we've done nothing. Please let us go."

Licinius jerked his head to his men. They dragged Faith and Ben out. Licinius grabbed Miriam roughly by her hair and wrenched her outside.

A soldier bound Ben's wrist until the biting rope drew blood. He then hooked the other end of the rope around Licinius' saddle. One of the other soldiers hoisted Faith on to the saddle, and pulled her tight into his arms. He fondled her roughly, and laughed when she weakly fought back. However, her fragile strength was nothing but a source of amusement to the Roman.

"You bastard," Ben cursed.

Licinius jerked the rope holding Ben and he nearly fell to his knees. Ben got the message. He stopped resisting for the time being. The other soldier lifted Miriam up to Licinius. He pulled her up sidesaddle and hooked his bleeding arm around her waist. He barked a command and they road back to Jerusalem.

CHAPTER XII

Daniel bounced about crazily as his horse tore down the teeming road. Travelers howled panic stricken, scattering out of his way. Frightened farm animals screeched and dashed into the countryside, chased by their owners. The boy, pitched far forward, frantically gripped both the reigns and the horse's mane. He had no control over the galloping horse. The moment he slammed his sandals into its side, he just hung on for dear life.

"Get out of the way! Look out!" he yelled repeatedly.

Several times, he thought they would crash into a group of peasants or barrel into a cart. His only response was to crunch his eyes shut and pray, trusting the horse to avoid the obstacles. The excited horse leapt a small donkey cart, nearly flinging Daniel off.

After several hair-raising minutes, Daniel started to regain control of the animal. He felt his body meld into the saddle, his tightening thighs gaining a grip. His head leveled out to the point where he felt confident enough to glance back. His eyes nearly bolted out of their sockets.

The Roman cavalry hurtled toward him like two nightmarish phantasms. They bowled over everyone in their path—man, woman, child, or beast. He could practically feel their hot breath on his neck. He dug his heels into the horse's flanks again and it surged even faster. In the distance, he could see Jerusalem getting nearer. That was the last place he wanted to go.

He stole another glance back. One of the soldiers had caught up, his hand reaching out to grab him. Daniel spasmed, jerking the reigns over. His horse made a violent bank to the right and dashed down an embankment. The soldiers, caught off guard by the sudden move, continued on for a few moments before pulling up. They swung their horses about and continued the chase.

Coming up fast were a mass of fig trees. Daniel drove straight for them, ducking under their claw-like branches that threatened to dislodge him. Once he was out of sight, he turned right to lose himself in the forest. The relentless thud of his pursuers' horses began to fade. Realizing his horse was nearly done, he slowed and ducked behind a clump of trees. Daniel's chest heaved, and his lungs burned after the frantic pursuit. He swayed from side to side in the saddle, peering through the branches for his pursuers. But there was no sign of them. Believing he was safe, if only for the moment, his thoughts turned to his mother and the others. What was happening to them? Maybe he should not have run away. But he knew there was nothing he could have done for them. His only hope now was to find the other stranger. Maybe he could help him somehow.

The two soldiers pushed through the grove of fig trees. They separated and completed a fruitless search for the boy. Meeting back at the tree line, they gazed in all directions with frustration and apprehension. They knew Licinius' punishment for letting a boy best them would be great. They were about to plunge into the grove yet again when one of them spotted a rider on the road.

"Wait! Look there!"

They galloped after the rider. Their swords flashed in the sunlight.

"Halt!"

The two soldiers converged on the rider, swords ready. The rider stopped and turned. The young man on the horse looked surprised. He was not the boy they had been chasing. He was much older. The soldiers growled and galloped on after another rider farther up the road. The young man grinned. He glanced down at caravan of goat carts struggling to get back onto the road. He nodded toward one of them. A small hand poked up between a half dozen goats. It gave a brief wave and then ducked back out of sight.

Daniel huddled low, hidden amidst the straw and manure in the crowded cart. He ignored the irritated goats shifting about, banging into him. He knew he was safe, at least for the moment. His mind then raced back to his mother. He knew she would be taken to Tribune Macro. He shuddered at what he would do to her.

After settling in the second floor room in the Lower City home, Jesus shocked his followers when he started to wash each of their feet. He began with Simon. A man of great passion, he protested this humbling act. He reached down to stop him.

"This is beneath you, Master," he said.

"An act of kindness is beneath no one, Peter."

Simon's eyes shifted to the others who were equally confused. He awkwardly sat back, and allowed him to wash and dry his dust-covered feet. Peter was the next disciple to have his feet washed. He also thought of objecting, but then accepted the kind act without a word of dissent. The other disciples uttered no words as Jesus washed their feet one by one. By the time Jesus finished the last of them, the homeowner's servants brought in their dinner.

The thirteen sat on the floor before the long, eighteen-inch high table that ran the width of the rented room. Jesus sat in the middle with his faithful companions to either side. The open windows facing the street allowed the clamorous tumult of the city to fill the room. Their meal before them was simple fare—fresh bread, assorted fruits, soup, and some wine.

The mood while they ate was almost jovial. Their concerns about returning to the city after the incident in the temple had passed. They joked that their concerns had been overblown. Then their master's calming voice interrupted the pleasant conversation.

"I tell you the truth that one of you here will betray me."

The twelve looked aghast, glancing at each other. Faces that moments ago were content twisted into shock and surprise. Jesus had not looked at anyone in particular when he spoke the stunning words.

"Not one of us!" Andrew exclaimed.

"No. No, of course not," others added.

Jesus looked left and then right. His face showed no emotion. It was strangely placid.

"It will be one of the twelve who has shared bread with me. The Son of Man will go, but woe is to the one who betrays him. It would have been better had he not been born."

The disciples turned to each other, gazing into their companions' faces as if expecting to detect some revelation of guilt. However, they found no answers with their taut faces.

Peter, impulsive as always, jerked to his feet, his knees striking the table. He ignored the sharp sting of pain. He did not address his master, but John, who sat alongside him.

"Ask the master which one he means."

Peter, always the first to act, was ready to strike down the betrayer.

John, sitting to the master's right, leaned in toward him.

"Master, who is this person? Name him so all will know."

Jesus tilted his head to a man on his left. His eyes seem to bore into his tightly-drawn face.

Judas, who had acted as surprised as the others, reacted with alarm, throwing up his hands. He reacted to the seething anger in Peter's face.

"Surely, it is not I, Master," Judas said, his face paling.

"Judas?" Simon said.

Murmurs of 'No', 'Not Judas' rippled through the room.

Jesus waited until the protests ended.

"Yes, it is you." Jesus' words were spoken quietly, barely above a whisper. "Do what you will and do it quickly."

Before anyone could react to the incredible accusation, Judas rose from the table and quickly hurried from the room. Peter and Simon made a move to pursue him but Jesus raised his hand.

"No, Peter. Simon, leave him. What is done is done."

Jesus returned to the food before him. He took one of the honey cakes and calmly ate it. The disciples became distressed, chattering among themselves. If what he had said was true, staying in the house was dangerous. Even spending the night in the city was risky.

"Master, we must leave at once," John suggested.

"Yes, we must. There is still much to do before my end."

Jesus and the eleven filed out of the room, descending upon the narrow staircase. On the first floor they met their host who had freely offered the room to them. He sensed their agitation.

"You are leaving so soon? Was not everything to your liking?" he inquired.

"Everything was fine. Many thanks for your generosity and hospitality, Abraham. Peace be upon you," Jesus said.

Jesus walked out. The disciples also thanked their host as they hurried after him. Once on the street their restless eyes darted left and right, expecting some danger to suddenly manifest itself. However, all they saw were fellow citizens going about their business. There was no sign of Judas.

"Where should we go?" Mark asked.

"We must return to Galilee. We will be safe there," Andrew suggested.

"We will go to the Gardens," Jesus said.

"Will that be safe?" Thomas asked.

"We must go farther away. The Gardens are too close to the city," James urged.

"We will go to the Gardens," Jesus said calmly.

The disciples looked at each other nervously. With the issue settled, they followed their master out of the city.

***

Miriam hung limp on Licinius' saddle. Barely conscious, she did not feel his rough, callused hands around her waist. Her eyes fell upon the darkening road in a monotonous up and down motion. Travelers looked up as they passed by. Their forlorn faces were just blurs to her.

Licinius sneered back at Ben who was stumbling to keep up. The twanging rope, cutting off circulation to his numbed hands, repeatedly jerked at Ben's arms, threatening to rip them out of their sockets.

Ben stewed in agony. His wrists burned. His straining

shoulders ached horribly from every jolt of the horse dragging him. His tortured legs seemed ready to desert him with every step. The sandals were practically useless now. His toes seemed to hit every loose rock on the road. Lightning bolts of pain shot into them and up his legs. Looking ahead, he managed a grim smile at Jerusalem looming up before them. He did not know what their fate was going to be, but at least this part would be over soon.

Ben stole a look back to his sister. Faith appeared to be unconscious, her raggedy body only supported by the strong, groping hands of the soldier. Her stringy hair matted her face. He could not even tell if she was alive.

"Faith," he called out. His voice was ragged. His throat seemed choked in dust. He growled to clear his voice.

"Faith!"

"No talking!"

Ben tumbled forward when Licinius jerked on the rope. Ben just managed to regain his balance. He glared up at the sneering centurion. Ben steeled his nerves. Whatever would happen, he was going to have to be strong for Faith and Miriam. But at least Daniel got away, if only for the moment. Maybe he could find Charlie. But even if he could find him, what could Charlie do for them now. All hope seemed lost.

***

After leaving Jerusalem by the Shushan Gate, Nicodemus led Charlie to the Garden of Gethsemane. It was a rather pleasant journey even under the dire circumstances that was awaiting the man Charlie had traveled back two thousand years to see.

With every step, an overwhelming sense of great anticipation, but also foreboding, seemed to dull Charlie's other senses. Sights, sounds, and smells faded in his mind. His beating heart quickened as they neared their destination. He desperately wished to rush ahead and get there as quickly as possible. Time was not on their side. If history was right, the Sanhedrin temple guards might already be on their way to arrest Jesus. However, Nicodemus' days of hurrying about were long over. Several times Charlie tried to quicken his step only to find himself waiting for the elderly man to catch up. He would apologize and they would proceed at a more leisurely, but also maddeningly, slow pace.

Nicodemus pressed Charlie continuously about him, Ben, and Faith. Of course, Charlie would not tell the man who he was, or how they arrived there. In the weeks leading up to their trip, he had created a simple biography for himself, and even for Ben and Faith, for such a moment. He explained they were living in Armenia when someone told him of the miracles Jesus had performed. He had spent many weeks traveling there to meet him in the hope He might heal his wife.

"I see," he said simply.

Charlie could see the man did not entirely believe his story. He questioned Charlie on how a recent arrival could know so much about the danger facing the Nazarene. This man seemed to know far more than a stranger should, having just arrived from such a far off land.

"There are many things I wish I could tell you, my friend. But you'd likely not believe my story. Is it far yet?"

"It's not far."

After crossing the river, they entered in the Kidron Valley. In the distance, Nicodemus pointed out the Mount of Olives. It was so named for the many olive groves that grew on the slopes. In the future, the mount would be the site of thousands of Jewish graves. But for now all Charlie could see was a sea of green trees swaying gently in the breeze.

They followed a narrow, upward path until they came to a rise. Below them was the Garden of Gethsemane. Paved paths moved between green olive trees. Carefully-laid stones lined the curving paths.

"Follow me," Nicodemus said.

He started down what appeared to be the main path.

The intense, almost painful, anticipation Charlie had been feeling since they left Jerusalem finally overwhelmed him. He froze, unable to move. In the next few minutes, answers to questions that had gnawed at him might be answered. When Nicodemus realized Charlie was not following him, he came back.

"Is there something wrong? Are you well?"

He could see the great anxiety plaguing the stranger. He placed a hand on Charlie's arm. Charlie looked into the man's face. The reassuring blue eyes seemed to smile at him.

"Yes, I'm fine. It's just that I've come such a long way to see him."

"I understand. Please. All will be well. Come."

Taking Charlie by the arm, he led him down the path into the shaded garden.

To the surprise of the disciples, the one-mile journey out of the city to the Gardens of Gethsemane was uneventful. At every turn they expected soldiers to descend upon them. But no one molested them. After exiting the Dung Gate, they turned north across the Kidron Valley. The orange sky was slowly dissolving into a majestic purple. The beginnings of stars began to prick the sky to the east. The mild warmth of the day was giving way to the cooling of the night. On any other day, the trek would have been a pleasant one, but the air was heavy with apprehension. Even the safety of being outside the city did not squelch their sense of foreboding. They had whispered to each other about Judas' betrayal and what it meant. Most of them refused to believe it. It had to be some kind of a mistake. The eleven stole frequent glances at their master whose normally peaceful nature seemed burdened with some great weight. Upon reaching the Gardens, the master asked the disciples to stand guard.

"Where will you go?" Simon asked. "We should stay as one."

"Yes. We should go far away from here," Matthew urged.

"We're still too close to the city," Philip added.

Jesus sighed, "I go to pray. My soul is overwhelmed with sorrow to the point of death. Keep watch. I will return shortly."

The master parted from the eleven. He slowly walked up Mount of Olives that was bathed in a wash of purple and crimson. Within a few minutes, he was lost to sight among the countless olive trees.

One by one, the eleven began to settle themselves on the ground, several taking refuge under the trees.

Peter and John watched them.

"Did you not hear the master? He told us to keep watch."

They shrugged off their counsel. They began closing their eyes. Then Peter and John sat down with their companions, resting against olive trees.

It did not take long for the heavy meal and long trek to takes its toll on them. Soon all were fast asleep.

People scattered as Licinius and his prisoners approached the Essene Gate. The rebellious murmuring of Jewish citizens watching this brutal treatment of whom they assumed to be some of their own was not lost on Licinius. He growled a command at them and they gave the patrol a clear path into the city.

Ben was close to exhaustion as he stared up at the gate. He had fallen several times over the last quarter mile. On the last stumble, Licinius dragged him over the dirt road. The rock-strewn path seared his bare arms and feet. He managed to keep his head up until he finally summoned the will to stand again. Fighting to remain conscious, he felt something shoved into his hand. He shook the sweat from his brow to see a young girl dash back into the crowd watching the column go by. He looked at the orange in his bruised hands. His fingers tore into it, dropping the rinds. His teeth ripped into the soft, moist flesh. The sticky liquid ran sloppily down his chin. The sweet fruit gave him an immediate surge of energy. When he saw Licinius glaring back, he quickly downed the rest of the orange, seeds, and all. The Roman jerked the rope almost sending Ben to the ground again. But he kept his balance this time and managed to give the angry Roman a defiant smirk.

After passing through the gate, Licinius turned toward the Upper City and the imposing building set against the west wall of the city. Although Charlie had given Ben a briefing on the layout of Jerusalem, his mind was reeling too much from exhaustion and sore limbs to remember any of it. But he realized their long, arduous journey was coming to an end. He suspected what awaited them was likely to be severe. With the sun dropping behind the mighty walls, the last part of their march would be in cool shade. No longer feeling the hot hammer blows of the sun on his head allowed him to clear his mind.

Ben could not see Miriam in Licinius' arms because his body blocked his view. All he could see were her feet dangling. One of them was bare. Somewhere along the trek, she had lost a sandal. He glanced back and stared up at Faith. Her eyes were open now, but they were glassy, unfocused.

"Faith," he grunted.

He said her name again, risking Licinius' punishment. Faith managed to lift her head, her squinting eyes showing recognition. She looked very feeble, but she at least she was alive.

Ben slammed into the hindquarters of Licinius' horse when he pulled up. He stumbled back and watched the Roman hand Miriam down to a waiting soldier. He dismounted and brushed his arms of dust. His harsh face was smeared with sweat and dust. He took the leather canteen from his saddle and poured the contents over his head. He shook his head, flinging water everywhere. He grinned at Ben's dry tongue distended from his parched lips.

He laughed as he drank deeply from the canteen.

Ben shook off his agonizing thirst. He turned back to see Faith had also been handed down to another soldier. He let go of her and she collapsed to the paved road. Ben fought to go to her aid but he was still tied to the horse.

"Cut me loose, you bastard," Ben demanded, glaring at Licinius.

Of course he did not understand the words, but Ben's meaning was all too clear. He stepped up to Ben and gave him the back of his hand. Ben fell to the hard pavement. A jolt of pain shot into his knees. He stared up at Licinius. For a crazed moment, he imagined wrapping his hands around the arrogant man's neck and crushing the life out of him. The Roman appeared to sense what Ben wished to do. He laughed as he unhooked the rope from the saddle and tossed it down.

Ben crawled over to his sister. He gently laid her head on his lap, brushing her oily hair off her haggard face.

"Faith? Faith, can you hear me?"

Her gummy eyelids managed to open. He stroked her cheek. It was clammy, almost cold to the touch. He hoped it was the cooling temperature, but he suspected it was not.

"Ben. Ben," she wheezed.

"Try not to talk."

He turned back to Licinius who was conversing with a soldier.

"She needs a doctor. A physician. She's very sick."

Licinius understood what Ben was saying but he showed no inkling of giving a damn.

"Get up," he commanded. He jerked his palm up. "Now."

Ben bit down on the urge to tell the man to go to the devil, but he knew defying him would gain nothing. He took several deep breaths, hooked his arm under Faith's shoulders, and struggled to his feet. Her limp body felt very heavy in his weary arms.

"Ben, I can manage," she said feebly.

"Relax. I have you," he said.

"Come!" Licinius barked.

He marched toward the large colonnaded, Romanesque building. Ben helped Faith along. A soldier was helping Miriam. She pushed him away defiantly. When he raised his hand to strike her, Licinius stopped him.

Seeing Ben struggling with Faith, she came over and helped

carry her.

"Thank you, Miriam," Ben said.

He glanced over at her. Her harrowing expression startled him. She looked like a person marching to her execution. Ben was racked by guilt over what they had done to this poor woman and her child.

"I'm sorry, Miriam. I'm so sorry."

As they approached the building, Ben suddenly recalled where they were going. They were entering Herod's Fortress. It was really two buildings. The one on the left was King Herod's Palace, and the larger one on the right was the Praetorium. The Praetorium was where prisoners were housed.

CHAPTER XIII

Upon reaching the Garden of Gethsemane, Nicodemus asked Charlie to wait while he went ahead to find Jesus. The priest delved deeper into the garden until he was lost from view. Charlie suspected he wanted to speak with Jesus first before allowing them to meet face to face. So, Charlie settled upon a small boulder near an olive tree. He checked his device. They were down to sixteen hours and four minutes. He glanced back at Jerusalem, now partly blocked by the many olive trees. The eastern walls of the city were in the shade now as the sun dropped fast in the west. The brightness of the day had now taken on a deep violent orange that seemed to presage ominous events. Long, claw-like purple shadows stretched out from the many olive trees in the peaceful, urban garden. Sitting there, he could understand why Jesus might find comfort here. Removed from the bustle and squalid life in the city, this was a place of serenity. At least for the moment.

Charlie's fingers tapped nervously on his knee. If history was right, time was running out for them. Temple guards might already be on their way to arrest Jesus. As he looked north, his thoughts turned to Ben and Faith. They should have been here by now unless something had gone wrong. But what could go wrong? Doubts invaded his thoughts. Maybe he should have gone with Daniel, and had Ben stay with Nicodemus. Then he realized that questioning his plan gained nothing. The issue hounding him was whether he had the courage to what he had to, regardless of the consequences, if Ben and Faith did not arrive in time. As if to reassure himself, he tapped the Glock under his robe. Did he have the will to use it if the need arose? The question went unanswered in his mind.

Several times Charlie jerked to his feet and nervously paced around before settling back on the boulder. He was shaking with great anticipation. He realized his pulse was racing wildly. His heart thumping in his chest was almost painful. He was about to go searching for Nicodemus when the priest finally reappeared.

"Come with me," he said simply.

Nicodemus escorted Charlie deeper into the garden.

"Jesus has gone to pray," Nicodemus explained. "His disciples are waiting for his return."

They walked down one of the paved paths. There the garden broke into rectangular sections of earth edged with small, colored stones. Gnarled trees and wildflowers growing within the rectangular patches were drenched in orange sunlight and purple shadows. At first, Charlie did not see them. But as his eyes adjusted to coming darkness, he could make them out. Scattered about on the ground were eleven men. They seem to be resting or sleeping. Charlie chest seized up for a moment.

The eleven disciples.

"He should be back shortly. Would you like to meet them?" Nicodemus said.

Charlie almost said, "Hell yeah," but checked himself. He nodded eagerly.

Nicodemus approached the nearest man. He was clad in a green robe with a simple sash around his waist. He appeared to be dozing.

"Peter. Peter?"

Simon Peter.

Peter's languid eyes flickered open. They darted about anxiously until they rested on the two figures standing over him. He moved up on his elbows, his eyes focusing on them.

"Greetings, Nicodemus," he said when he recognized him.

He seemed wary. His eyes probed the darkness beyond the two men. Then they turned back to them.

Charlie smiled to himself. Simon Peter himself. A man destined to be declared a Saint one day; a man who would be crucified by Emperor Nero in Rome many years hence.

"What brings you to the garden on this pleasant evening?"

"This man has come a great distance to meet your master.

His name is Charlie."

Peter did not stand. He gave a curt nod to Charlie who returned the greeting. Even in the dying light, he got a sense of him. Peter was a large man, perhaps four inches taller than he was. His face was equally large, his eyes deep set, his brows dark. His black hair and beard were unkempt. His penetrating eyes were an intense cobalt blue. There seemed to be great strength in the man's thick body. That was to be expected of a fisherman. Charlie was anxious to ask him so many questions, but Nicodemus stopped him before he could ask them.

"He has a loved one who is gravely ill. His wife. He's hopeful Jesus can help her," Nicodemus explained.

"You've come far, have you?"

Charlie nodded. For a moment, he had lost the power to speak.

"You have not met my master before then?"

Nicodemus nudged his head at Charlie.

"No, I've never met him. But he's well known in my land," Charlie said rapidly.

"Yes," Peter nodded, pleased to hear this. "The news of his work has spread far."

Charlie slowed his breathing, getting control over his conflicting emotions.

"Yes, his work has spread. The day will come when all will know of him," Charlie said cautiously. He nearly said many will know of Simon Peter as well, but stopped himself.

Peter did not react with surprise by Charlie's revelation. He simply nodded as if he understood the power of his master's message.

"You've put much hope that my master will heal your wife," Peter said.

"Yes. Everything," Charlie said.

"If it is God's will, I am certain he will," Peter said. "Would you like to meet some of his other disciples?" Nicodemus asked.

"Yes, I would," Charlie replied anxiously.

***

After entering the Praetorium, the guards led the prisoners down several steep flights of stairs into the dark bowels of the cellblock. It was tough going. The only illumination came from lit torches mounted in the walls. Negotiating the steps would have been hard enough without having to assist Faith as well. It did not help when the last soldier prodded them along with his short sword.

"Faster."

"Suck it," Ben grumbled under his breath.

A sharp thrust nearly sent all three tumbling down the steps. Ben turned his head back to fire a tirade that had been building all day. However, Faith shook her head, her pale eyes pleading.

"Please, don't provoke them, Ben," Faith gasped.

"Okay, Faith. Okay. I won't. Hell, they wouldn't understand 'drop dead dick wad' anyway."

Upon reaching the dungeon, they saw two dank passageways. The guards shoved them down the left one. They passed one cell after another. The mournful, heart tugging wails reaching out to them from each iron door seemed to come from the pits of hell. The agonized begging of tormented men and women had the effect of fingernails clawing at a chalkboard. They glanced at the human skeletons reaching out through the bars. Their wretched pleading was undecipherable, but the meaning all too clear.

"Ben, I can't go any further," Faith whimpered bleakly.

Ben hugged Faith closer when he sensed her legs go wobbly. Her body shuddered. Her left arm tightened around him. Her fingernails dug deep into his side.

"It's okay. I got you."

The ground under their feet was slick. Their sandaled feet created dull splashes in the occasional puddle. The air was moist and damp with a thick odor of human filth. When a rat scuttled over their feet, Miriam screeched, jumping away.

"Keep walking," a guard commanded.

The lead guard stopped and cracked open a cell door. He motioned them inside. Ben and Miriam helped Faith into the cell. They set her down on the uneven ground strewn with straw. The guard slammed the cell door with a dull, ominous thud that felt like an icy hand gripping their hearts. The keys jangled in the lock and he turned to leave. Ben hurried to the door and reached out to the steely-eyed guard.

"Please. We need water. Water? Do you understand?" he pleaded, making a drinking motion.

The guard understood what he wanted, but all he did was smirk and walk away.

Ben turned about and looked down at his sister and Miriam. They were squatting on the ground, leaning against the bare stone wall. There were no beds or furniture of any kind. There was a bucket in a corner near the cell door. From the odor drifting from it, he knew its purpose. Opposite the door, a small-barred window about six feet above the floor let in light and air.

Ben approached the far wall. He jumped up and grabbed the bars. He groaned as he pulled himself up enough so he could peer out. He was overlooking the front of the fortress. Roman soldiers patrolled the area. Ben dropped back down. He slowly sunk down onto the ground. He looked to Faith and Miriam folded up on the cold earth. He wanted to say something hopeful to them, but when he saw their doomed expressions, he knew it would be a waste of time. A wave of exhaustion suddenly struck him like a body blow. He surrendered to it, shutting his eyes.

Charlie felt almost as if he were in a sort of daze as he met the disciples. When he originally thought up this plan of coming back, he had not anticipated this meeting. He had spent weeks studying the movements of Jesus during his life. But he had not spent much time studying his faithful disciples. He knew some of their history of course, but he also knew much of it was guesswork at best.

All of them had to be awoken out of a sound sleep. Several times Charlie almost allowed his growing frustration to explode at them. How could they be resting while their master pondered his coming death? Then he realized they did not know what he knew.

Andrew, brother of Peter, the one who had introduced many of the disciples to Jesus, was modest and soft spoken. He looked nothing like his brother. He lay under the low branches of an olive tree, his crossed arms cradling his head.

"I have not seen Judas among you, Andrew. Is he here?" Nicodemus asked.

Andrew's pleasant attitude suddenly turned somber. His narrowing eyes shifted briefly to Charlie. He shook his head.

"No. He is not with us this night."

Charlie saw Andrew's mood shift but said nothing. Nicodemus appeared to miss it.

"Was there talk in the temple about our master today?" he asked, shifting the conversation away from the missing disciple.

Now it was Nicodemus' turn to flash apprehension.

"There is always the wagging of tongues in the temple, Andrew. Priests gossip like old women," he replied evasively.

"Did it involve our master, Rabbi?"

"Why? Have you heard something?"

Andrew shook his head. Then the two glanced at Charlie, not wishing to air dirty laundry in front of a stranger. Little could they suspect that Charlie knew more than either of them.

"Come along now, Charlie," Nicodemus said.

"Peace be with you," Andrew said to Charlie.

Charlie replied in kind, smiling wistfully at the amiable man.

Little did Andrew know that he, like most of the others, was destined to be crucified and martyred after converting so many to the new faith. It was strange to meet someone and know their fate but not being able to tell him.

"And this is James and John. They are brothers," Nicodemus said, looking down at the two men resting against the thick trunk of an olive tree.

James, half-dozing, nodded somberly to Charlie.

"Greetings," John said, looking Charlie over closely.

Charlie could see that they were brothers. They shared the same wide-set brown eyes and thick black hair. Fishermen by trade, they were both thick bodied and very darkly tanned. They appeared to be men of action.

Charlie quickly recalled their biographies. James, unlike the others, spent the rest of his life in Judea preaching the new Christian faith until Herod beheaded him in 44 CE. He would be the first to become a martyr.

John, like his brother, came from a well-to-do family. Destined to write the Gospels of John, of all the disciples, he would be the only one to die of natural causes.

"You are not from Judea?" John asked cautiously.

"He is from Armenia," Nicodemus explained.

"You are from Bethsaida I believe," Charlie said.

John perked up.

"Have we met before?"

"No, we have not. But I have heard of you. All of you in fact."

Nicodemus brought Charlie to Bartholomew.

"Greetings, Bartholomew," Nicodemus said.

"Greetings, Rabbi," Bartholomew replied.

Bartholomew was resting against a boulder. Suspected of being of royal birth, his robes certainly reflected that belief. They were of the finest linen; the sandals were well crafted. He was stocky in build. Handsome, clean cut, his hands did not display the weathering of the others who mostly toiled as fishermen.

"This is Charles. He's come to see your master."

He nodded politely to Charlie.

Charlie so wished he had a chance to learn more about each

of these men who were to have such a profound effect on the world in the years to come. Bartholomew was possibly the most adventurous of the disciples. Some historians believed he preached as far away as India where he too would eventually die a martyr's death.

"Why do you wish to meet our master?"

"My wife is very ill. I hope He can help her."

"He has come all the way from Armenia," Nicodemus explained.

"So far. I was not aware word of his works had traveled as far as that," Bartholomew commented.

"It's traveled farther than that, Bartholomew."

Charlie's words seemed to please the disciple.

"May our master ease your wife's suffering."

"Many thanks," Charlie replied.

Nicodemus then took Charlie by his arm and brought him to where three more of the disciples rested side by side on the ground. One of them sensed their presence and woke the others.

"Rabbi Nicodemus," the middle one said.

"Greetings Thomas," he replied, and then introduced Charlie.

Doubting Thomas. The pessimist of the group. Of all the others, he was the man who needed to see something before he would believe it. *Ben would probably like him*, Charlie thought to himself.

Nicodemus then introduced Phillip and Matthew. The three were cordial to Charlie, but seem more interested in resting than talking. Charlie once again wanted to alert them to the danger their master faced, but Ben's warning rang in his head.

Nicodemus shrugged and guided Charlie toward the last of the eleven. This had to be the brothers, Jude, and James, the Lesser.

When their shadows fell over them, they became alert, jerking up. It took them a moment to recognize Nicodemus. They relaxed, lying back down.

The brothers wore identical light brown robes. They looked

to be in their mid-twenties. While little is known about them, they were believed to have fiery personalities. But Charlie could see little of that in their rather listless attitude. Jude would go on to preach the Gospel in what is present day Iraq before achieving martyrdom. His brother would meet his fate in Egypt. Charlie was suddenly struck by the courage and strength of character these men possessed to strike out alone to spread their message to a world not ready to welcome it.

"Rabbi Nicodemus, what brings you to the Garden?" Jude asked with a sigh.

"Were waiting for your master to return," Nicodemus said.

"Oh, he went up to the Mount of Olives to pray. He will return presently," James mumbled, going back to sleep.

The two turned and walked away. When they stepped into a patch of shadow, a threatening voice called out.

"Watch where you are walking!"

They stumbled back and stared down at the burly man resting in that shadow.

"Oh, my apologies, Simon," Nicodemus said earnestly.

Simon, the Zealot.

Charlie stared down at the man stretched out on the ground. He could make out none of the man's stature or features. He was just a large, dark silhouette.

From what little Charlie remembered, Simon the Zealot was a man of mystery compared to the rest of the disciples. Very little was known of him, other than his abiding hatred of Rome. But that hate had been blunted by his love for his master.

"What brings you to the garden, priest?"

"I bring a man who seeks help from your master."

"A Roman?" he asked.

"No, not Roman," Charlie declared.

"You look Roman."

"He is from Armenia, Simon," Nicodemus assured him.

"Is he? He doesn't look like any Armenian I've ever seen."

Charlie became nervous at Simon's belligerent demeanor. He looked to Nicodemus to calm Simon down.

"Rest assured, Simon. This man is not from Rome."

"I'll have to take your word on that priest," Simon said and then closed his eyes.

Charlie and Nicodemus retreated to a large stone and sat down. Charlie so desperately wanted to warn them. But Ben's admonitions restrained him. What impact would there be if this moment was changed in some way? How might accepted history itself be altered? But maybe accepted history was wrong. The idea did not seem so crazy now that he was there. Had the past two thousand years been so wonderful for humanity? How many wars and misery had consumed the human race the last two millennia? A billion? What if he changed the course of history tonight? Could things really be any worse than they were now? He possessed the knowledge and the means to make that change. He thought hard on whether he dared. Maybe they did not just come to save Faith. Maybe they came to save everyone. If Jesus survived this night, was it possible things might change for the better? Charlie found himself shaking almost feverishly. It felt as if every organ in his body was ready to burst. He struggled to breath.

Nicodemus observed him closely as they waited. He seemed to sense Charlie's internal travails but said nothing to the stranger. Then he looked off toward the Mount of Olives.

"It's him. He's returned."

Charlie twisted around to where Nicodemus was staring. At first, he did not see anything. Then the figure coming down from the Mount of Olives cleared some trees. The man wore an off-white robe that reached down to his ankles. He walked slowly as if a great weight was pressing down upon him. Charlie knew what that weight was, of course.

"I'll introduce you to him," Nicodemus said.

He took Charlie by the arm, and together they walked toward him.

The master stared down at his sleeping disciples with reproach.

"Could not one of you keep watch for one hour?"

The awakened disciples had no reply. A few looked up, ashamed by their lethargy.

Jesus was still staring down at his disciples when He saw the two figures approaching. His somber expression managed a smile when he recognized Nicodemus.

"Rabbi," Nicodemus said.

"Greetings, Rabbi Nicodemus," Jesus said.

Charlie thought his voice was surprisingly calm considering he knew what was about to happen.

Staring at him, Charlie recalled the many paintings that could only guess at what Jesus really looked like. He resembled them, and he did not. He was a tall, lean man, an inch or two over six feet. His hands were rough, as one would expect from a carpenter. His long brown hair framed a tanned face many would describe as handsome. Dark piercing brown eyes that now looked burdened looked frankly into Charlie's eyes.

"I would like to introduce a new arrival. He's been searching for you all day. His name is Charles."

Jesus nodded pleasantly to him.

"Greetings. You have come a great distance have you not?"

Charlie cleared his throat, "Ah, yes, I have."

Nicodemus looked from Charlie to Jesus, and then back again at Charlie. He seemed to sense that something unspoken had passed between the two. He realized Charlie was hesitant, or maybe too overwhelmed, to speak.

"Charlie has someone very close to him who is very ill," he explained.

"Yes. My wife," Charlie uttered.

Jesus sensed Charlie's apprehension. He stepped closer and set a comforting hand on his arm. It was a strong hand that gripped his elbow. Charlie felt a warm shiver go up his arm. With that touch, he felt a surge of hope that everything was going to be all right.

"You must love her very much to have made such an arduous journey."

"Yes, I do."

"To truly love another is God's greatest gift, is it not?"

Charlie nodded, "Yes, it is."

"To sacrifice oneself for another is man's greatest gift."

Charles and the Nazarene smiled at each other in a private understanding that was lost on Nicodemus.

"Is your wife here?"

Charlie shook his head, looking anxiously around in the hope that he would see them entering the garden. But there was no sign of them.

"She's been delayed."

Charlie realized time was running out. Faith's only chance now was for Charlie to act. He realized what that could mean to history. But he decided to risk it. History be damned.

"It's not safe for you to be here. You are in great danger," Charlie said.

"You know then?" Jesus asked, surprised.

Charlie nodded firmly. He seemed ready to burst out everything he knew. Jesus sensed his quandary.

"Then you must know I must stay."

His firm voice had the ring of one who finally, after much turmoil, had accepted his fate.

"Must you?" Charlie said.

Jesus nodded fatalistically.

"But there's still time for you to get away. I can help you."

"You would risk your life to save me?" He asked.

"Yes," Charlie replied without hesitation.

He nodded, his gentle face moved by Charlie declaration.

"You are a brave man, Charles, to risk so much for someone you've only just met. But I have to be brave now as well. I have to be brave to save you."

"But the world needs you more than you can know."

"Yes, I know. But I'll still be here with all of you even after I'm gone."

Charlie became despondent.

"But there are so many things I would like to know; to ask you."

Frustration racked Charlie now. To be this close to so many answers and be denied them infuriated him.

"The answers are right before you. Continue on the path you are on and you will find all those answers. Believe me," Jesus told him.

Nicodemus looked past Jesus and showed alarm. Charlie followed his eyes and stiffened. In the distance, men with torches were entering the garden.

"No. No. Not yet," Charlie said.

As the band of men came closer, they were revealed to be temple guards. There were ten of them. A robed figure led them.

Charlie stepped forward, placing his body between Jesus and the approaching band.

"You must leave here. They've come to arrest you," Charlie warned.

"Arrest him? But why?" Nicodemus protested.

"So I can fulfill my destiny, Rabbi. My time has come."

Jesus' words were edged with angst.

The armed contingent stopped about thirty yards away. They stared at the scattered disciples, and then at Jesus, Charlie, and Nicodemus. They appeared uncertain as to their next step.

Charlie thought if they acted quickly they could still get away. It was night now. They could escape into the darkness. There was still time to save Jesus and Faith. But before Charlie could act, Jesus stepped around him and looked to his followers who were still resting.

"Rise," Jesus told them.

At his command, the confused disciples roused themselves,

getting to their feet. They spotted the armed guards and mumbled to each other in confusion. Even in the muddled light, Charlie could see the fear in their eyes.

Charlie considered the guards. They bore spears or short swords. *He could take them*, he thought to himself. He had never shot anyone before, but what better reason could a man have than this one. He swallowed hard, choking down his fear. His jittery hand fumbled under his tunic. His twitching fingers settled over the Glock in its holster. He found the safety, and after two attempts, flipped it.

The leader of the guards stepped forward staring at the men. They all looked the same to him. He turned to the robed figure who was staring at Jesus.

"Which one is the Nazarene?" the leader asked.

Judas strode past the disciples and headed straight for the three. He flashed a thin, poisonous smile at Jesus. Charlie and Nicodemus placed themselves in front of the Nazarene.

"No, do not interfere," Jesus said, setting his hands on their shoulders. He gently pushed them aside. He took a step forward, away from their protecting bodies.

"Greetings, Rabbi," Judas said.

His voice was pleasant enough, but his expression was dark. Then, like some Mafia chieftain, he kissed Jesus on both cheeks.

Jesus stared blankly at Judas. He showed no anger. The smile Judas had displayed now became a frown when his betrayal did not generate the reaction he had hoped.

"Do what you came to do," Jesus said simply.

Judas regained his composure and turned to the temple chief. He raised his voice so all could hear.

"Who do you seek?"

The leader moved forward.

"We seek Jesus of Nazareth," he said in an officious manner.

"I am he," Jesus said simply.

The temple chief signaled one of his men with a hand gesture. When he stepped forward with a pair of manacles, one of the disciples lunged out swinging a small sword. The wild stroke struck the man by the ear. A spray of blood gushed forth. The man cried out, falling to his knees, his hand cupping the bloody wound. The disciple then confronted the other temple guards, waving the sword in a threatening manner.

"No. No more. Lower your sword, Peter," Jesus commanded.

Peter stood in the glare of the torches, the dripping sword raised up. Seeing the reproach in his master's face, he reluctantly lowered his weapon. Some of the other disciples, having summoned their courage, stepped forward, interposing their bodies between the guards and their master.

"No more violence. Step back, my brothers," Jesus told them.

The confused disciples saw admonishment in their master's face. They reluctantly stepped away.

Charlie knew it was up to him now if he was to save Faith, and maybe save Him as well. He grabbed the Glock and started to slide it free when Jesus turned to him. He stared at him with displeasure. He set his hand on Charlie's chest. At his firm touch, Charlie felt a great release, as if all the volcanic anger that had been building in him passed.

"No, brother. For those who live by the sword, must die by the sword," he warned him.

Charlie leaned forward, his clenched fist around the gun. "But I can stop them. I can save you."

"How many lives would your wife want you to take to save her?" he asked.

Charlie stared hopelessly at him. What to do? He glanced at Nicodemus who looked confused at this shocking turn of events. He would get no help from him. It was his decision now. He thought about just wounding several of the guards figuring they would run away at the magic power of his terrifying weapon. But they would likely return with an overwhelming force before they could get very far. People would be killed. Charlie groaned inwardly, his body going limp. He left the gun in its holster.

"Fear not. Your faith will be rewarded," Jesus said, smiling.

Jesus then stepped over to the wounded man who was still on his knees, moaning. The guard's bloody hand was pressed hard against the vicious gash.

"Rise," Jesus said simply.

The temple guard looked up at Jesus. He struggled to his feet. His hand never left the side of his head. Jesus placed his hand over it. Within moments, the guard's mask of agony gave way to one of calmness as if some soothing balm had been applied to his wound. Jesus removed his hand and stepped back. The guard stood there like a statue for a long moment. Cautiously he removed his hand to reveal to all that his ear was completely healed. Shocked muttering erupted from the other temple guards. Several stumbled away. The now healed guard kept touching his ear in amazement. Then he cried out and fled into the darkness.

The leader of the temple guards stood his ground. While as amazed as all the others, he remembered his orders.

"Manacle the prisoner," he commanded.

None of the temple guards moved. They shifted nervously on their feet. Several stepped back even farther.

He issued the command again. Seeing that they would not obey, he stepped forward and manacled Jesus' wrists himself. He looked up at the prisoner expecting some rebuke for arresting him.

However, Jesus merely nodded passively.

The leader of the guards motioned with his hand toward the city. The temple guards formed a ring around their prisoner.

"Back to the city," the leader ordered.

They marched off. Charlie watched helplessly as history once again played out before him. He glared at Judas. The betrayer's face was no longer jubilant. He appeared numbed by the turn of events he had engineered. When Charlie lurched forward to strike him, Nicodemus restrained his arm.

"No, my friend. No. No more violence. Come. Come."

Charlie, Nicodemus, and the disciples followed the cohort of guards back to Jerusalem.

CHAPTER XIV

As sunlight retreated from the hellish cell, a silver moon glow slowly crept in. The flickering torches in the cellblock corridor failed to combat the grim darkness. The dancing red-orange glow lashed feebly at Faith and Miriam resting against the wall. They were not sitting together now. Miriam had moved away. She curled up in a ball in the corner alone with her misery. Even the mournful begging from the other prisoners had finally exhausted itself.

Ben checked his device for the tenth time since their imprisonment. He was not even sure why he bothered. There could be no escape or parole for them. In a little over thirteen hours the Eight-ball would power up and leave them in the past. He clenched his fists in frustration. What the hell was he thinking to let Charlie talk him into this? He should never even have told him about the discovery. If he had only maintained the secrecy of the project, they would still be home, safe and secure. What would Sidesh do when the Eight-ball returned and they were not inside it? He had told him to erase the drives and security footage so no one would know what they did. Would he do that? Or would he try to help them somehow? He was not feeling particularly hopeful.

"We never should have come here," he muttered.

Faith looked up at hearing his exasperated lamentation.

"You're right, we shouldn't have come, Ben," she said. Her words came out garbled.

Ben came over and slid down the wall next to her. Her head tilted into his shoulder. He took her clammy hand and tried to rub some warmth into it.

"Look, we haven't done anything wrong, Faith. They'll have to let us go. They have to."

He did not sound as confident as he had hoped. But he was sure they would be released at some point. Even the Romans had a legal system. They had committed no crime. But that could be days or even weeks. How long could Faith endure in this pit?

"Ben, I'm not talking about us. I'm talking about Miriam and Daniel. We're responsible for her being caught. By our coming here, we've changed things. Not in a history changing way maybe but we've changed things."

Ben looked at Miriam. She stared gloomily at the cell door. Faith was right. He wanted to do something to help her but he could not even speak to her.

Faith cleared her throat and lifted her head up.

"Ben, do you think Charlie is all right?"

Ben was about to say something and thought better of it. He suddenly got the crazy idea that maybe Charlie could get back to the Eight-ball, return to the present, and somehow get some help. The absurd notion of a company of U.S. Marines breaking into the prison and rescuing them in Hollywood fashion flashed into his sleep-deprived mind. He grunted, realizing he was getting weak in the head. The cavalry was not going to come to the rescue them this time.

"Remember when we used to watch scary movies as kids, and you would ask me if I wanted you to hold my hand, and I said no, that I wasn't scared?"

"Yeah, I remember."

"Well, I am scared now. Hold my hand, Ben," she asked.

Ben looked at her left hand still cupped tightly in his own. "Sure thing, sis."

He held her hand up to show her he was holding it. She smiled weakly.

"Oh, you were. I can barely feel it," she said.

***

Night greeted the temple guards as they passed under the great arch of the Water Gate. The great flow of humanity entering the city just a few hours earlier had slowed down to a trickle. The many clamorous sounds of the city in daylight had subsided with the arrival of darkness. The few individuals still about watched the procession with little interest. Charlie and the disciples still followed them from a discreet distance.

Once they cleared the gate the temple guard did not strike out to the temple, or Herod's palace, but for the home of the high priest, Caiaphus, located in the Upper City.

Nicodemus, who had gone on ahead, returned to Charlie.

"I believe they mean to put the Nazarene on trial," he said.

Charlie nodded. He decided to reveal the truth to him. It did not really matter now anyway. Nicodemus would be witness to the show trial that was about to begin.

"He will be convicted, Nicodemus."

Nicodemus grabbed Charlie's arm, partly turning him.

"What?"

"He's to be crucified."

The priest gasped. Then, watching the procession, he realized where they were going.

"For what crime is he to be crucified?"

Charlie was about to tell Nicodemus everything he knew, to hell with history. But before he could speak, a figure broke out of the shadows, startling them. Then, Charlie recognized him. He grabbed Daniel around the shoulders.

"Daniel!"

He looked past the gasping boy who had been in hiding most of the afternoon near the city gate hoping to spot Charlie.

"Where are Faith and Ben? Where are they?"

The boy's chest heaved as he fought to catch his breath.

"Where are they?" Charlie repeated, calming his voice.

"They've been taken," he panted.

"Taken! Taken where?"

Charlie squeezed the boy so hard he groaned. Realizing he was hurting the boy, Charlie released his grip. He dropped down to look straight into his eyes. Even in the low light, he could see the stark fear in them.

"The Romans took them," he said.

He briefly revealed how the Romans had followed them back to their home and how he managed to escape.

"Why? Why were they taken?"

Daniel hesitated.

"Tell me, Daniel. Why was your mother taken?"

"My mother and I are escaped slaves."

"Slaves?"

Charlie stood up. He turned to Nicodemus who had heard their conversation with interest.

"Who was your master, Daniel?" Nicodemus asked.

The boy hesitated again.

"Tribune Gaius Macro."

Nicodemus stiffened when he heard the name. His mouth tightened as he looked to Charlie.

"Who is Gaius Macro?" Charlie asked the priest.

"I know of him. He was badly wounded by one of his slaves several months ago in Joppa. The accused woman is called Miriam. It was said a boy was also involved," he said, staring down at Daniel.

Daniel looked away.

"Miriam, a slave" Charlie muttered.

Now it made sense why they reacted with such terror when the Roman patrol rode by the house.

"Tribune Macro has offered a great reward for the woman and her son," Nicodemus added.

Daniel's face turned up. Tears were running down his cheeks.

A multitude of thoughts raced through Charlie's disconcerted brain. He had to do something. But what could one man do against an entire city. His eyes darted around, looking over the sleeping metropolis. He watched the temple guards as they turned and were lost from sight. But he knew where they would Him.

He bent down to Daniel and lifted his chin up. He wiped the tears staining his cheeks.

"Daniel, where were they taken?"

Daniel pointed toward the palace in the distance.

"They were taken to the Praetorium. My mother as well," he said.

Charlie nodded grimly.

The Praetorium. His first guess would have been the Atonia Fortress. He sighed with relief. Getting in and out of the Fortress would have been a daunting task. He might have better luck with the Praetorium. At the very least they would have to be charged. They had committed no crime so the odds were they would be released. But that could take days, or possibly weeks. They only had hours. In any case, that would not help Miriam. She had wounded a Roman tribune. Her punishment, if convicted, would be severe. Rome executed convicted criminals for lesser offenses. Roman execution methods were incredibly brutal, even for a woman. If memory served him, stoning was the preferred method in dealing with women.

"Who can we speak with tonight about my wife and brother-in-law's arrest today?" Charlie asked the priest.

"Tonight? No one. Roman justice can be fair, but it is never swift, my friend," Nicodemus said.

Charlie was well aware of how Roman justice operated during these times. It was agonizingly slow in a far off province like Judea. If he waited for the legal process to play out, they would be trapped forever, two thousand years in the past. He realized that could be their fate regardless. But he refused to surrender to that possibility unless there was no other alternative. There was only one option left for him now.

"I need to get them released. Miriam too," Charlie said to Nicodemus.

"Released? You seek the impossible. While bribing officials is not unusual, even Roman officials, I cannot see Macro letting Miriam escape him."

Charlie stared at the great palace. Lights burned in several of the open windows. While not as well-guarded as the Fortress, the palace would be well protected with Pontius Pilate visiting the city. He took a breath and recalled the layout of the Praetorium. A desperate plan quickly took shape in his mind, but he knew he could not pull it off alone. He glanced down at Daniel. The boy looked terribly frightened. But there was nothing else to be done now.

"I need your help, Nicodemus."

"To do what?"

"To get them out. To help them escape," Charlie said plainly.

The priest was appalled at his proposal. His head shook, his hands rising in protest. Nicodemus' alert eyes darted into the murky darkness, alarmed that their conversation might be overheard by someone. Other than several of the disciples who were talking in hushed whispers, no one else was within earshot.

"Escape! What are you suggesting? The Praetorium is too well guarded. No one has ever escaped from there."

"I know the Praetorium and the palace well. There is a way to get them out. I will need a couple brave men. Men who can be trusted."

Nicodemus stared at Charlie. He could not believe what he was hearing. This stranger was mad to suggest such a scheme. His first impulse was to hurry away in case someone was eavesdropping on them.

"It cannot be done," he stated with finality.

Charlie reached into his robe and produced several gold coins. He held them up.

"I have gold. I have a lot of gold. Nicodemus, with or without your help, I have to try to save them. One of them is my wife. Do you understand? I will not leave them in that hellish place. Even if I die trying, I'm going to do this."

Nicodemus could see Charlie was determined to go through with this madcap scheme. Despite his better judgment, he decided to help him.

"Very well. Wait here a moment. I think I know some men who might be willing to help you."

Nicodemus stepped over to the disciples. There were only two present. It appeared the others had taken off into the night. From the historical accounts Charlie recalled, the disciples apparently went into hiding after the arrest of Jesus.

Charlie watched Nicodemus speak to them. In the meager light Charlie could not identify them. He looked down at Daniel and set a comforting hand on his shoulder.

"Don't be afraid, Daniel. We're going to get all of them away. I promise."

Daniel looked up grimly.

Macro made his way down the flight of steps to the main dungeon beneath the Praetorium. Dozing guards at first ignored the figure coming down, and then they snapped to attention when the lit torches revealed Macro's scarred face. He stopped before the chief guard on duty.

"Where is she?"

"This way, Tribune."

The chief guard led Macro down the dim corridor to the last cell on the left. Macro waved him away. He saluted and drifted back into the darkness.

Macro stared into the cell. His piercing eye locked on the three huddled figures one by one. It finally fell upon Miriam. Her face was partly hidden from view but he recognized her all the same. Then, as if sensing his presence, she lifted her head and stared up at Macro. She shuddered. She quickly shifted over, pressing her shaking body into Faith.

"Who is he?" Faith asked, trembling under that hateful stare.

Ben had come around from a restless sleep. He saw the Roman now. The man's massive hands clenched the iron bars as if ready to rip them apart. Ben shuddered at the pure hate coming from the cyclopean eye.

"He's no friend, that's for sure," Ben said.

Faith hooked a protective arm around Miriam. Her body

continued shaking despite Faith's support.

"Did you really believe you could escape me, Miriam? There was no place in the Empire I would not have searched to find you. I've endured so many sleepless nights hoping for this day to come. Now you and your bastard boy will soon learn the true measure of pain."

Macro's guttural promise sent Miriam into another series of convulsions. She buried her face into Faith's bosom. Faith hugged her tighter.

Ben struggled to his feet. He approached the cell door. Macro's eye tore itself from Miriam and bore into Ben. He reached out to grab Macro's tunic.

"I know you can't understand a word I'm saying pal but we've done nothing wrong. You have to let my sister and I go," he pleaded.

Macro seized Ben's hand and crushed it, forcing him to his knees. Ben tried to fight back but the Roman outweighed him by at least fifty pounds. Once he had Ben on his knees, Macro twisted his hand and flung him to the ground. He snorted with derision.Macro turned his harsh gaze back to Miriam.

"Do not look to your God to save you again, Miriam. He has abandoned you."

Macro snorted, striding off into the inky blackness.

Ben crawled back to Faith and Miriam. Miriam was whimpering, her chest heaving with intense seizures. Faith rocked her body against her own, stroking her head. Ben wanted to do something, or say something. But there was nothing that he could do. He dropped back against the wall and buried his head in his dirty hands.

Charlie checked his device. Eleven hours and twenty-one minutes remained. His thoughts shot back to Faith and Ben locked up in some prison cell not more than a hundred yards from where he was hiding. From the shadows, he watched several guards patrolling ceaselessly.

Charlie slid out the Glock pistol from his holster. He examined it under the light of a nearby oil lamp. It was his ace in the hole. Daniel, who had nodded off, suddenly awoke and stared up at the strange object. Seeing Daniel was alert now he jammed the Glock back under his tunic.

"What is that?" he asked in fascination.

"It's nothing. Are you worried about your mother?" he asked, wanting to change the subject. "I'm sure she's safe."

Daniel's long, pale stare back was not reassuring. He was a smart kid. He knew where his mother was and how hopeless the situation looked. He could hardly blame him. Their situation looked bleak.

"Daniel, we're going to get her out," Charlie promised.

Daniel managed a grim smile, nudging his head up and down. Charlie set his hand on his shoulder.

They both turned when Nicodemus returned with the two remaining disciples. It was the brothers, John and James.

"John and James wish to help you." Nicodemus said.

The brothers nodded to Charlie.

"The Romans are holding your wife?" John asked.

"Yes. And two others. My wife's brother and a woman," Charlie said. "Are you sure you want to help? It will be very dangerous."

"We are beyond helping our master now," John said morosely.

"He would want us to help you, I'm certain," James added.

Charlie looked them over more closely now. John had a sun burned, determined face, and was stocky of build. He had muscular, almost apish arms. James looked like a younger version of John. His determined eyes twinkled in the torch light. They appeared to be men who could handle themselves if they got into a tough spot.

"How do you plan to enter the Praetorium?" Nicodemus asked.

"Right through the front gate," Charlie revealed.

Nicodemus shook his head at his boldness. John and James traded looks. They both grinned with eagerness.

"You're a brave man," John stated.

"We are brave also," James promised.

Charlie felt a surge of confidence from their zeal.

"Thank you."

He offered the disciples a gold aureus each.

"Keep your money," James said

"You insult us with the offer," John added.

"I'm sorry. I meant no offense," Charlie said, pocketing the two coins.

The two disciples accepted Charlie's apology.

"I must go now," Nicodemus said. "You were right. The elders mean to put the Nazarene on trial. I go to speak up for him. I will do everything I can."

"Good luck," Charlie said, knowing the outcome was a fore gone conclusion. "Thank you for your help."

Charlie gripped the man's hand.

"Good fortune. I will pray for your success," he said. He turned and hurried off into the darkness.

Charlie gazed at the Praetorium. His thoughts drifted to Faith, Ben, and Miriam in their cell. He turned back to John and James. He felt a great surge of excitement knowing they had his back.

"We will need a cart and a horse," Charlie said.

James leaned toward John. They spoke in hushed tones.

"We don't have much time," Charlie said.

John signaled Charlie.

"We know someone who can help you. Come with us."

Annas, son of Seth, was a thick, stocky man in his early sixties. His silver hair and beard framed a bloated face and deep-set gray eyes. His eye-catching ceremonial robe was of blue and purple. While his son-in-law Caiaphus held the title of High Priest in the temple, he was the true power in Judea despite being removed from power by Gratus some fifteen years earlier.

He stared at the man before him. Normally such an interrogation would take place in a more official location, not inside his palace. However, this was no normal interrogation. Usually a prisoner was expected to genuflect before him but Jesus was no ordinary prisoner. He did not appear to be the kind of man who would kneel to anyone.

"Do you know why you have been brought here?" Annas asked.

Jesus did not respond.

"Well?"

"I have only spoken openly, teaching in the synagogue, or the Temple, where all can come together. I have never spoken in secret. Why have you brought me here for your questions?"

Suddenly a blow landed across his face, stunning him. Jesus reeled from the strike, but kept his feet under him. Then, he stared at the sneering temple guard. There was no anger in his eyes.

When the guard readied another blow, Jesus calmly raised his hand.

"If I said something wrong, testify as to what is wrong. But if I spoke the truth, why strike me?"

Annas waved the guard back. This was not how he wished to begin the proceeding.

One of Annas' aides entered the open courtyard, leading several dozen robed figures. As they walked in, they split into two groups encircling the lone figure.

Jesus said nothing as the members of the Sanhedrin entered. He watched as Caiaphus stood alongside his father-in-law, Annas. They nodded to each other.

Among the almost sixty members were two who seemed to stand apart from the others. Nicodemus was still in a state of shock at what he was witnessing. He spotted the trickle of blood running down from the Nazarene's mouth. He looked to the man alongside him, Joseph of Arimathea.

"They have beaten him."

Joseph stepped forward boldly and pointed to the prisoner.

"By what right is the prisoner being mistreated?"

Annas reacted with a shrug.

"He was being obstinate."

"Is that a crime? What is this man's offense, Annas?" Nicodemus questioned.

"There are many charges, and many witnesses," Caiaphus said, stepping forward, officially taking charge of the trial.

"Then let them step forward and speak. But I will permit no more assaults on this man. We're not Romans or barbarians," Joseph declared.

The other priests nodded in agreement.

Caiaphus bowed in acquiescence, "Very well."

Caiaphus nodded to another priest. He brought forth a middle-aged man whose excited eyes darted about nervously. His body shook with all the priests glaring at him.

"Your name?"

"I, I, I am called Aran, Son of Nachum," the man stuttered.

"Go on."

Aran stepped toward Jesus cautiously, pointing his crooked finger at him.

"This man said aloud to all who could hear, 'I am able to destroy the Temple of God and rebuild it in three days.'"

The priests turned to one another and whispered to each other. Jesus looked at the accuser who quickly retreated.

"Well? Will you not reply to the accusation?" Caiaphus asked.

Jesus had no reply. He stood passively in the light of the many torches that sent flickering shadows in all directions.

Caiaphus stepped forth, opening his palms up, trying to get the prisoner to respond.

"I charge you by the living God; tell us if you are this Messiah, the Son of God."

Jesus looked to the entourage waiting on his reply. He had not wiped away the trickle of blood from his chin, but the wound had stopped bleeding.

"Speak man!"

"You will not believe me, but from now onward the Son of Man will sit alongside the power of God," he said.

The words, plainly spoken, held no passion or anger. It was as if He were stating a simple truth.

There was a gasp from the priests. A few stepped forward, and then, all of them, in a discordant cry, spoke:

"Are you then the Son of God?"

"You say that I am," he replied.

Caiaphus grinned, nodding to Annas.

For most of the priests, this was all they needed to hear. One of the priests lurched forward and in a fit of rage, ripped his robe open.

"Who needs more witnesses? We've heard him say it himself. He speaks blasphemy! He condemns himself with his own words," the enraged priest exclaimed.

Charlie and Daniel followed them into the Lower City. At this hour there were few people walking the streets. They passed homeless people huddled between buildings, trying to stay warm in the cooler temperatures. John and James had them twisting and turning down one secluded alleyway after another until Charlie was totally lost. They stopped at a rundown shop and knocked on the door. Getting no response, they knocked harder until the door shook.

"Who's out there?" a perturbed voice growled from inside.

"It's John and James. Open up."

"I don't open my shop to anyone at this hour. Go away and come back in the morning."

John, a man of action, banged on the door once again.

There was a frustrated grunt, and then the door opened. The grumpy man held out a small oil lamp with one hand while rubbing his gummy eyes with the other. The bearded man's scowl made every line in his face look like deep scars.

"What is it that can't wait until morning, John?"

The man then fixed his squinty eyes on Charlie and Daniel. John pushed his way into the man's shop. The others followed.

"Abraham, we need to borrow your cart and horse," John said.

"At this hour? What for?" he asked with suspicion. "Who are your friends?"

"We don't have time for dilly dallying," Charlie said.

"Dilly dally? I don't understand," Abraham said.

"Can we borrow your horse and cart?" John asked again.

"Why?"

John looked at Charlie. He shook his head. He did not want him to know of their intentions.

"We can't tell you, Abraham. But it is very important."

"What are you two up to now? No good I'll bet. Are you still following that rabbi? What a waste your lives have become. You should go back to being fishermen. Fishing is an honest profession."

Abraham set the lamp down on a table. He lit another lamp hanging from the ceiling. It was a small room with a desk and chair. A few saddles, a broken cart wheel, and some harnesses for horses were scattered about.

"How much must I pay to use your cart for the day?" Charlie asked.

He opened his palm and flashed a silver denarius.

Abraham stepped up and examined the coin. He then displayed two fingers. Charlie opened the other palm, showing a second coin. He dropped it into Abraham's hand.

"You two are up to no good again. You're such a disappointment to your mother," he said.

"Uncle, we're trying to help this man find his wife. She's...lost," James said.

Abraham stared at them in disbelief. He shrugged and pocketed the money. He led them out the back where he kept his cart and horse.

"Don't look at me. You want them, you get them ready. I do not work during Passover. And neither should you."

"We're not working, Uncle. We're...helping," James said evasively.

John and James harnessed the horse and dragged out the cart.

"Is this true? Are they trying to help you find your wife?" Abraham asked.

"Yes, it's true," Charlie said.

"Really. Hard to believe they told the truth. They are the biggest liars in the city."

"That's not true," John protested.

"Well, not I," James added.

"They really are," Abraham whispered to Charlie.

They climbed aboard after the horse was secure to the cart. John settled onto the narrow seat and took the reins. Charlie sat alongside him. James and Daniel sat in the back.

"You will bring it back, won't you?" Abraham asked Charlie.

"Yes. We'll bring it back. Thank you."

John tugged on the reigns and the horse jerked forward. After leaving the shop, John swung the cart toward the main road.

"Where are we going?"

"Out the Essene Gate. I'll direct you after we leave the city," Charlie said. He checked the device again. There was still time.

CHAPTER XV

Caiaphus raised his hands, silencing the agitated priests clamoring for death of the prisoner. The shouting and cursing finally faded to angry murmurings. Caiaphus, feeling confident in his power over the proceedings now, stepped up to Jesus.

"You stand condemned, prisoner. The sentence for your crime is death," he stated boldly.

Nicodemus and Joseph, who had watched the grotesque proceeding in almost stunned silence, stepped forward, standing close to Jesus.

"Wait! There must be a vote. Every man here must state his decision for all to hear," Nicodemus stated. He wanted every leader of the Sanhedrin to be on the record openly. He did not want any of them to claim innocence later.

"Nicodemus is right. All members must cast their vote before a sentence of death can be passed," Joseph added.

The priests did not respond as Caiaphus had expected. They murmured back and forth to each other at being compelled to openly declare the prisoner guilty. Caiaphus twisted back to Annas who stood there stoically. He did not find any help there. He was on his own. Thinking quickly, he signaled for quiet.

"That will not be necessary. All that is required is a consensus. Those in favor of guilt call out."

A great roar of approval echoed in the courtyard.

"Those opposed," Caiaphus called out, staring at Nicodemus and Joseph.

Both men raised their hands. Their eyes searched the faces of the sixty-odd priests around them. Not one joined them. Many averted their eyes.

"It is death," Caiaphus said.

He turned his gaze to Jesus who looked back without showing any emotion but that infuriating placidity that unnerved the temple leader.

"We do not have the power to condemn a man to death, Caiaphus," Nicodemus reminded him.

"Rabbi Nicodemus is correct. Remember what happened to Annas when he condemned and executed a man many years ago. Procurator Valerius Gratus deposed him. The Romans do not grant us the power to execute a prisoner," Joseph added.

Annas turned red-faced with annoyance at having his infamous removal from office recalled before the Sanhedrin. He seemed about to speak to it but thought better of reopening an old embarrassment that still stung him deeply to that day.

Caiaphus smiled at the agitators' foolish attempt to stop him. He stepped toward them with a look of false earnestness.

"Of course, Roman law must always be followed," he agreed. "We shall proceed there forthwith. Manacle the prisoner."

***

After leaving Jerusalem Charlie directed John to an area just west of the city, directly opposite Herod's palace. As it was still night, there was no one else on the road that ran parallel to the city. It was slow going as there was little moonlight to guide them. The last thing they needed was to lose a wheel in an unseen hole or ditch. Looking back, Charlie saw Daniel and James were fast asleep. Watching them made Charlie aware of how exhausted he was. He had not slept in over twenty-four hours. He was also starving, having little food since their arrival. John offered him some leaven bread that he devoured in a few minutes. He then washed it down with some poor wine. It was not much but it helped settle his stomach. He suspected Faith, Ben, and Miriam would be getting little food or water from their Roman captors.

"Why are we traveling outside the city when your companions are inside the Praetorium?" John asked.

Charlie glanced at him. He could just make out his features in the pale moonlight. John's face had a bluish cast, his eyes probing

Charlie's face for an answer.

"I'm not concerned about entering the Praetorium. It's getting out that will be the tricky part. We're almost there."

Charlie looked right to the great wall that encircled Jerusalem. Against the star-filled sky, he could make out the irregular shapes of buildings behind the wall. When they came abreast of what he believed was Herod's palace, he told John to roll the cart off the road and into an empty field. Charlie's eyes followed the thirty-foot wall down until it met the slope of a hill that continued right on down to the road. He was confident he had found the right spot. But there was only one way he could be certain.

"John, hand me that oil lamp," he asked.

John lit the lamp and handed it over.

"Wait here. I need to check on something."

Taking the lamp, Charlie crossed the road and started up the slope, reaching up to the wall. Wild, waist-high grass covered the steep incline. John watched him struggle, stumbling occasionally over scattered pits and rocks. Charlie waved the lamp back and forth, peeking around gnarled trees and thick bushes. Finally, he turned around and navigated his way along the same path he took going up. When he reached the cart, he blew out the lamp and handed it back to John.

"What were you looking for up there?" John asked.

"Nothing. Just looking around," Charlie said cryptically.

Charlie turned his body away from John and checked the device again. Looking back to the wall, he could now see the faintest change in the night sky that was slowly giving way to the coming sunrise. He considered going back to the city, but he knew he would stand a better chance getting inside at dawn when the Praetorium was dealing with matters that were more important.

He turned to John.

"We can rest now for a few hours."

John nodded. He looked tired as well.

Not wanting to disturb James or Daniel, they found a bare

piece of earth and stretched out their tired bodies. Charlie stared up at the dome of stars twinkling down at him. The last time he saw so many stars was on a camping trip he was on as a kid. An occasional shooting star streaked overhead.

"Why did the Romans arrest your wife and companions?"

"One of them is an escaped Roman slave."

"Your wife?"

"No."

"You are not from here?"

"No. It's our first time to Judea."

"I've lived my whole life here. My brother, too"

"You were a well-to-do fishermen, John. Why did you decide to give that up and follow your master?"

"Being a stranger, how do you know so much about my brother and me? That we were fishermen?"

"Nicodemus told me," Charlie lied.

John said nothing for a few moments. Charlie could sense him reflecting on the question.

"Brother John introduced us."

"John the Baptist?"

John nodded. "Yes. Before we met him, all we thought about was fishing. And other things. But he told us our true charge in life was to be fishers of men. He believed men required more than fish to live. After hearing his words, the thought of going back to the sea became impossible for us."

"I heard a story about the Nazarene."

"There are many stories about him. What do you wish to know?"

"Did he really walk on water?"

John fought back a chuckle.

"You heard about that?"

"Yes. A story like that travels far."

"Yes, it would. What would you have me say? That he did indeed walk on water? Would you believe me if I told you it was true?"

"I guess I would," Charlie replied.

"I have seen him do many amazing things. Is that not why you have come all this way? So he could help your wife?"

"Yes. But now it appears my journey may have been for naught."

"We will see. There may yet be time. You are not from Armenia, are you?"

"No, I'm not."

"Rome?"

"No. Farther."

"Gaul"

Charlie grunted, amused.

"No. Farther than that even. A place you have never heard of because it doesn't even exist yet. And it won't for a long time," Charlie revealed.

John turned his head to Charlie.

"But how can you come from a place that does not exist?"

Charlie turned his head to him and smiled. Part of him longed to tell him the truth. The man was about to risk his life to help him. He owed him the truth, or at least part of it.

"It's a long story; one that might be hard for you to believe." Charlie said.

"I'm not very tired, and I am well educated. I even speak some Greek."

Charlie rested his head back on the bare earth and turned his gaze back up to the ocean of stars that were slowly beginning to fade.

"Have you ever laid out like we are now and stared at the stars, John?"

John nodded, folding his arms under his head.

"Yes. I have. Many times. Fishing often leaves a great deal of time to gaze at the sky."

"Do you know how many stars there are? More than there

are grains of sands in the world."

John grunted in amazement.

"How many is that?"

"Someone suggested there might be seventy septillion stars."

"Sep-til-lion? Is that a lot?"

Charlie grinned. "Yes."

"People say stars are lights from heaven. Is that true?"

"No. Every little star you see is like the sun that rises each morning, but they are very, very far away. In fact it takes thousands of years for their light to be seen."

John wrestled with that idea for a moment.

"Does that mean then there are places like this up there?"

"Maybe. No one really knows the answer to that."

John was quiet for a moment.

"Are you from up there?" he asked cautiously.

Charlie laughed, "No. I'm from here, just like you."

"From a place that has not been born yet."

"That's right. You see, from where I live, we want to know what's up there. Are there places like this out there? We've even built machines that can explore some of those places."

"Where is this place that you can do such things?"

"It exists in another time."

"Another time?"

"John, I have traveled from thousands of tomorrows that have not yet seen the rising sun."

John turned his head and stared at Charlie. His face registered confusion.

"How can you travel from tomorrow?"

"It wasn't easy."

"Are your companions from...tomorrow?"

"Yes. That's why I have to save them. If I can't rescue them by tomorrow we will not be able to go home."

John did not speak for a long moment.

"Is it good where you come from? Are there Romans in

your...time?"

"No. Where I come from the Roman Empire ended thousands of years ago."

John grinned at that.

"So, we will be free of the Romans?"

"Yes. Some day."

"That will be a great day."

"Yes, John, it will."

John lowered his head and stared up at the stars as he imagined a world without Rome.

***

Pontius Pilate grimaced when his aide, Julius Quintus, entered his office and informed him that Caiaphas was demanding an immediate audience. He had hoped he would be spared the constant annoyance of Jewish leaders during their Passover observance. From what he understood about their demanding faith, no Jew could enter a Gentile residence or building during this important celebration. Apparently, if they were to do so, they risked becoming 'unclean' and could not eat their sacred meal. Why couldn't these people simply adopt the Roman gods who had no rules to speak of and demanded nothing but the odd offering? Life would be so much simpler for him.

"What do they want now?" he asked.

The aide stepped up to the desk. The rhythmic clinking of his dangling sword echoed off the vaulted ceiling

"They want you to pass judgment of one of their own apparently. A rabbi."

Pilate sat back in his chair and stared at his aide with incredulity. He then gazed down at his desk overflowing with paperwork. He had hoped for a few peaceful few days of respite from the troublesome Jewish population.

"A rabbi? One of their own?"

"I believe the Sanhedrin see him as a renegade rabbi who

operates outside their control. There was an incident in the temple the other day that greatly upset them."

Julius did not seem confident about his belief. As if to underline that, he rolled his shoulders.

Pilate considered putting Caiaphus off and ordering him to come back later to show he was not at his disposal. However, he reconsidered that option. For the leader of the Sanhedrin to bring this to his attention meant this was a serious matter.

"Very well."

He got up and followed Julius out.

When they reached the palace grounds, Pilate was surprised by the unruly crowd that had gathered. He did not only have Caiaphus waiting, but a dozen other richly-dressed priests, and a number of other citizens. However, his attention turned to their prisoner. He was a tall man in a simple brown robe. His face showed bruising. Dried blood stained his chin. However, despite the mistreatment, he stood erect, almost defiant.

"Blessings upon you, Governor," Caiaphus said.

The priest's normally arrogant, if not superior, attitude seemed oddly passive this morning. Pilate did not like that for some reason.

Pilate returned the greeting, and stepped forward to get a closer look at the prisoner. He regarded the governor with no emotion, but he had a calm, melancholy look about him.

"So, what charges do you bring against this man?"

Caiaphus glanced at the other priests uncertainly.

"Pilate, if he were not a criminal, would we have brought this man before you?"

Pilate, a guarded man, and experienced with the political machinations of the day, sensed a trap as he stared into the priest's eyes.

"If this man has not broken Roman law, deal with him yourselves. You have your own laws."

Caiaphus looked to his fellow priests once again. But they

offered him no support. He was on his own.

"Roman law prevents us from executing this man."

"Execute? You wish this man killed?"

Pilate feigned astonishment. Of course they wanted to do away with this renegade rabbi. Why else would he have been brought here? These Jewish leaders wanted to use him, and his office, to do their dirty work. And he thought Roman politics were vile.

"Has this man broken Roman law that risks death?"

One of the other priests finally summoned up the courage to speak. He stepped forward, joining Caiaphus. He was younger than their leader.

"He causes mischief among the people by his preaching. He started in the city of Galilee, and now stirs up the people here."

Pilate smiled now, happy that his first assumption had proven correct. This prisoner had become popular among the people. The priests clearly feared him and his message. But rather than risk their reputations, they wanted to use him to avoid taking blame for his death. However, he would not allow them to manipulate him.

"Do you mean to say this man is from Galilee?"

Caiaphus delivered a sneer at the priest. The young priest fell back to the others, lowering his head.

"If you want to prefer charges against this Galilean, you must go to Herod Antipas. Galilee is under his control. This is not my concern. Go to him for your justice."

Before Caiaphus could respond, Pilate turned and strode back into the palace. He grinned with satisfaction with how he handled what might have been a messy scandal. Let Herod handle this little problem.

Caiaphus, stung by Pilate's abrupt command, ordered his party to turn around and march to Herod's palace only a short distance away.

***

The sun had finally risen over Jerusalem. A formation of gray clouds blocked most of the early light. In the west, the last of the night was dissolving to a murky blue-gray. Donkey-driven carts over flowing with produce were already meandering up the road to Jerusalem. Clouds of singing birds wheeled overhead.

Charlie stared at the great wall towering over them. It was now or never. He looked to his companions awaiting his orders.

"James, I want you wait here."

"I can't go with you? I wish to help."

Charlie looked at the eager man who was ready to risk his life to help him. If only there was more time. But time was the one thing he did not have.

"I know you do. You are a brave man. But I need you to wait here until our return."

James nodded.

"When will you return?"

Charlie smiled grimly.

"If we're not back by noon, we're not coming back."

James looked to his brother. They embraced and said something to each other Charlie did not hear.

"Don't wander off if you see a farm girl," John warned him.

"Only if she's a very pretty farm girl."

They laughed.

Charlie waved down one of the men driving his donkey cart headed for the city. The driver pulled up.

"Come on," Charlie said.

John and Daniel followed him to the cart. Charlie produced a sisterius coin and offered it to the man. He nodded pleasantly and waved his hand at the rear of the cart. They settled on the tailboard. The driver flicked the reins and the cart started up the road, back to Jerusalem.

***

Herod Antipas laughed with delight after Caiaphus laid his case before him. His round belly quivered and his jowls puffed up in amusement. He sat lazily back in his bronze curule chair, thrusting his thick legs out, enjoying this little bit of Jewish theater. He had sipped his wine as the high priest listed the many 'crimes' committed by the prisoner standing before him.

Finally, Herod waved Caiaphus into silence. The high priest bowed slightly, stepping back, confident that he had made his case before the ruler of Galilee.

Herod turned his gaze to the prisoner who had listened to Caiaphus denouncing him for fifteen minutes without uttering a word in his own defense.

"You've been accused of making miracles, Nazarene."

"Is making a miracle a crime?" he finally said.

Herod grinned, looking to Caiaphus to see his reaction. He had none.

"That is a good question. I suppose it depends on who is making the miracle."

Herod the Tetrarch, which means ruler of a quarter, stared to Caiaphus for a reply. Not getting one, he looked back to the prisoner. His large smile pushed his cheeks up to his eyes.

"Perhaps you would care to make a miracle here and now for our benefit," Herod said.

Jesus stood there silently.

"No? Surely there must be some magic trick you could conjure up for us."

The prisoner simply stared passively at Herod.

Herod nodded, impressed by the man's wisdom. If he were to perform some trick, he would be condemning himself.

Herod sat back down and sipped some more wine, reflecting deeply. The last thing he needed was to involve himself in a political clash between these religious leaders and Rome. He was still haunted by his rash decision to execute that preacher called John the Baptist several years earlier. He had no desire to make the same mistake again. Let it be on Pilate's head to decide this man's fate.

"Caiaphus, step forward."

The high priest stepped up to Herod, grinning with anticipation.

"You have made no case against this man with that I can condemn him to death. You weary me with your accusations. I will have nothing further to do with this. Go. Go now."

Caiaphus frowned. He was about to protest Herod's pronouncement and then thought better of it. He signaled his followers.

"Take him away. We will go back to Pilate."

***

When they reached the Essene Gate, Charlie had Daniel cover his face with his robe. But the Romans guarding the entrance paid them no mind as they rolled into the city with other people.

"We'll get off here," Charlie called out.

The man stopped the cart letting the three drop down. They waved thanks and pushed on into the Upper City that was already coming to life.

It was a short, uneasy walk to the Praetorium. Charlie could feel his stomach tightening with every step as the ominous structure grew larger. He could only imagine what Daniel and John were feeling. He stopped when they were fifty yards from the guarded entrance. He shut his eyes and said a personal prayer.

"Dear Lord, please help us now in what we are about to do. Do with us what you will."

Charlie made a quick cross. John took notice of it.

"Is that motion you make a call to your God?"

"Yes," Charlie said simply, realizing he was looking at one of the men who would give birth to his faith.

Charlie glanced down at Daniel, setting his hand on his bony shoulder. He could sense the coiled tension in the boy's skinny frame. He was taking a great risk with the boy, but this was going to be their one and only chance to save Faith, Ben, and Miriam. Daniel sensed Charlie's eyes on him and looked up. The corners of his mouth formed a smile that barely masked the apprehension in his hesitant eyes. Charlie hoped he would be up to their desperate gambit, or they would be lost.

Charlie dropped down to one knee and stared into Daniel's pale face. His chest heaved with every breath. He was glad he had not revealed his plan to him earlier. It would have been too heavy a burden to place on the boy.

"Daniel, I need you to be brave now. To save your mother, I'm going to need your help. Can you do that?"

Daniel fought down his fear and nodded. He was one tough kid. Charlie cupped his pale cheek tenderly.

"Good boy."

Charlie ripped part of his robe away and used it to mask the lower part of his face. Seeing this, John did the same. Charlie patted his shoulder, getting an intense sense of confidence when it touched the pistol. He took a deep breath. It was now or never.

"Ready?" he asked John.

"Yes. I'm ready."

He placed his hand around the back of Daniel's neck and marched him toward the Praetorium. John walked alongside as they approached the main gate. There was more activity than he expected. The whole garrison had been called out. He knew with the trial, and the coming crucifixion of Jesus, the Praetorium would be on high alert. He was actually counting on that.

The Roman commander at the gate stared at the three. He took notice of the masks on Charlie and John. Two vigilant guards behind him came alert. They hitched up their swords as if anticipating trouble.

"What do you want?" the commander growled.

His sharp question sounded more like a demand.

"We wish to see Tribune Macro," Charlie said.

Charlie then shoved Daniel forward. The boy looked

terrified. Charlie did not think he was acting. He could hardly blame him. He was scared as well.

"The Tribune has been searching for this boy. We've come for the reward."

The commander glowered at the boy, and then thoughtfully considered the masked men. He appeared to be wary for a moment. Finally, he turned to the guards.

"Stay alert."

He turned back to Charlie.

"Come with me."

Charlie, John, and Daniel followed the commander into the Praetorium. They passed a strident mob that was assembling off by the main courtyard of the palace. Guards were pushing back against them. Still more guards issued out to help control the growing horde.

John, seeing all the soldiers and the flustered crowd, leaned in toward Charlie.

"My master is in there, isn't he?"

Charlie nodded, "Yes, John. He's before Pilate. If you wish to go I will understand."

John stared off at the gathered crowd. He looked back to Charlie. He could see the great turmoil eating away at John's heavy heart.

"Is there anything I can do for him?"

"I'm sorry. There isn't anything anyone can do for him now," Charlie said somberly.

The words startled John for a moment. Then he nodded his head in resignation.

"That is what I thought. He would have helped you if He could. Since He cannot, I will."

Charlie choked down his own anguish.

"Thank you, John," Charlie said.

CHAPTER XVI

Pilate was just finishing a most satisfying breakfast when a shadow fell over him. Julius' long face was grim with portentous news. Staring up at it, Pilate guessed he had returned. He hoped he was wrong.

"They have returned, Governor," Julius said, exasperated.

"Who has returned?"

"The Jewish priests with their prisoner; and there are more people with them. There may be trouble. I've called out the garrison."

Pilate pushed his empty plate away, rolling his head tiredly.

"These annoying priests will be the death of me, Julius," Pilate groaned. "What happened?"

"Herod refused to listen to the priests. Apparently he spoke to the prisoner and found he had committed no crime for him to pass judgment."

Pilate managed a tired grin. Herod was a very shrewd individual for a non-Roman. Why risk breaking Roman law by convicting a man for the benefit of some troublesome priests? He clearly did not fear the Sanhedrin. That spoke well of him. *Well, two can play that game*, he thought to himself. He would not let Herod get the better of him.

"Very well."

Pilate stood and followed Julius out.

A much larger mob had gathered just behind the gates leading to the main courtyard. However, unlike the earlier assemblage, this one appeared near riotous. Pilate glanced back and signaled Julius. He hurried forward and took personal command of the soldiers. He immediately ordered them to drive the crowd back.

Pilate stepped up onto the platform glaring down at the high priest and his minions pressing their faces against the bars of the large gate. He was in no mood to deal with their inter-religious quarrels.

"Why are you back, Caiaphus?" Pilate called out.

Caiaphus gripped the bars of the main gate. His fellow priests stood behind him. Just beyond them, the surging mob pushed against the line of soldiers.

"Herod refused to convict our prisoner."

"That is hardly surprising, priest. You have not yet revealed this man's crime against Rome."

Pilate realized he needed to tread carefully here. The emperor had strict rules for governors on not interfering in the religious laws of states like Judea. Doing so risks rebellions. And in the Empire, it seemed the Jews, unlike most Roman subjects, were always on the brink of open rebellion.

"He claims he is the King of the Jews," Caiaphus announced.

Pilate looked to the prisoner who stood there almost defiantly indifferent to the proceedings. A king. That was a different matter altogether. Declaring oneself a king was a direct threat to the power of the emperor and his rule over Judea. Maybe there was more to this prisoner than he originally thought.

"I will speak to this 'king'. Julius, bring forth the prisoner," Pilate said.

Julius took the prisoner by the arm and escorted him into the courtyard.

Caiaphus was about to follow when he realized Passover forbid him from entering the palace, or any Gentile place. Pilate smiled at the high priests' discomfort.

A guard brought Jesus up to Pilate's platform. Caiaphus and the crowd could only observe from behind the gates. The floor of the courtyard was paved with diamond shaped flagstones. The thick stonewalls on either side soared up some twenty feet. Along the right wall, narrow stairs ran up to the battlement where Roman soldiers marched back and forth, carefully observing the crowd. There was no roof or ceiling, thereby allowing the early morning sun to fill the courtyard. A number of staff, having heard about the hearing, eagerly watched the proceeding.

Pilate sat back in his chair that was resting upon an elevated platform. Being higher up allowed him to look down upon his subjects, and those he would pass judgment on. He took this opportunity to study the man who was causing all this turmoil. Unlike Caiaphus and the other priests who invaded his morning in fancy dress, this rabbi was clad in a simple, ankle length robe, and dirty sandals. Despite the mistreatment at the hands of his own people, he displayed a regal dignity in his posture. His intelligent eyes seemed to regard Pilate with polite detachment.

"Is Caiaphus right? Do you consider yourself King of the Jews?" he asked almost mockingly.

A ripple of amused guffaws burst from the staff.

"Is this your idea, or did the others speak to you about me?" the prisoner said.

The prisoner's firm voice carried easily across the space between himself and Pilate. It was as if he were standing alongside him on the platform.

"I am not a Jew. It is your own chief priest who has brought you to me for judgment. What do they think you have done that requires my attention?"

"My kingdom is not of this world," he stated plainly. "It is of another place. But, if it were, do you not think my servants would have allowed those men to deliver me to you?"

Pilate smiled. He leaned back, his hands caressing the armrests.

"So, you are a king then?"

Pilate now felt more confident in dealing with this man. Any man who proclaimed himself to be above the emperor could rightly be judged an enemy of Rome.

Jesus glanced at the others in the courtyard before looking back to Pilate.

"That is why I was born. To give testimony to the truth. All men who hear truth hear my voice."

Pilate reflected on his words. Unlike many pompous religious leaders he had dealt with as governor, this man seemed no more threatening than a shepherd tending his herd. But he had to be careful. Wolves can often hide in sheep's clothing.

"But what is truth?" Pilate asked, genuinely wanting to hear the man's reply.

Jesus simply stared back, saying nothing.

Pilate grimaced, hoping the man might convict himself by his own words. However, he wisely remained mute. Knowing he could not convict a man of preaching truth, he looked past Jesus and fixed his gaze on the Jewish priests on the other side of the gate who had been closely watching the proceeding.

"This man has committed no crime," he announced.

The indignant crowd roared with disapproval.

"Do you wish me to release this 'King of the Jews'?"

A roar of 'No' and 'Crucify him!' overwhelmed the few who begged for him to be released.

"Crucify him!"

Pilate finally realized he had greatly underestimated the volatility of the situation. Clearly, the Sanhedrin priests had whipped up the crowd into a blood-fever pitch. However, he knew he still could not convict a man who had committed no crime against Rome. Of course, there have been exceptions. But if word was to reach Rome that he acted against a priest without cause, Emperor Tiberius might find offense. Thinking quickly, he realized a way out of his predicament. Three convicted killers were to be crucified that day. Maybe his answer lay there.

"I will give you a choice then. I can release this man of peace, or the murderer Barabbas. What do you say?"

"Give us Barabbas! Give us Barabbas!" they screamed.

Pilate fell back in astonishment.

Barabbas, the worst of the three men sentenced to die, had committed crimes of murder and robbery in numbers that appeared endless. The crazed fools preferred him spared to terrorize them again rather than letting this man go free. He now realized how much hatred, or was it fear, that the Sanhedrin had for this preacher. What could he have done to them to strike such fear?

As Pilate listened to the raging crowd demanding the man before him be crucified, he searched for a way out. There were other considerations. Perhaps this simple rabbi had a large following. If he crucified him, they might rebel, causing him no end of problems. Rome held governors in low regard who could not keep their subjects under control. Then another idea occurred to him. Maybe there was a way to pacify the mob's thirst for blood.

Pilate rose from his chair and raised his right hand. The yelling slowly subsided.

"You have offered me no proof that this man has incited the people to rebel against Rome. Therefore, he has done nothing to deserve death. Silence!"

The crowd that had erupted again became subdued.

"I will punish him, and then I shall set him free. That is my judgment."

The crowd flared up once again. Some pushed against the iron gates until Roman soldiers, brandishing swords, struck at probing hands reaching between the bars. After several arms were sliced open, they fell back.

Pilate pointed to his aide.

Julius signaled two Roman soldiers. They grabbed Jesus and escorted him toward an adjoining courtyard for punishment.

Pilate dropped back tiredly into his chair and turned a deaf ear to the clamorous mob. He watched the soldiers strip the robe from the prisoner and manacle his hands to the scourging post. The two huge men then produced wood handled whips. They pulled back and struck the ground several times. The leather tips, with lead weights on the ends, triggered sharp explosions and sparks. Pilate, a weak man, despite his reputation for ruthlessness, shuddered with each crack. He had witnessed a whipping only once before, and he had no wish to see another. He jerked to his feet, displaying as much dignity as possible under the circumstances. He turned to Julius.

"Bring me wine, Julius. I need a moment to think."

Julius nodded as Pilate exited the courtyard.

***

A thickening shaft of dusty sunlight invaded the dreary cell. It created a small patch of light on the ground. Ravenous fleas darted in and out of the shimmering beam. The persistent wail of hungry and thirsty prisoners began once again. Barks from irritated guards, or the clang of swords against their cell doors, did not make them more compliant. While the coolness of the night gave way to the warming sun, it did nothing to dampen the stench of human excrement and rot.

Miriam lay scrunched up in a corner, sleeping restlessly. She twisted and turned, occasionally mumbling aloud some inner nightmare.

Faith lifted her head up from Ben's shoulder. She looked weakly at him. Her face wore a deathly pallor now. Only a few hours in this hell had taken a terrible toll on her already failing health. She looked many years older. Somehow, their great trip through time had accelerated her disease. Even if they somehow got back home, what could they do for her?

"Why did you really come with us, Ben?"

Her voice was frail as if coming out of deep well.

"What do you mean? You know why I came, sis."

She squinted, studying his face as if expecting to see a different answer than the one he gave her.

"Do I?"

"Of course. What are you getting at?"

"Oh, poor Ben."

"What?"

She frowned, resting against him again. Her head felt so heavy now, as if her neck could no longer support it. The dull muscular twinges she had been feeling sporadically never ceased now. Her chilled body felt almost alien to her.

"It's okay to have doubts about what you believe, Ben."

It was his turn to try to read her face. Tilting his head down, his eyes gazed at her withering body.

"Do you? Have doubts, I mean?"

"Yes. Sometimes."

Ben showed surprise. He never thought to hear her express a thought like that. She always threw up a brave front, even when they were kids. He reflected for a moment.

"Like when you found out you were sick?"

He asked the question cautiously.

Faith struggled to bring her knees up close to her chest. She wrapped her arms around her legs before resting her chin down upon them. She sighed, recalling all of the things she wanted to do with her life. Now they felt as if they belonged to a stranger from a long time ago.

"Yes. We had so many plans. Things we wanted to do. Then to have that taken away seemed so...unfair. I got so angry, Ben. I got so angry. At everything...Everyone. Charlie. Me. The world...God, even."

Ben stared at her. This was shocking to him.

"I never...you never said anything."

"I know. I guess I was ashamed."

"Faith-" Ben started to say, but her headshake stopped him.

"I was. Not then. That came later."

"I'm sorry."

"It's okay. You know, you tell yourself why you should be any different from the person with cancer across the street, or the starving kid in Ethiopia. What makes you so special that bad things shouldn't happen to you? Then you realize how silly that sounds because you're not. You're no better or worse than anyone else is. So we tell ourselves there must be a reason for it. It's all part of God's plan, until you find out your plans and God's are a little different. And your plans go out the window, and you begin scrambling to make sense of everything."

"Einstein said, 'God doesn't play dice with the Universe.' Someone reminded me of that recently."

"I like that. He was a pretty smart man."

"Yes, he was."

Faith played with her wedding band, turning it on her finger. It was loose now. Several times, she had almost lost it.

"If it were not for Charlie, I think would have given up. But he wouldn't let me. Not for one damn second. He always believed we'd find an answer. He held onto his faith when I almost lost mine."

Ben looked around their cell and grunted.

"I don't think he saw this coming."

Faith grabbed Ben's hand. However, there was no real strength in it. Her cold fingers did not seem to work.

"Don't worry, Ben. He'll come for us."

Ben flashed skepticism.

"How can you be so sure?"

"Because he's the one thing I never lost faith in."

Ben nodded, not wanting to point out all of the problems of one man delivering them from their desperate predicament. For all they knew, Charlie could be dead, or in one of the other cells ten feet away. But he would never suggest such a possibility to Faith. Charlie was her last hope.

"You know I didn't like Charlie at first. I didn't think he was good enough for you. I even told him so. We almost had a big fight about it."

"Yeah, I know," she said.

"He told you?"

Ben was shocked. Charlie outweighed Ben by thirty pounds. Ben suspected he would have been pounded him into pulp.

"Charlie told me everything. Almost word for word."

"Really? I guess, maybe, I was wrong about him," Ben ventured reluctantly.

"No maybe, Ben. You were."

Faith pressed herself against Ben's warm body.

An explosion of noise from outside triggered a reaction from them. Ben got up and moved to the barred window above. An angry cacophony of indecipherable voices reached them. He jumped up and grabbed the bars. He pulled himself up until his eyes could just look out. Off to his left he saw a large crowd had gathered. Beyond them, he could see a robed figure on a large platform. The distinguished man was trying to speak over the angry voices. Then he spotted another figure near the platform. He was a tall figure with long brown hair.

"What is it?" Faith asked.

Miriam was awake now and standing up. She looked up at Ben peering out the barred window. She said something. It was likely the same thing Faith had asked.

Ben felt his fingers losing their grip on the bars. The burning in his arms became too much and he dropped back down to the ground. He massaged his sore shoulders.

"I don't know for sure."

He thought for a moment. Then he had a revelation.

"I think it's him, Faith."

Faith struggled to her feet. She swayed uncertainly, a flash of dizziness forcing her to lean against the slimy wall to keep her balance.

"What? Charlie!" she said, almost panic-stricken.

Ben shook his head. He debated telling her what he thought was happening. Faith crept over, her chest heaving.

"No. *Him*," he finally said.

Faith needed a few seconds to understand what he meant. It startled her. She grabbed his arm tightly, showing renewed strength.

"Are you sure?" she asked.

"I think so."

The sharp crack of a whip startled all three of them. Their eyes shot up to the barred window, as equally loud cracks came, one after another. With every crack, the crowd groaned excitedly.

Ben took a breath and jumped. Grabbing the bars, he was just able to pull himself up to the window. Looking beyond the crowd, he saw a man manacled to a wood post being violently whipped. The man made no sound; at least any sound he could hear from where he looked. Ben lost his grip and dropped back down to his knees. He gasped, out of breath.

Faith leaned against the wall. She stared up at the barred window as the whipping continued. It banged like gunshots. She gasped with every explosion.

"Oh, Ben, help me up! Help me! Help me see!"

Her outstretched hands clawed up to the barred window. Ben came up behind her. He placed his hands under her arms and tried to lift her but he barely got her off the ground. He just was not strong enough. He finally gave up.

"I'm sorry, Faith. I can't do it," he muttered.

The two of them slid back down the wall. Faith, shaking now, fumbled for something under her robe. She pulled out the chained crucifix. She wrapped her hands around it and prayed under her breath.

After the barbarous whipping mercifully ended, Jesus was unchained from the vertical post. He staggered forward and dropped to his knees.

"Stand up, prisoner! Get to your feet!" one of the two soldiers commanded.

Seeing he could not obey, they jerked him to his feet. More than his back had been brutalized. The deep lacerations ran down both thighs. In some places, muscle and bone were visible, as rivulets of blood ran down his body. Every step he took was an ordeal in excruciating pain. Suffering now from both dehydration, and shock, his vision swam, the world about him a murky gray. The crowd watched in morbid fascination as he faced Pilate again.

In the crowd, Peter looked on helplessly. In the chaos of the last few hours, he had lost track of the other disciples. He suspected they were somewhere in the great clamorous crowd, or they had gone into hiding. He wanted to act, to do something to help his master. But alone, what could he do against the might of Rome? As he watched his master dragged off, he reacted to a threatening voice that screeched over the angry crowd.

"Here is one of his disciples! Here is one of them!"

Bursting from the crowd, the accuser, a woman with a red visage, pointed a bony finger at Peter.

"Look! Here is one of his followers!"

Peter's eyes darted from the accusing woman toward others in the rapacious crowd who demanded a new target for their hateful venom. A horde of foaming citizens launched their fists trying to strike him down. He threw up his arms in self-defense, blocking their wild blows.

"No! No! I am not one of them. I do not know that man!" he cried out, looking for an avenue of escape.

"I've seen you with him! You are one of them!" another woman, attired in a teal blue robe, cried out.

"No! You are mistaken. He was another man. I know not this Jesus! Get away!"

Seeing a gap in the crowd, Peter pushed his way through before the accusers could attack him again. After he was clear, he ducked between two buildings. His lungs burned as he tried to catch his breath. Then he suddenly recalled Jesus' warning about how he would deny him. The words rang in his ears like body blows until he dropped to the ground and wept many bitter tears.

CHAPTER XVII

Charlie, John, and Daniel sat stiffly on the wood dais in the main hallway. Roman soldiers stole glances at them as they strode past. From their raw chatter, Charlie knew what was happening not more than a hundred yards from where they were sitting. As much as it pained him, he was helpless to do anything about that now. Daniel kept looking up fearfully whenever a soldier appeared. After they passed, he sighed, his lungs deflating with relief. Charlie patted the boy's knee and gave him a reassuring look. He could sense the boy was close to panic at just being in this building.

"There are so many soldiers," John commented.

"I know," Charlie agreed.

Charlie stared at him. John looked almost as apprehensive as Daniel did. Then he suddenly realized what he had done. How could he have been so foolish? By bringing John along, he was taking a tremendous gamble with the future of Christianity itself. If something were to happen to him in trying to save Faith, Ben, and Miriam, the consequences could be incalculable. He was far more important than they were; at least in the eyes of history yet to come. But they were all committed to this course of action. Now, not only did Charlie have to rescue the others, but he had to make certain nothing happened to John. It was just one more burden he had to carry. He heaved a sigh.

"Is there something wrong?" John asked, reacting to Charlie's fixed stare.

"No," he replied evasively.

"The way you look at me sometimes. It is as if you know me," he said curiously.

"Do I?" Charlie said.

John nodded, "Yes. Do you know me?"

Charlie smiled. How could he answer that question? There were so many things he could tell John about his future, so many great adventures ahead for him, and the others. Their odysseys in the decades to come would ripple through time for the next two thousand years. Tempted as he was to reveal a small hint of that future, Charlie finally decided he had no right to interfere in his destiny.

"No, John. I only met you this day. But you remind me of someone I know," Charlie explained.

"I see."

John did not look as if he believed Charlie, but the appearance of more Roman soldiers marching by diverted his attention.

Charlie stole another look at his device. They only had a little over four hours or they would be lost in this time forever. His eyes gazed down the long hallway. In his mind's eye, he recalled the layout of the Praetorium that he had studied for weeks. There was a lot of conflicting information about the Praetorium. Few could agree on the actual structure of the building because no part of the Praetorium exists in the present day. After the great rebellion by the Jews in 67 CE, the victorious Roman army leveled most of Jerusalem. And over the succeeding centuries, further wars destroyed even more of the city, until very little remained from this time.

John spotted him first. He uttered a grunt to Charlie.

Tribune Macro strode down the corridor toward them. He was alone. Daniel saw him a moment later and his body spasmed. He pressed himself instinctively against Charlie.

Macro looked down at them with his one dark eye. He ignored the two men and scowled at Daniel who seemed to shrink in terror before the giant. An ominous leer cracked his gaunt face like a rotten egg. He then turned his penetrating gaze upon the two masked men.

"Who are you?"

"Does it matter who we are? We brought you the boy you've sought for many months," Charlie said.

The two men aroused Macro's natural suspicion. A gut

feeling warned him there was something off about them. He jabbed a thick finger at Charlie, who he believed was the leader.

"Why do you wear masks?"

Charlie was ready for that question. He stood up confidently. John followed him.

"We do not want anyone recognizing us for bringing you the boy."

Macro flashed a knowing smile. A Jew who betrayed another Jew, especially a child, could find his life at serious risk. He glowered at Daniel.

"Stand up, boy," he commanded. "Stand up!"

Daniel stood on shaky knees, staring at the vengeful centurion. This was no act on his part. He was terrified.

"Come with me, boy. Your mother is waiting to embrace you," he said coldly.

He grabbed Daniel roughly and started to drag him off. Charlie stepped out in front of the centurion. He threw his palm out expectedly.

"Wait, Tribune. We want our reward."

Macro stared at Charlie's outstretched hand, surprised by the man's impudence. Then he nodded and signaled them to follow him.

***

The roar of many Roman soldiers coming up the corridor drew Ben over to the cell door to investigate. Pressing his face against the bars, he could see a mass of dark figures coming their way. They appeared to be shoving a stumbling figure along. Whenever the figure hit the ground, one, or several of them, would kick him vigorously. He would then struggle to his feet and stagger forward a bit.

"Release Barabbas," a chief guard ordered.

"Release him? He was to be executed this day," a guard replied with confusion.

"Orders from Pilate. This prisoner will die in his place," the chief guard snapped. "Release him."

"What is it Ben?" Faith asked from the corner of the cell where she had not moved since the whipping.

"I'm not sure," he replied.

"Come along King of the Jews," a rancid voice barked.

Finally, the figure collapsed right before their cell. His long, stringy hair cloaked his face. The man's bare back had been torn apart by a horrific pattern of bleeding lacerations.

"My God," Ben muttered, horrified, realizing who it was before him.

"Ben, what is it? What's happening?" Faith gasped.

"Don't come over here, Faith. Just stay where you are. You don't want to see this. Do you hear me? Just stay back."

Faith and Miriam ignored him. They staggered over, joining Ben. Faith pressed her face into the iron bars. They stared in shock at the beaten man on the ground. Faith instantly understood who she was looking at. She uttered a gasp and felt her heart lurch in her chest so violently she grabbed her bosom.

"No. Oh God," she whimpered.

The brutish soldiers gathered around, leering at the sprawled figure who could only lay there utterly exhausted. They jeered and laughed at him unmercifully.

"Look at the mighty king," one of the soldiers joked.

A soldier pushed his way through holding something in his hands. From Ben's point of view it was ring shaped, like intertwined wires. The soldier thrust it into the light. Now he understood what he was seeing. It was a twisted crown of thorns. The soldier held it up proudly for all to see.

"What is a king without a crown? Ha! Here is your crown, king," the soldier spat.

He dropped down to one knee and shoved the thorny crown into Jesus' head. He grimaced, his bloody back arching violently, forcing more blood from the many gashes. Almost immediately, trickles of dark blood ran down his head, mingling with the blood running down his back. The barbaric soldiers cheered the bloody coronation. The joined roar boomed like the howling of predators feasting on a fallen prey.

"Now you truly are a king!" he roared.

He kicked him, forcing a horrific grunt from him.

"You bastards!" Ben yelled, shocked at the horrific brutality he was witnessing. For the first time in his life, he really felt as if he was capable of killing another human being. Not that Ben believed these jackals to be human beings. He seized the bars and violently shook them. For a fleeting moment, he almost felt he possessed the strength to rip them away.

Faith fell down to her knees, gasping, as a torrent of tears poured down her cheeks. Her tremulous hand reached through the bars toward him. As she leaned forward, her crucifix spilled out from out of her robe hanging by the thin chain. It dangled there, twinkling in the torch light.

"Stop hurting him. Please," she mumbled weakly.

"Leave him alone, God dammit!" Ben yelled.

Jesus turned up and met Faith's anguished eyes. His expression was gaunt, pale; his bloodshot eyes twisted with great pain. He wheezed spasmodically. A single thin line of blood from his tortuous crown trickled down his forehead and cheek.

"I'm sorry. God protect you," she said weakly. "Oh Ben, what can we do?"

Ben shook his head impotently. He never felt so utterly helpless in his life. If this had taken place in the present, he would have called the cops to stop this brutality. Then he realized these were the cops. At that moment, he despised the world and everything in it.

Faith reached out nervously and caressed his face, her fingers smearing the blood on his cheek. She shook as a great tremor shot up her arm, the electrifying sensation warming her whole body. A comforting sense of peace coursed deep into her. For an instant, her unrelenting pain of hopelessness was driven from her heart.

Jesus' tormented eyes dipped down from her gaunt face and focused on the crucifix dangling there. He stared at it for a long moment, not sure he was seeing it. Then he looked back up to Faith. Her hand finally found his and squeezed it tight. Suddenly some of his excruciating pain seemed to pass from his weary eyes. There was a renewed vigor in his face.

A sharp command from down the corridor triggered an immediate reaction from the guards. They bent over and jerked Jesus to his feet, pulling his hand from hers. She tried to grab it again, but it was too far away now.

"Come along, King. You are wanted by Pilate," a Roman barked as they dragged him away.

"No! Stop it! Leave him be," Faith begged.

"Damn you. Damn all of you," Ben cursed repeatedly as his hands shook the bars.

A guard struck the cell bars with his sword, sending them sprawling to the hard ground. Ben crawled over to Faith. He took her into his arms and held her. Shaking uncontrollably, she buried her face into his chest and sobbed.

***

Macro led the three into a smoky office crudely furnished with a simple desk and chair. One wall consisted of shelves stuffed with rolled papyrus. The opposite wall displayed a small arsenal of swords and spears. A beam of dusty sunlight poured through the large casement. The tribune grabbed a small chest hidden behind some papyrus and set it down next to a jar of wine and several tin cups on the desk. He unlocked the chest and withdrew a small sack that clinked. He weighed it in his hand, opened it, and checked the contents. He stared at Charlie.

"Your reward, Jew," he said.

He was about to fling it at Charlie when he noticed Daniel was pressing his body protectively into the masked man's side. His eye narrowed with reflection. For a betrayed boy, he seemed oddly trusting to the man who had just sold him out.

"You are holding two prisoners who were taken with Miriam. We wish to see them," Charlie said.

Macro fixed a long stare at the masked man. His natural cynical nature became aroused.

"Who are they to you?"

"They are...friends."

"Friends? You've chose dangerous friends."

Macro's gaze turned back on Daniel who was looking up at Charlie, not with anger, but with expectation. The Tribune's rising sense of suspicion flashed in his cyclopean eye. He set the sack of coins down. He crossed his arms.

"Remove your masks. I want to see your faces," he commanded.

Charlie's eyes darted to John. He realized the game was up now. John seemed to pale under the penetrating gaze of the Roman.

"Well?"

When the two did not remove their masks, Macro grabbed the hilt of his sword in a threatening manner.

"I want to see your faces. Show me your faces."

Charlie shuddered inside when he saw his scarred hand grip the sword hilt. This was literally the moment of truth. There was no going back now. He reached into his robe. His jittery fingers tapped the pistol grip nervously. The sensation of cool metal seemed to settle his nerves. He slowly pulled out the pistol. He released the safety and pointed it at Macro. Although his guts were churning over fiercely, his hand held steady.

Macro showed surprise at the strange metal object pointed at him. He squinted at it, turning his head to get a better look at it. It was not a knife, or short sword. It also did not look like any bludgeon he had ever seen before.

The oblong thing in Charlie's hand also perplexed John and Daniel. John's right hand was under his tunic fumbling for his blade. He would not surrender without a fight.

"What is that?" Macro inquired, clearly fascinated by the thing.

"You're going to take me to your prisoners, Tribune," Charlie ordered.

Macro cracked an amused smirk, revealing a missing canine tooth. He unsheathed his short gladius sword and raised it high. The sharp blade reflected the sunlight. He held it up as if to say, "mine is bigger than yours is".

Charlie knew he had to demonstrate the futility of resisting him. He considered a warning shot but dismissed it. He did not want to risk it. It was possible Macro could strike him down before he could fire another shot. He took careful aim, held his breath, and squeezed the trigger.

There was a sudden sharp crack. The pistol jerked up in his hand. Macro stumbled back, slamming into the wall and sliding down. Charlie circled the desk and stared down at the bleeding hole in Macro's right arm. The gladius sword had clattered to the floor. When Macro's hand instinctively reached for it, Charlie kicked it away. Macro stared up in shock. Then he glanced at his wounded arm. He winced at the burning sensation shooting into his shoulder.

"God protect us," John mumbled.

Charlie stole a look to John and Daniel. They had identical open mouth expressions. He stared back down to Macro.

"We're going to try this again, Tribune. You are going to take us to the prisoners."

Macro stared back stubbornly. He was a brave man. The idea of taking an order from anyone, particularly a Jew, turned his stomach. He shook his head. Maybe that thing was like a bow and arrow, and could only fire once.

Charlie sensed what he was thinking. He took careful aim again and fired. This time the bullet just missed Macro's ear, burying itself into the paved floor. Charlie pressed his sandaled foot into Macro's bloody arm. Macro grimaced, a guttural grunt escaping his frothing lips.

"Right now," Charlie said, aiming the pistol right at Macro's forehead.

Macro nodded, realizing the futility of further resistance for the moment. Later he might get his chance to turn the tables on them.

"Get him up."

John hurried around and jerked the tribune back to his feet.

"John, bind his wound."

John tore off another part of his robe and wrapped it around Macro's arm. As he worked, he stole looks at Charlie's magical weapon that spit fire.

"What is that weapon?"

Charlie considered some glib reply but nothing came to him.

"It's a new weapon from far off. Make sure the arm doesn't bleed. We don't want anyone to see he's been wounded."

"This will be my pleasure."

He tightened the tourniquet forcing a grunt from Macro. John enjoyed seeing the Roman in pain.

"It's done."

"Good. Ready, Daniel?"

The boy nodded, still dumbfounded by the excitement of the last couple of minutes.

Charlie got right up in Macro's face. His fear was gone. Firing the gun had somehow cleared away all of his apprehension. He was ready to shoot and kill anyone who tried to stop them now. It was a strange, yet exhilarating sensation.

"Shall we go, Tribune?"

CHAPTER XVIII

Pilate slumped back down onto his throne just as the prisoner returned to the courtyard. Pilate felt exhausted, and the day had barely begun. The besieged governor watched the prisoner stagger up to his podium. He slowly raised his head and gazed up at him. Pilate choked down the bile racing up his throat when he saw the vulgar crown of thorns pressing down on the beaten man's head and the crimson tears rolling down his pale cheeks. He considered chastising the guards for their brazenness but changed his mind. Criticizing them might make him look weak in the eyes of the population. Weakness was something a Roman must never show a subjugated populace.

As Jesus stood before Pilate, his face showed neither anger nor pain. His shoulders were hunched forward a little, his head tilted down, while his chin was pressed upon his breast. However, he still displayed that almost annoying intransigence from earlier.

"There is your king," Pilate announced boldly to the people, unable to look at the prisoner anymore.

He had hoped the terrible beating the guards had inflicted upon the priest would satiate the inflamed crowd. But he still did not comprehend the terrible fear the prisoner had ignited in Caiaphus and the other priests, nor how much the Sanhedrin had whipped up the people against him.

"Take him and crucify him!" the bloodthirsty mob chanted together as if well-rehearsed.

Pilate stared, listening, the maddened chanting ringing in his ears. Finally, unable to bear it anymore, he rose up and waved them to silence.

"Shall I crucify your king? Shall I?"

"We have no king but Caesar!" someone in the crowd screamed.

Others joined in, repeating the phrase.

Pilate was aghast. He was well-versed in the Jewish faith to know that the declaration of Caesar being their king was heresy. Now leaders of the Sanhedrin eagerly joined the mob in declaring their fealty to Rome.

"What crime has this man committed?"

"Crucify him!" they yelled repeatedly.

Pilate felt himself beaten down by the mob's enraged demands. They had finally whipped him into total capitulation. He turned to Julius and ordered him to bring a small bowl of water. Holding it before him, Pilate dunked his fingers into the warm water, ritualistically cleansing his hands submissively before the mob. Then he faced them, displaying his hands.

"I declare myself innocent of this man's blood. I now make his fate your responsibility," he told the roaring mob.

"Take him away."

The crowd exploded with glee as the Roman soldiers closed in on Jesus and escorted him away. He moved slowly, his bare feet leaving a trail of blood across the courtyard.

Pilate watched his guards escort the condemned man out with the vile taste of bitterness in his mouth. He cursed his weakness in allowing the mob to wear him down and manipulate him. As he turned to leave, he caught sight of Caiaphus. The high priest was smiling at him with grim satisfaction.

***

A recalcitrant Macro marched down the hall. His tunic carefully hid the crude arm bandage John had hastily fastened. John and Daniel walked on either side of him. Charlie was right up behind the Tribune with the Glock pressed right up into his spine. Passing soldiers saluted, but Macro did not reciprocate. Charlie prodded the weapon into his back.

"If you try and warn them they will all die. Not just you."

Reaching the stairway to the lower dungeon, Charlie looked around. He told John to go first and Daniel to follow behind himself.

With Macro sandwiched between Charlie and John, they started down to the lower level.

Macro breathed hard, feeling disorientation from the hot piece of metal still embedded in his arm. He darted looks around as they descended. He contemplated calling out but he thought it prudent to be patient and wait for them to become careless.

"Keep going," Charlie said, giving him a shove.

At the bottom of the stairs they stopped. Several guards were throwing dice in one corner to pass the time. Spotting Macro, they scrambled to their feet and saluted. When Macro did not respond, Charlie dug the Glock into the back of his head.

"You saw what this did to your arm. Imagine what it will do to your head. Nod if you understand," Charlie said, trying to sound as menacing as possible.

The Tribune nudged his head in acknowledgement.

"Good. Take us to the prisoners."

Macro turned left and led them down the long passage of the cellblock. The stench of death drifted in the air like an invisible fog. The sickly sweet smell stung Charlie's nostrils. The mournful cries of prisoners begging for their lives clawed at his heart as cold shivers ran up his spine like sharp knives. The thought of Faith being in this hellish place, if even for only a day, steeled his nerve.

Hearing the approaching footsteps, Ben came to the cell door. Somehow he had to get the guards to give them food and water. He spotted Macro, followed by three other shadowy figures.

"Hey, we need food and water in here. What kind of place are you running here? Did you hear me? We want food!"

The moment Macro reached the cell, Charlie shoved him face first into the nearby wall. The Roman grunted when his injured arm slammed into the facade.

"Don't move. Watch him," he told John.

John grabbed Macro around the neck with one hand while pressing his blade hard against Macro's back.

"I have him."

John leaned into Macro, twisting the blade.

"Please do something so I can stick this in your spine, Roman."

Ben recognized Daniel when he came to the cell door. He was aghast at seeing the boy again. He dropped to his knees and reached through the bars.

"Daniel! How did you get here?"

At hearing Ben mention Daniel's name, Miriam struggled to her feet and stumbled over. She cried out in excitement and horror at seeing him in this dreadful place. Her arms shot between the bars and wrapped around her son. She pulled him tight against the bars and kissed him.

"Daniel! Daniel!" she cried.

"Momma!" Daniel cried back.

Both were in tears at their reunion. He felt his ribs almost breaking from the power of her embrace, but he did not care. He was just happy to know she still lived.

Macro turned his head to see.

"Don't move," Charlie told Macro.

John forced Macro to look straight into the wall.

Charlie stepped over into the light, revealing himself to Ben.

"Ben, where's Faith?"

Ben shuddered when he saw Charlie standing there. He could barely speak.

"Char-Charlie?"

Faith looked up at hearing Ben's voice. She pushed herself to her feet and limped to the cell door. Ben slid over as she pressed her face against the bars. She looked at Charlie in amazement.

"Charlie? Charlie?"

"I'm here, Faith. I'm here, darling," he said, overwhelmed.

He pulled the mask down and kissed her through the bars.

"I knew you'd come," she gasped.

Charlie was shocked at how weak and ghostly pale she looked since the last time he saw her. Faith's lips were cold. Her voice was hoarse. She struggled to breath.

"Everything is going to be okay," he promised.

"Please, tell me we're getting out of here, Charlie," Ben said.

"Yeah, we're getting out. Right now."

Macro took his chance to try warning the guards, but the sharp jab of John's knife made him reconsider.

"I will skewer you like the pig you are if you call out," John warned him.

Charlie pulled the mask back up and faced Macro.

"Open the cell," Charlie commanded.

When Macro hesitated, John drew blood with his blade. Macro barked a command to the closest guard. He hurried over, whipped out the keys, and unlocked the door.

"Tell the guard to withdraw," Charlie whispered.

Macro ordered the guard to leave them. He saluted and withdrew.

Charlie opened the cell door. Miriam lifted her boy into her arms and embraced him, showering him with kisses. Faith came into Charlie's arms. Even though she was weak, she felt renewed strength at getting out of that hellish cell.

"Faith, can you walk?"

She nodded, "Yes. I think so."

Ben noticed the Glock in Charlie's hand.

"Damn, Charlie. I never thought I'd live to see you go all Dirty Harry," Ben said.

"Here, you take it, Ben," Charlie said.

He handed the weapon over. He could not support Faith and hold the gun at the same time.

"Can you handle it?"

"Damn right I can."

Even though Ben had never actually fired a gun before, he felt no insecurities holding it in his hands. He was more than ready to shoot anyone who tried to stop them from getting out of this hellhole.

Charlie turned to Macro, pressing his thumb into his bandaged bullet wound. The Roman groaned. Ben pressed the weapon into Macro's side.

"You're now going to walk us out of here. If you make one sound to warn anyone, you will die instantly. Do you understand me?"

Macro's defiant gaze bore into Charlie for a moment and then he nodded simply. He realized he would have to bide his time for the present.

"Good. Go," Charlie said.

With John leading, they started down the passage at a slow, measured pace.

***

Licinius strode into the Praetorium with Lucan yapping at his heels like an obedient dog. He clawed at the Roman's cloak.

"I brought the woman to the tribune, didn't I? He needs to pay me for that at least."

Licinius ignored him. He had more than enough to deal with today with the coming executions without having to deal with this greedy weasel harassing him. Lucan seized the Roman's cloak, tugging on it. Licinius stopped suddenly and confronted him. Lucan stopped and fell back when he saw Licinius' raised fist.

"Please I meant no offense," Lucan pleaded. "I only want what was promised. A man has to eat, doesn't he?"

Licinius flung several silver denarius coins at him. The coins clinked on hitting the ground, rolling off into the shadows. Lucan scrambled after them almost tripping over his raggedy robe.

"You get the rest from Tribune Macro."

***

Upon reaching ground level, Macro made a turn to the right in the direction of the exit. The thud of approaching footsteps froze Charlie and the others. His eyes darted about as his mind came alive with memories of the Praetorium's layout.

"Wait," Charlie said.

He spotted a side corridor. He pointed to it.

"This way. Move."

Charlie led them into an antechamber. Ben shoved Macro inside with the others. Charlie dragged the woolen drape back as Licinius marched past. He took the stairs to the dungeons.

Charlie peeked out. He watched Lucan hurrying to catch up to Licinius. Ben touched Charlie on the shoulder.

"What's wrong? Is there a problem?" Ben asked nervously.

As Charlie expected, there was a great deal of activity in the Praetorium with the trial and coming crucifixion of Jesus. Just walking out the front gate was full of risks. Shooting his way out against the whole garrison was really not an option. He only had one clip of ammunition. He stared at Macro. Under the circumstances, he appeared oddly confident.

"I don't like this. We can't risk going out the way we came in. There are too many soldiers."

"Do they know about us?" John inquired restlessly.

"No. Three men are to be crucified. The whole troop has been turned out in case of trouble."

Faith tugged at Charlie when he mentioned the crucifixions. "Jesus?"

Charlie nodded somberly.

She sighed.

"Well we can't hide in here. They are going to find our cell empty any minute now," Ben said.

"I know another way out of here," Charlie said.

He checked the corridor again. It was empty for the moment.

"This way. Stay close to me."

He stepped out and grabbed a torch off the wall. He led them down an obscure corridor that seemed to lead nowhere. In his mind's eye, he recalled the plans of the Praetorium again. They turned left, and then right, before coming to a closed door. He tried it. It was unlocked. He held out the torch revealing a steep flight of steps vanishing into blackness. A rush of cold air with the foul odor of rank water enveloped them. They all winced at the smell. Faith suffered a severe coughing fit.

"Faith, are you okay?"

She recovered and nodded.

Ben looked over Charlie's shoulder, staring down the flight of stairs leading into the black abyss below. He looked appalled.

"We're going down there?"

"Down there is the way out," Charlie said.

He handed the torch to John.

"This can't be the way out," John said.

"Trust me. This is the only way out now. You lead the way, John. It'll be okay. Go on."

Macro flashed surprise, his dark eye meeting Charlie's.

"Who told you about this?"

"If I told you, you would never believe me," Charlie said cryptically. But Macro's question removed any doubt that they were in the right place.

Charlie shoved the Roman against the wall. He stripped off part of his robe and blindfolded him. Charlie then removed his own mask and shoved it into Macro's mouth so he could not call out. Charlie did not catch was Macro stripping off part of his own tunic and dropping it on the floor.

"John, go on. Watch your step. It's a deep descent," Charlie warned.

John started down cautiously. He held the torch high so the others could see their way down. Miriam and Daniel followed close behind him.

"Ben, you keep an eye on our friend," Charlie said.

Ben pressed the Glock into Macro's back, maneuvering him onto the first stair.

"My pleasure. Watch your step, asshole. It would be a real shame if you fell all the way down there and cracked your skull open."

Charlie turned to Faith who was resting against the wall. Her blue eyes were almost pale gray now. He hooked his arm around her shoulder. She looked up at him weakly with an expression that she could not walk much farther.

"That man, Charlie. Who is he? You called him John," she asked.

"His name is John Boanerges, son of Zebedee."

She reflected on the name for a moment. Her eyes grew when she realized who he was.

"He's one of the..." she started to say.

"That's right," Charlie said, nodding.

Her leaden eyes turned down the long flight of steps. She shook her head.

"I'm sorry darling, but this is the only way out. I'll help you down."

"I'm all right. I can make it on my own," she said bravely. While confidently spoken, her words came out in painful rasps.

"It'll be dark, and the steps could be slippery. We'll go down together. Just lean on me."

She finally nodded.

Charlie closed the door behind them. They went down together, taking one step at a time. The stench rising from the blackness below was almost as bad as the dungeon. Faith fought down the bile building in her empty stomach. Her legs ached terribly now. Every arduous step triggered nasty stabbing pains in her ankles that raced up to her hips.

Charlie whispered in her ear, one two, one two, for each step. Several times Charlie had to signal a stop so Faith could rest.

"Charlie, are you sure you know where we're going?" Ben asked. The flickering torchlight silhouetted his dark form, hiding his face.

"Ben, I wrote my Master's thesis on this city, I know what I'm doing," he said plainly.

Ben grunted, unconvinced.

Charlie turned to Faith. She struggled to breathe as if some great weight was pressing down on her lungs. He held her close, warming her shivering body with his own. Her skin was cold and clammy.

"I'm sorry, Faith. I'm sorry about all of this," he whispered in her ear.

"I saw him, Charlie. He held my hand," she gasped.

Even in the feeble flicker of the torch, Charlie could see the dried blood on the hand she held up. She could see the anguish in his face.

"It's all right. I'm not afraid anymore. I'm not afraid of anything anymore."

"Neither am I," Charlie replied.

***

Licinius and Lucan reached the dungeon. The guards came to attention. Licinius gazed down the dimly lit hallway.

"Where is Tribune Macro?"

"He was here not a quarter of an hour ago," one guard said.

"He was here? What happened?"

"The Tribune came here with several men and a boy. Then he released the other prisoners and then they all left together."

"What?"

Licinius looked incredulous, not believing the guard's report. He quickly strode down the passage and found the cell empty. He slammed the cell door and glared at the guard.

"Why did he release them?"

The guard shrugged. Guards do not ask tribunes questions about prisoners. Orders are given, and they obey.

Licinius shoved the guard aside. He hurried back through the passage and raced up the steps. Lucan scurried after him.

"Does this mean I won't get paid for the woman?" Lucan asked breathlessly. All this running about was incredibly draining to the informer.

Upon reaching the top, Licinius made for the main entrance. Reaching the courtyard, he scanned the area. The grounds were deserted now. The enraged mob had hurried off to harass the three convicted men about to be crucified. Licinius stepped over to the two soldiers on duty. He grabbed one roughly.

"Legionnaire, did you see Tribune Macro leave?"

The soldiers shook their heads.

"We have not seen the Tribune for some time."

"Call out the garrison and search everywhere for him. Go!"

The soldiers raced off.

CHAPTER XIX

John's flickering torch finally revealed the bottom of the deep stairwell. Upon reaching the ground, his sandaled feet sank into cold mud. The flaring torch created rippling light patterns of orange and yellow across the moisture running down the walls.

"I've reached the bottom," he announced as his eyes probed the darkness. It looked like a dead end to him.

The rest of the group joined him in the narrow grotto. An unpleasant cold pressed in upon their tired bodies. They huddled close to John's torch to gain what warmth it grudgingly gave.

"How could you have known about this? You said you have never been to Jerusalem," John asked.

"I read about it," Charlie replied cryptically.

"Now what?" Ben asked, his voice echoing dully. His eyes tried to penetrate the gloom, but all he saw was a forbidding blackness.

Charlie took the torch from John. He pushed forward and probed the fog like blackness beyond. Daniel and Miriam gasped when they found themselves back in the dark. Macro took this moment to try to slip away, but Ben was one step ahead of him. He grabbed his tunic and jerked him back with some effort. He pressed the gun hard into the Roman's back.

"Oh no, pal, where do you think you're going?"

Macro stiffened as the barrel dug into his spine.

"Charlie?" Faith called out.

Charlie found what he was looking for about thirty feet from the stairs. His torch revealed a long, grim tunnel about four feet in height. The tinkle of dripping water echoed with an almost gloomy precision. He bent over and took several steps inside. He swung the torch about revealing curved walls coated with slimy moss.

"Charlie?" Ben called out.

Ben missed the warmth of the torch. Their rudimentary clothes were not suited for keeping out the cold and dampness.

Suddenly the pulsing glow of the torch returned. Charlie stopped and looked them over. He could see their relief at his return.

"Okay, follow me. We're almost home free."

Charlie led the way back up the way he came. John helped Faith along now, followed my Miriam and Daniel. Ben pushed Macro along. They stopped at the low tunnel.

"Where does this lead?" John asked.

He did not sound too anxious about exploring the tunnel.

"It's a secret way out," Charlie said.

"Secret way?" John asked nervously.

Charlie probed the tunnel with the torch. The feeble light could only penetrate a few feet down the tunnel. Beyond was ominous blackness. He turned back. They all looked frightened. All except Macro. He just stood there, blindfolded, but still defiant.

"Listen to me. If the palace was ever overrun, this was the escape route for the governor and his staff. Very few people know about this for obvious reasons."

"I guess I shouldn't have slept through all those boring history classes," Ben said.

John turned to Charlie, not understanding the words exchanged by the strangers.

"Charlie, what language are you speaking? It's not of Armenia. I have met people from there and their language is nothing like yours."

"Well, it's a rare tongue, John. Only a few people today speak it."

Charlie stepped up to Macro.

"Tie him up," he told John.

John handed Faith over to Ben. He seized Macro and shook his head. He whipped out his blade and pressed it against the Roman's neck. His head recoiled at the sharp sensation of cold steel on his skin.

"We should just cut his throat. I will do it if you can't. There is nothing I would like more."

Faith stirred when she saw John press the blade against Macro's flesh. She immediately understood what he wished to do. She grabbed Charlie's arm.

"No," Faith croaked. She then glanced at Miriam who seemed to share John's desires.

Charlie stared at the Roman who was now looking left and right probably wondering if this was where his life would end. He wanted to kill Macro. He was shocked at how thirsty he was to spill a man's blood, even this man's blood. It would be simple to take him back into the darkness, away from the others, and shoot him. Leaving him behind, even tied up, was very risky. He stared at Macro who seemed to sense how close he was to death. But if he was afraid, he showed no sign. He stood there, his arrogant head held high.

"Ben, give me the gun."

Ben handed it over.

"Charlie," Faith said.

Charlie looked at her. Her pale eyes showed disapproval, but she did not say another word. It was his decision to end this man's life. He aimed the gun at Macro's chest.

Miriam had no idea what Charlie's was about to do. She had never seen a gun before, but instinctively she knew it dealt death somehow. She embraced Daniel and turned his face away. The boy had seen far too much killing.

Ben stared at Charlie. He did not know what to say. He was a non-violent man at heart. The idea of killing someone, or even hurting another person, turned his stomach. But, somehow, two thousand years in the past, in this dark cave, killing an unarmed, blindfolded man, he felt oddly ambivalent. And after Macro had viciously abused Faith, Miriam, and himself, he had no thought of compassion or forgiveness. He had a good idea of what Macro planned to do to all of them.

Charlie grabbed Macro's robe. He pressed the barrel into his chest in the hope the roar of the gun would be muffled. Macro stiffened when he felt the barrel. He started to take a step back, but Charlie held him in place.

"Don't move."

They all stood as still as trees as Charlie's finger started to tighten on the trigger. He shut his eyes, not wanting to see what happened next. With his eyes shut, a strange light lifted the darkness. The light slowly coalesced into a man's face. He recognized the face as belonging to the man he had come two thousand years to see. It stared at him as plain as day. He suddenly felt a gentle hand settle on his wrist holding the gun.

"For those who live by the sword, must die by the sword," he reminded him.

The alarming hatred strangling Charlie's body drained off. Soothing warmth enveloped him. Exhaling, he lowered the gun, releasing his grip on Macro's tunic.

He turned to John.

"No. I won't kill him. Tie him up, John. Go ahead."

John reluctantly removed the rope belt tied about his waist. He moved behind Macro.

"On your knees, Roman," he said.

John grabbed Macro by the neck and forced him down. He fought hard until John kneed him in the back. His knees sank into the mud. John quickly bound his wrists tightly until it triggered a grunt from the Roman. He then pushed him face down into the mud, and proceeded to bind his ankles.

"He's secure. If you wish, I will kill him for you."

"No, John. Your master would not want you to."

John reflected for a moment and nodded.

"You are right, he wouldn't."

"Let's go," Charlie said.

Using the torch, he led the way into the dripping tunnel. Ben helped Faith along. John, Miriam, and Daniel followed. Icy water dripped on them as they splashed through chilled puddles. The ground was much firmer but the cold water numbed their exposed feet.

"I wish someone would have invented boots for this time period," Ben remarked.

Charlie had to keep the torch swinging about to avoid the water. The last thing they needed was to lose the only light they had. He carried no matches or lighter. He considered asking Ben for his small flashlight, but he had already shown the others enough future technology.

After traveling some thirty or forty yards, the torch cast a gloomy yellow glow over what was clearly a man-made stone block about six feet in diameter. A thick, rusting, iron ring dangled from the center of it.

"Take the torch, Daniel," Charlie said.

Daniel grabbed it, holding it up with both hands. The heat of the flame warmed his face and arms.

"Give me a hand Ben. John."

"Will you be okay?" Ben asked Faith.

She nodded weakly.

Miriam came over and supported her.

Ben and John joined Charlie. Together they grabbed the iron ring and braced their feet.

"How much does this thing weigh?" Ben asked.

"No idea. It's likely hinged in some way."

"Let's hope so."

"Ready? Go!"

They grunted.

"Pull! Pull! Come on! Pull!"

The three strained on the ring, pulling with all their might. At first, nothing happened. It felt immovable. Then it gave just a little. That tiny shift emboldened them.

"Again! Pull!"

They set their feet and heaved until every quivering muscle in their body was ready to burst. The thick slab groaned, dirt and rocks spilling from the top and sides, as it reluctantly pivoted on the hidden hinge. A gloomy crack of crescent light flashed. When they saw that light, they doubled their effort. The crescent became a quarter letting in more light that crawled into the chamber. With the light came a rush of warm air like a mother's embrace. The three men released the iron ring and collapsed to the ground. Their chests heaved as lungs drank in the fresh air.

***

A Roman soldier held up the cloth Macro tore from his tunic. Licinius snatched it away, recognizing it as part of Macro's tunic.

"Where did you find this?"

"Down there," he pointed.

He followed the soldier to the closed door. He threw it open and looked down. Other than Macro, Licinius was the only other centurion who knew where the stairs led.

"Get more men!" he barked.

The soldier ran off.

After rolling and twisting on the muddy ground, Macro struggled onto his knees. He grunted furiously through his gag as he fought to break the rope cutting the circulation to his hands. Not getting anywhere, he braced his knees together and stood up. He nearly lost his balance in the disorienting cave. He hopped over to where he thought the stairs were and slipped in the mud. He banged his head into the lower stairs, and cursed. Turning his back, he brought up his arms and started rubbing his bonds against the edge of one of the steps.

***

Charlie helped Faith toward the streaks of sunlight coming from the opening. The others followed, stumbling over rocks and debris. The coldness was gone now. Sweet morning warmth gave them delicious shivers.

Upon reaching the mouth of the cave, Charlie pushed aside the tall, waist high weeds concealing the opening. After looking around and making sure it was safe, he helped Faith out into the daylight. They stood on a steep slope. Beyond was the sunlit valley that went all the way to distant hills of green and gold. Below them, Charlie spotted James and the horse drawn cart. He sighed with relief that he had not deserted them.

"We're clear. Come on out," Charlie called.

John, Ben, Miriam, and Daniel ventured out of the cave. They embraced the warmth of the sun, swallowing deep breaths. Looking north, however, their mood changed. A boiling mass of dark clouds was forming over the city. The rumble of distant thunder shook the sky, and even the earth under their feet.

"Be careful going down. It's very slippery," Charlie warned everyone.

Charlie ran his arm around Faith's waist, and they awkwardly started down the slope to the road below. It was slow going. Finally, against her feeble protests, he scooped her up in his arms and carried her down. Ben, holding Miriam's hand, followed with John and Daniel right behind them.

***

Macro flung the torn ropes away and ripped off the gag. He ignored the blood flowing from the cuts in his wrists from getting free. He bent down and clawed at the bonds around his ankles. Finally free, he groped in the darkness, feeling the steps. He crawled onto them and carefully reached to his right until his hands hit the supporting wall. Using it as a crude railing, he started up. The climb up the steps was awkward and treacherous in the stygian blackness. With each step, his mind burned with his plans for the men who did this to him.

***

James stared with amazement as the five people reached the cart. He embraced his brother. Upon seeing the retched condition of the others, he grabbed a water skin from the cart and offered it to

Ben. He allowed Faith and Miriam to drink before he took his turn. Water never tasted so good to him.

"I never thought to see any of you again," the disciple said.

"This is James," Charlie said to the others.

Faith and Ben nodded respectfully.

Charlie stared up at the seething ocean of clouds spreading in all directions from the center of Jerusalem. Faith pressed herself into his body.

"It's started hasn't it?" she asked, already knowing the answer.

"Yes. We need to go," Charlie said.

"You got my vote," Ben replied.

They helped Faith, Miriam, and Daniel onto the cart.

"Which way?" James asked.

"North," Charlie replied as he pointed the way.

James turned the cart and headed north.

Ben tugged at Charlie's arm.

"You recruited two of Jesus' disciples to help us, didn't you? Do you even remember all of those timeline conversations we had?" Ben whispered.

"I know, I know," Charlie replied tiredly, knowing where Ben was going with this.

"Suppose something had happened to either of them. You could have changed history, Charlie."

"You don't have to remind me, Ben. But without their help, you'd still be in that cell with Faith and Miriam. Have you thought about that?"

Ben's mask of criticism fell away.

"Oh yeah. Good call."

"You're welcome. How much time do we have?"

"Two hours twelve minutes," Ben replied after checking the device. "Think we'll make it?"

Charlie did not reply. With the exhilaration of their escape faded, he felt a great weight of despair start to overwhelm him.

Looking down at Faith, resting her head on his shoulder, there was part of him that hoped they would not make it back in time. What did she have to look forward to back in the present? They had gone through all of this for nothing. In fact, it was worse than nothing as far as Faith was concerned. He could feel her life slowly ebbing away, and there was nothing he could do about it.

***

The murmur of voices and the flicker of a torch alerted Macro. He stopped and waited as the bobbing torch came toward him.

"Licinius?"

"Tribune?" Licinius called back.

Licinius and three soldiers emerged out of the glow of the torch.

Macro ripped the torch away from his subordinate. He turned around and scrambled back down the stairs. He hurried through the tunnel until he reached the opening in the cave. He looked out to the road below. All he could see were farmers in the distance tending their crops and herding their animals.

Macro hurried back up the tunnel to Licinius.

"Come! Hurry!"

He dashed back up the long flight of steps. Licinius and the soldiers raced to keep up with him.

***

After crossing the road to Joppa, James turned the cart northeast. Overhead the sky flashed and thundered until the ground trembled almost continuously. They could feel the dull booms in their bones.

John and James looked up. The strangeness of the sky disturbed them. They whispered their uneasiness to each other. There was no rain. However, you could feel it coming.

Charlie gazed right at the great wall that encircled Jerusalem.

The wall bent east about fifty meters before it again turned back north. He knew where they were when he spotted the crowd scattered across the stunted gray hill that sprouted like an afterthought in the corner niche. A sudden cold chill clawed up his back. Faith sensed it as well. She turned to Charlie, feeling numb all over.

"Oh my God," she muttered breathlessly.

Before the great wall of Jerusalem, the pitted hill looked more like the surface of the moon than anything on earth did. The flock of onlookers that had collected all along the slope of the hill stared up at the three stark wood crosses silhouetted against the obsidian sky. They had reached Golgotha. The skull.

"Charlie, is this-," Ben muttered, stopping when he saw Charlie's grim nod.

A great flash of lightning whited out the sky for a moment revealing three gaunt figures nailed to the crosses. Some of the people on the slope retreated down in terror. A squad of Roman legionnaires, the death squad, stood before the crosses, admiring their handiwork.

Faith grabbed Charlie's arm so tight it nearly drew blood; but he did not feel it.

"James, stop here please," Charlie said.

James pulled back on the reins, stopping the cart. The horse neighed, twisting its head at the thunder that was continuous. The agitated animal did not want to be there. John and James gazed at the crucified figures. The faces of the three men were hard to make out in the dim light when a sudden flash of lightning revealed them. Their stunned eyes fixed on the center figure.

"John!" James exclaimed, seizing his brother's arm. "It's our master."

"I know, I know," John gasped, wanting desperately to believe his horrified eyes were deceiving him.

Charlie and Faith stared, numbed to the bone, choking down their emotions. It was shockingly surreal to witness this extraordinary event. Their breathing stopped as if someone was smothering them. Charlie grabbed Faith's hand. His mouth opened to speak, but he had no words.

A Roman soldier climbed up to the middle cross. He seemed to be speaking to Jesus, and then glanced back to his compatriots. He laughed at them. Brandishing a long spear, he pressed it against Jesus' ribs and plunged it in. A gush of blood ran down his lean, straining body. A wail erupted from several witnesses almost as if they could feel the weapon was penetrating their bodies.

Charlie and Faith shook violently, finally letting out their long held breaths.

Ben watched this mind-numbing spectacle spellbound. He wanted to do something, anything, to stop what was happening. But he realized he was helpless to stop it.

"Charlie, what can we do?" Faith gasped. Unable to watch anymore she buried her face into his chest and wept.

Charlie could only shake his head impotently. He then looked at John and James. The horror in their gaunt faces devastated him.

"John, we never should have deserted him," James said.

"I know. Why would they do this?" John turned to Charlie, anger sparking in his eyes. "You knew this was going to happen, didn't you? Why didn't you stop it?"

John's accusation struck Charlie like a body blow. What could he possibly say to him? Unable to meet his dark gaze anymore, he looked away.

A hooded figure not far from the three crucified men looked back, gazing at the onlookers. He stopped and reacted with recognition to the people on the cart. He strode toward them with slow, labored steps. Finally, the hood turned up, revealing Nicodemus' gaunt face.

"Greetings," he said to Charlie and the others.

Charlie nodded.

Nicodemus looked at Faith pressed against Charlie.

"You succeeded?"

"We did. Many thanks."

"How could you let this happen, Rabbi?" James asked Nicodemus harshly.

"I did all that a man could do, James," he replied sadly.

Nicodemus bowed his head in shame. His distressed face had a lifeless gray pallor. His sunken blue eyes were bloodshot with fatigue. He was a broken man. He turned back to the grim hill, his shivering hand pointing to the silhouetted cross and the central figure fixed upon it. Then his hand dropped as if heavily weighted.

"I do not understand why this is happening. He committed no crime. Maybe I have lived too long."

"I'm sorry, Nicodemus, that you had to witness this."

Nicodemus studied Charlie's face. Understanding flashed in his somber eyes.

"You knew this was going to be the Nazarene's fate? You warned me. How could you have known?"

Charlie could almost feel the great sorrow weighing down upon the old man. He was sorely tempted to reveal the future to him. He suspected he would get some comfort from it. He glanced back to Ben who sensed his temptation. He gave a look of disapproval, slowly shaking his head. Charlie set his hand on the rabbi's shoulder, as he addressed the two brothers as well.

"My friends, in a few days you will hear an incredible story that will lift away your sadness. Then you will finally understand why this had to happen. Try to keep your faith. Believe me, it will be rewarded."

Their eyes widened with questions. Charlie desperately wanted to tell them more, but he suppressed the desire.

"There is nothing more I can say. I'm sorry."

Macro strode out of the Praetorium. He marched up to Licinius and four mounted legionnaires. While they were saddling the horses, Macro had taken time to clean himself up, wiping away the filth and mud of the cave. He ignored the great disturbance overhead. The soldiers, however, could not tear their eyes from the violent sky. It triggered an uneasiness these veteran soldiers could not explain. Macro leapt aboard his horse, kicked it in the side, and rode off. Licinius and his men followed.

CHAPTER XX

A blinding light suddenly rended the sky as if the sun had gone supernova. Moments later came the thunderous echo that shook the earth. Most of the people on the hill turned and fled in panic, racing back to Jerusalem. A small group, including several women, remained, moving closer to the limp figure nailed to the center cross.

"It's over now," Charlie said simply.

Charlie and Faith crossed themselves.

John and James looked on, stricken, unable to move or speak. John then pulled his brother into a tight embrace.

No one spoke for what seemed ages, but was only a minute or two. Faith raised her head, the tears running down her face mixed with the falling rain.

"It's time for us to go home, Charlie," Faith said.

He looked down at her. He knew what she meant.

Ben stared at Charlie's despondent face. Everything he had done, all his hopes and prayers, were gone now.

"She's right, Charlie. There's nothing else for us here now," Ben said.

After thinking for a few moments, Charlie realized they were right. He reluctantly nodded to James.

"We should go."

"Wait. I have to stay," John said.

Charlie looked at John and nodded in understanding.

"Look after them James. Take them where they wish to go. I'll see to our master," he promised his brother.

John dropped off the cart next to Nicodemus. Charlie climbed down and joined them. There was so much he wanted to say, but there was no time.

"I'll never be able to thank the both of you for what you did," Charlie said as he embraced both of them. "Take care. Find peace, brothers."

"You as well," John said.

"Safe journey home. I wish things could have ended differently for you both," Nicodemus added.

John and Nicodemus strode slowly up the hill. Charlie watched them for a moment, and then climbed back onto the cart. James flicked the reins and the cart jerked forward.

***

After galloping out the Essene Gate, Macro rode west. They rode pass the Serpent's Pool, and headed north until they were abreast of the escape tunnel. Looking about, Macro spotted a boy and a herd of goats. The boy and goats had taken refuge from the storm under a large cypress tree. He galloped over to him. The frightened boy gazed up at the Roman cavalry towering menacingly over him.

"We're looking for three men, a woman, and a boy who came down from up there," Macro barked, his finger pointing toward the distant slope.

The boy froze with fear. His goats bleated nervously, instinctively pressing closer to the shepherd.

"Well?" Macro asked again, ripping out his sword.

Seeing the monstrous blade, the boy cried out for mercy.

"I saw them get on a cart and go north," he finally muttered, his finger pointing the way.

Macro stared, thinking the boy might be lying, trying to send them the wrong way. He did not trust the word of a Judean. Then he saw the genuine panic in the boy's face.

"If you're lying, boy, I'll cleave you in two," he threatened.

Macro yanked on the reins, swung his steed about, and galloped north. Licinius and the others hurried after him.

***

It was deathly quiet in the cart as it bumped along the road leading back to Miriam's home and the cave. James stole looks to the strangers in back. Daniel rested his head in Ben's lap, completely exhausted. Miriam leaned against him, feeling safe for the first time in ages. He hooked a comforting arm around her.

Ben looked over to Charlie. He was staring impassively at the passing countryside. Faith rested against him, his arms supporting her, fingers stroking her head.

"I'm really sorry, Charlie. To come all this way. I almost believed we might pull this off."

Despair overwhelmed Charlie. Everything he had hoped and prayed for had gone for naught. He looked back to Golgotha which was now lost in the misty sheets of rain. Faith placed her hand on his face and turned it toward herself. Her wet face was so pale, almost white.

"Faith..." he started to say.

"Charlie, I'm, I'm fine. Really I am. I'm gla-glad we came."

"Are you really?"

She nudged her head up and down.

"I don't want you to be sorry about how this turned out. We all knew what a gamble this was going to be. I'm not sorry we took it. Not for a second."

Charlie pulled her failing body tighter against his own. The cart bumped and weaved over the muddy road. He looked ahead. In the distance, he could see Miriam's home. Not far from there, he saw the cave they had stepped out of the day before. The day before. It seemed like ages ago. If all went well, they would be back home in less than an hour. But then what?

Charlie turned to Ben. He knew the answer to the question he was about to pose, but decided to ask anyway.

"Ben, is it possible to come back, but do it earlier?"

Ben grimaced, shaking his head.

"We can't. I told you before this was a one shot deal. It would take forty-eight hours to prep and program the Eight-ball for a return trip. Even if we could look what the first trip did to her. Another trip might kill her."

Charlie had already thought of that.

"By Monday, if not sooner, the DOD will be shutting down the lab and the program," Ben added. "Charlie, it's hopeless."

Charlie closed his eyes and allowed the exhaustion he had been keeping at bay overwhelm him.

***

Macro and his men halted before Golgotha. They spotted several horse-drawn carts. The tribune barked orders to his men to check all of them. They dropped off their mounts and searched every cart for the escaped prisoners.

Macro and Licinius looked up at the three crucified men. They were unmoved by the horrific sight. They had seen many crucifixions. They had seen far worse ways for a man to die. They reacted to a jarring rumble and stared up at the boiling black clouds blotting out the sun.

"What is this sky?" Licinius asked with apprehension. He was a man who feared little, but there was something different about this sky. "I've never seen it so dark in daylight."

If Macro was spooked by the sky, he did not voice an opinion. He scanned the area. The thick sheets of rain had birthed a thick, rolling fog that shrouded everything within a few hundred yards.

The soldiers returned and remounted their horses.

"They're not here," they reported.

A sudden flare of lightning lifted the shifting haze for a moment. Macro lurched forward in his saddle, and probed far down the road. He caught sight of a horse and cart moving ghostlike about a mile ahead.

"There! It's them! It must be them!" he yelled.

Licinius and the soldiers tore their eyes from the sky and turned to where Macro's long arm pointed. The cart was just a blurry gray mass for a moment and then it was gone.

"Are you sure? I think that shepherd boy lied," Licinius

suggested.

"No. I want all of them, Licinius! All of them! And alive!"

Macro kicked his heels into the horse's ribs when the very air shuddered from an explosion of thunder. The ground under their horses shifted violently. The terror-stricken horses reared up as if shot with a thunderbolt. The powerful jolt was so sudden that none of the riders could hold their positions. Violently thrown off their mounts, the stunned soldiers grunted when they slammed hard into the earth. When Macro landed on his head, hammer blows of stars blinded him momentarily.

The hysterical horses bucked wildly, racing off in all directions. Macro struggled to his feet. He swayed dizzily, his eyes still blinded by the aurora borealis swirling before him. He ripped off his helmet and rubbed his eyes. With his vision partly restored, he glared down at his stunned men scattered about on the ground. He then spotted the frenzied horses running off.

"Get those horses! Move!"

The soldiers gathered their wits and stumbled after their panic-stricken mounts already fifty meters away. Judeans nearby laughed at the running soldiers.

Macro fumed, his heaving chest ready to burst. With the cold rain stinging his bare arms, he looked back up the road. The cart was now out of sight, lost in the fog of rain, but he refused to let them get away. As he slowly reclaimed control of his anger, he felt an odd, prickly heat on the back of his neck. The rest of him was cold. Over many years, and many campaigns for the Roman Empire, he had a developed a keen sense of when he was being watched. It had saved him many times. He felt it now, but it was subtly different. He turned around, probing the people scattered on the hill. But the person watching was not among them. Then, his eyes turned up to the man on the center cross. The man's head, wearing a bloody crown of thorns, hung limp, his chin pressed into his chest. He was clearly dead, but his eyes were still open; and they were staring right at him. A sudden chill of feat struck Macro. It was something he had never felt before. The cold shudder seemed to clutch at his beating heart. The pain was so intense he had to tear his eyes from the cross and look away.

***

James stopped the cart near the well not far from Miriam's home. Everyone climbed off the back. The rain had lightened considerably. The sky over them was not as dark. The clouds were more blue-gray with the faintest rays of sunlight streaking out. When they looked back, the frightful storm appeared anchored directly over Jerusalem. Flashes of punishing lightning and thunder still pounded the darkened city. They looked at each other, glad to be far away from the citadel.

Ben checked the device. Thirty-eight minutes remained. It was a very close thing, but they were going to get back home. He walked over to Charlie and Faith who were still staring at the city. They had their arms around each other.

"It's time to go guys. We have thirty-eight, no, thirty-seven minutes left. Come on."

Ben showed the device to Charlie and Faith. Charlie turned to Faith. There was nothing for them to do now.

"I guess he's right," he told her.

Charlie turned to James. The poor man, soaked to the skin like them, was still reeling by the death of Jesus. He was a man lost now.

"I wish there was something I could do or say," Charlie said.

"Will you all be safe here?" he asked.

"We'll be all right. But you should not remain here."

"I know."

"You will return the cart?"

He promised he would. He stared out at nothing in particular.

"I'm not sure what happens now. Where do we go? What will we do?"

"You will know soon, James. Believe me," Charlie promised.

"How can you be so sure?" he asked gloomily.

Charlie smiled furtively and threw his arms around him. As he hugged him, he whispered in his ear. James stiffened and pulled away, his eyes filled with astonishment.

"Peace be upon you and your brothers," Charlie said. "Thank you for everything."

Faith stepped up to James and embraced him.

"Thank you," Ben said, embracing him.

"God go with you," James said.

He climbed back on the cart and rode off.

Ben again signaled to Charlie that time was running out.

Faith stared at Miriam and Daniel. Miriam had her arms tight around her son. They looked helpless, unsure of what to do. Faith felt that overwhelming surge of guilt again. They had put their lives in great danger in their hope of saving her life. It was not fair that they should suffer for it.

"Come on. We need to amscray. There's nothing left for us to do," Ben said, motioning toward the cave.

Charlie started to follow him. Then they both realized Faith had not moved from where she stood. She was still staring at Miriam and Daniel.

Ben came back to her, setting his hand on her arm as if to help her along.

"Faith, what are you waiting for? Let's go," Ben said.

"But what about Miriam and Daniel, Ben?" she asked.

Charlie and Ben looked at Miriam and Daniel. They both now realized what a horrible fate awaited them when, or if, Macro found them. Ben looked back to Faith. He shrugged helplessly.

"What can we do about that?"

"You can take them with you," she said simply.

"What? What are you talking about?" Ben said in shock.

Faith made eye contact with Charlie and started one of those husband-wife silent conversations that only they could understand. Charlie did not like what she was saying with her eyes. He shook his head. But she would not budge. She was adamant in her decision.

"Are you crazy, Faith? We're going home," Ben said.

He tried to pull her along, but somehow she had found the strength to resist him.

"Ben, if they stay, they'll be killed. You know that."

Ben grabbed Faith's arm more forcefully, ready to drag her away if necessary. He leaned in close.

"We can't take them, sis. There's only room for three," he reminded her.

Faith nodded knowingly, "I know that. Take them."

"No. No way. I'm not doing that."

"She's right, Ben," Charlie said.

Charlie knew there was no point in arguing with Faith. He had been married to her for too long. When she made up her mind there was no changing it.

She smiled at him.

"Look, we can come back," Ben said.

"You know we can't do that. You said so yourself," Charlie reminded him.

Ben released his grip on her arm. He pressed his hand against her back, his face almost touching hers.

"Faith...please. Don't do this."

Faith took his hand. She stared into his pleading eyes. She smiled weakly. Even in her weakened state, there was a glow to her cheeks.

"We'll be all right, Ben. Really. We've had our miracle."

She turned her eyes to Miriam and Daniel who had no idea what was being discussed.

"It's time for theirs."

Ben could not believe what was happening. He shook his head. He was not going to let her do this. He jabbed his finger insistently toward the cave.

"Faith, we can be home in five minutes. Five minutes. It's right in there. Please, sis."

Faith shook her head. There was no defiance in the shake. She had simply made up her mind and that was that.

"Charlie, please talk some sense into her."

He turned to Charlie and realized he was not going to get any help from him. For a second he considered throwing her over his shoulder and forcibly taking her back. But he knew Charlie would never permit that. He checked the device again.

"We'll be okay, Ben," Charlie said.

The more Charlie thought about it, the more he knew Faith was right. What would they be going back home to anyway? At least some good would come from all this if they could save Miriam and Daniel.

Faith took hold of Ben's arm. Her eyes were misty. She knew this was the right thing to do, but that did not make it any easier. She could see how stricken Ben was by her decision.

"There isn't much time, Ben," she said, her voice trembling.

Ben could see this was hopeless now. He looked to Miriam and Daniel. They looked resigned to their fate.

"Okay," he muttered finally.

He turned to Charlie and pointed to Miriam and Daniel.

"But you need to tell them Charlie. They have a right to know what the deal is."

Charlie sighed, "You're right, Ben. They do have a right to know."

Charlie walked over to Miriam and Daniel. They looked utterly helpless.

"Macro will not give up trying to find you."

The mention of his name sent a shiver through both of them. Their eyes swung down the long road to Jerusalem.

"We can help you get away from him. Far away where they can never hurt you again."

"Where can we go where the Romans can't find us?" Miriam said despondently.

Charlie glanced back to Ben. He shrugged. Trying to explain

what they had in mind could take hours, and even then they might not be able to understand it.

"Ben, I don't think we have the time for a lecture on time travel."

Charlie looked back to Miriam. He smiled warmly.

"Miriam, we can take you where they can never find you. Ever. But it's a long way. It will be unlike any place you have ever seen. Ben will look after you there. Faith and I are staying behind."

Miriam and Daniel did not understand what Charlie was trying to say. He decided to cut to the chase.

"Do you trust us?"

They both nodded.

"Then you must trust us now."

Daniel looked up to his mother. He nodded to her.

"I will trust you," Miriam said.

"Good. Come with us."

They started toward the cave. Miriam and Daniel stopped before the entrance. She shook her head, reconsidering her decision.

"We won't be safe in there."

Charlie took her arm gently.

"It's going to be all right. Please."

They entered the cave. Ben switched on the penlight and led them up the dark tunnel. The thin beam of the pen light played over the ground and walls. Miriam kept a tight grip on her son.

"Where are you taking us?" Miriam asked.

She had warned her son about staying out of these caves, as there were a number of dangerous dead falls that had injured several children.

"It's not far," Charlie assured her.

When the beam of the pen light struck the Eight-ball Miriam and Daniel froze, their eyes widening in amazement.

"What is it, Momma?" Daniel gasped.

Miriam shook her head. She grabbed hold of her son and stepped back away from the alien object.

Ben triggered the device. The hatch folded open. The interior lights switched on. The machine began to power up. Miriam and Daniel bent forward and looked into it with stunned curiosity. They turned to the others.

"It's powering up," Ben said.

He sounded relieved. He had not been one hundred percent sure the Eight-ball would start up again. He checked the readings on the device.

"Is it working?" Charlie asked.

"Yeah. All green. We're good. The program is loading."

Ben turned to Charlie and Faith. The light from the Eight-ball shined on their faces. He still held hope Faith might change her mind. The faint smile she showed dashed any prayer of that happening.

"Faith, I-"

Faith stepped up and embraced her brother. He held her close, not wanting to let go.

"We'll be okay, Ben," she said softly. She kissed him on the cheek. "I don't know. Maybe it was all supposed to work out like this. I love you."

"I love you," Ben said, choking down a sob.

Ben pulled away, fighting down his emotions. He went to Charlie and handed him the Glock.

"You better take this. You might need it."

Charlie slid the weapon back into his shoulder holster.

They stared at each other. All they could do was nod. Ben finally embraced him.

"Dammit, you look after her," he said.

"I will, Ben. Every day."

Ben stepped over to Miriam and Daniel. He could see the apprehension in their eyes. He set his hands on their shoulders. They stood frozen to the ground, unwilling to get any closer to the Eight-ball.

"Charlie, tell them it's going to be okay."

Charlie told them as simply as he could to trust Ben and that everything was going to be fine.

Reassured somewhat, they stepped toward the machine. Ben helped Miriam into the machine first. After she settled in the middle seat, Ben buckled her down. Then he did the same for Daniel. Their eyes gazed about the fantastic interior.

"Now don't touch anything," he warned them.

By the way they sat stiffly in their seats, he knew that was the last thing that was on their minds.

Ben stood at the hatch, taking one last look at Charlie and Faith.

"Goodbye," Faith said. "God bless."

Ben rubbed his swollen eyes and climbed into the Eight-ball. The hatch closed and locked.

Charlie and Faith backed far away.

A few seconds later arcs of white flame encompassed the black sphere. There was a sudden burst of blinding light and when their vision cleared, the machine was gone. Charlie took Faith by the hand and helped her out.

When they exited the cave, the rain had stopped, and the sun had begun to break through the fading clouds. It was good to feel the warmth of the sun again.

They gazed over their new world. Charlie pulled her close. She was shivering. He did not know if it was her illness, or the apprehension about how they were going to survive there.

"We're going to be okay," he assured her.

"Will we?"

"Yes," he promised.

Charlie realized he was very thirsty all of a sudden. He saw a group of people gathered by the well drawing up buckets of water.

"Are you as thirsty as I am?"

She nodded.

He helped her over to the well. They calmly waited their turn. Faith listened to the Judeans talking among themselves. She leaned into Charlie. He put his arms around her.

"Can we make it here, Charlie?"

"Of course we can. I have plenty of money. We'll do fine. Maybe we'll become farmers. We can grow olives. Or maybe I can teach. If I'm careful, I might even be able to parlay some of my historical knowledge. Not enough to alter the future, but just enough so we can survive."

"Farmers, hmmm," she said. "Why not? You'll have to teach me the language."

Charlie was about to respond to her when he spotted Macro and his men. They were galloping up the road right toward them. Faith spotted them a moment later and shuddered. They both breathed with relief as they shot past them. Then they pulled up at Miriam's hovel on the other side of the road. Several soldiers dismounted, drew swords, and hurried inside.

"Charlie," Faith whispered nervously.

"It's okay. We'll be fine."

Charlie tapped the Glock in his shoulder holster for Faith's benefit. That seemed to reassure her. He pulled her robe up over her head, hiding her face. They blended in with the others drawing water from the well. Glancing back, Charlie spotted the soldiers exit the hovel and shake their heads at Macro. The tribune pivoted his horse around, his eyes probing earnestly in every direction. When he saw the gathering by the well he galloped over. Startled people stumbled back. A frightened old man dropped the bucket, spilling the water.

Macro glared down at the fearful peasants. He dismounted and began checking each person in turn. When he was done with one, he pushed them aside and moved to the next one.

"Charlie," Faith whispered weakly.

He wrapped one arm around her while the other one slid under the robe to grab the pistol. His heart pounded in his chest as they waited their turn.

Macro finally came to them. His hand caressed his sword. He stared at Charlie for a long moment. He showed no sign of recognition. Charlie expected that having worn a mask when they first met. Macro then turned his focus on Faith. She kept her back turned away from him.

"You! Turn around!"

Faith shuddered. She knew he would recognize her at once. Her hand gripped the crucifix so tightly it nearly drew blood.

"God, please help me," she whispered.

Charlie slid the pistol out but kept it out of sight. His finger fumbled to release the safety. He suddenly found it hard to breath.

Macro unsheathed his sword and pointed it at Faith. The tip pressed into her back. While he had been checking the people, Licinius and the soldiers had ridden up and were watching now. Charlie wondered if he could shoot all of them before they could strike him down.

"I said, turn around. Face me!" he commanded.

Faith pivoted slowly about. Her veil cloaked her face from the Roman. Charlie was pulling the pistol up when her hand settled upon it, stopping him.

Macro lifted the sword up against the veil. He flipped it up and over, revealing Faith's face. His planned look of elation became a grunt of surprise. It was not Miriam. His narrowing eyes showed no recognition of the face staring back at him.

Charlie, seeing Macro's reaction, turned to Faith. The amazing sight before him stunned him. Her face was no longer pale. She was radiant. The hand clutching his that was clammy and cold only a few moments earlier was warm to the touch. Her eyes now shone brightly. Her lips were red and full. Her cheeks glowed from some internal light. She smiled pleasantly at the stunned Roman.

Macro stared at her for a long moment. His tense body heaved with frustration. He shoved his sword back into its scabbard. He remounted his steed and barked a command to his men.

"Back to the city!"

They rode back south.

Faith sighed with relief. She turned and smiled joyfully at

Charlie. She took his hand and set it on her cheek. What had been pale and ghostlike was now warm, full of new life. He pulled her into his arms and crushed her body against own. She gasped, not from pain but in utter contentment. He smothered her face and lips with kisses. As they kissed, Faith took the Glock from his hand and dropped it down into the deep well.

CHAPTER XXI

Sidesh stared at the Eight-ball as it bled off the heat from its long spatial journey. For him the machine had only left a few minutes earlier. He cautiously stepped closer to it. He held his breath as the hatch finally gasped open. Bending down and peering inside, Sidesh did not know what he would find. He half expected it to be empty. He audibly sighed with relief as Ben climbed out. His taut face was grimy, his clothes ripped and muddied. Otherwise, he looked no different from when he left.

"Wow," Sidesh muttered.

Ben smiled with relief at Sidesh. He was not sure what he was going to find when the hatch opened. For all he knew they could have arrived at any time or place. He grabbed Sidesh's hand and shook it.

"Doctor Livingstone, I presume."

Sidesh grinned with relief at Ben's reference to journalist H.M. Stanley's famous first meeting with explorer Livingstone in Africa a hundred and fifty years prior.

"How did it go?"

Ben shook his head grimly. He turned and looked back inside the pod.

"It's all right. You can come out."

Ben quickly realized his passengers were too terrified to budge from their seats. He really could not blame them. Ben stepped into the Eight-ball and unbuckled their harnesses. He helped Miriam out first, and then Daniel. It was impossible to say who displayed more amazement—Sidesh or the two new arrivals.

Sidesh leaned into Ben.

"Who are they?" Sidesh asked softly.

"There's no time for introductions, Sid. I need to go back. Start reprogramming the computer," Ben said.

Sidesh did not appear to hear Ben. He was too busy staring at Miriam and Daniel. They were looking around the lab with an incredible combination of awe and dread. Miriam held Daniel close against her body, whispering something to him in Aramaic.

"Did you hear me, Sid?"

"I can't, Ben. We have unexpected guests," Sidesh finally replied, jerking his head back.

Sidesh stepped aside revealing the three men standing behind him. Two were clad in black suits. They had the inscrutable faces of government bureaucrats. Ben immediately made them out to be from the NSA or some clandestine government agency. Neither option bode well for him. The other was a more familiar face, although it now displayed an unfriendly scowl. He wore the uniform of an Air Force General.

General Jack Wellman stepped forward. In his late fifties, he was lean of build, and flashed laser blue eyes that could drill right through a man when the moment required. This was one of those moments.

"General?" Ben said with surprise.

Wellman stared at Ben, and then directed his penetrating gaze to Miriam and Daniel. He looked very somber.

"Ben, I think we need to have a serious talk."

He considered Ben's raggedy clothes and smirked.

"Ah, but you better put on some decent clothes and clean up first."

Ben stared at the general and then to the two suits. Ben turned back to Sidesh. He shrugged helplessly.

"Don't look at me like that. They literally arrived a few minutes after you left," he explained.

"Go on, Ben. We'll wait for you in the conference room," Wellman said.

Ben nodded. He came over to Miriam and Daniel who were oblivious to what was happening. Miriam grabbed his arm nervously. He smiled as one might to a scared child.

"It's okay. Come with me, Miriam."

Of course, they did not understand him. He took her hand

and gently stroked it.

"You're going to be fine. Come on. Sidesh, want to help us?"

"No, not really," he said stiffly.

Ben threw him a look.

"Okay, okay."

Ben and Sidesh escorted the two out of the lab. When they reached the locker room, Ben found Faith's clothes. To Miriam, of course, they were unlike anything she had ever seen before. However, as she examined them, a light came to her eyes. She nodded that she could manage.

"Sidesh, what do we have for Daniel?"

Sidesh thought a moment, still in a state of shock.

"Well, we can give him Freddy's lab pants and coat. He's a small guy."

"Would you get them please?"

"Yeah, sure," he said. "What's with them, Ben? Where's your sister and her husband?"

Ben waved tiredly. "Later. It's a long story. A really long story. I'll tell you everything, but let's get the boy a change of clothes first."

"Sure thing."

Sidesh went to a nearby locker. He pulled out the white lab coat and pants. He handed them to Ben.

"Can you manage? There are a couple things I kind of have to do about the thing we discussed before you left."

Sidesh whispered to Ben. Who knew if the walls had ears?

"Good idea. You, you go do that."

Sidesh darted out.

Ben looked down to Daniel whose wide eyes seemed to be darting from one strange sight to another. The light fixtures above fascinated him. But so did everything else. Ben realized Miriam and Daniel were going to have a lot to learn and experience in their new world. He felt rather sorry for them.

He rubbed Daniel's head.

The boy smiled anxiously.

"It's going to be okay, Daniel. I promise."

He seemed to understand the gist of Ben's words. He then helped Daniel discard his old clothes and helped him dress. He led him to a sink and filled it with water. The amazed boy watched as hot water flowed from the faucet. Ben washed his own face and hands, and then handed the soap to Daniel. He started to scrub his face and hands.

"Help you mother, Daniel," Ben said, pointing to where Miriam was dressing.

He nodded eagerly and hurried off.

Ben returned to his locker. He stripped off his tattered clothes and flung them to the floor. He quickly threw on his own clothes. He stared into the locker mirror and sighed. What he really wanted now was a long, hot shower. Taking a deep breath, he could still smell the foul odor of goats and the stink from his stay in that putrid cell. Unfortunately, a shower would have to wait until later.

When Miriam reappeared wearing Faith's clothes, Ben froze. He stared at her for a long moment. She looked so different now in modern clothes. In a way it made her look even more lost and helpless. He could not even begin to imagine what she was thinking right now. She regarded Ben's gaze and became anxious. She shrugged her shoulders as if asking him if she had put the clothes on properly.

"No, no, you look fine," he said, smiling gently.

She managed a smile somehow.

"Daniel?"

Daniel came around clad in the loose fitting white lab pants and shirt that hung on his lean frame. Ben looked down to see he was still wearing the ratty sandals. However, there were no shoes for him there. New footwear would have to wait.

They stared at him for some reassurance that everything was going to be okay. Even if he could communicate to them, he did not know what he would have said considering the circumstances. He was as unsure about the future as they were, so he just smiled and nodded. He then took them by the hand and escorted them to the company conference room.

***

The two men were from the National Security Agency as Ben suspected. They looked as if they were pressed out of the same mold, right down to their coldly-detached personalities. They robotically flashed their IDs to Ben who barely had time to read their names. General Wellman introduced them, but as far as Ben was concerned, they were Agent A and Agent B. They sat stiffly on one side of the polished mahogany conference table like two hanging judges. General Wellman sat at the far end as if he were afraid he might catch some contagious disease from them. Sidesh sat opposite the agents trying hard not to show how freaked out he was feeling. He was already imagining being kicked out of the country.

Ben paced the width of the spacious room. He glanced occasionally at Miriam and Daniel. Their amazed faces pressed against the panoramic window that stretched the width of the room. It provided a stunning view of the San Gabriel Mountains. A passing jet triggered a torrent of amazing adjectives Ben could only guess at.

"You're not listening, Ben," Wellman said patiently. "This is not my call. This comes down all the way from the Oval office. It's done. It's shut down. Can you really blame them? Can you even imagine the chaos that would result if word leaked out about this little discovery of ours?"

Ben stopped and leaned on the table. He directed his stare at the general. He knew he there was no point in talking to the men in black.

"General...Jack, please...I just need a little time. A day. Twelve hours."

"The General has no say in this now, doctor," Agent A said flatly. "We're taking over the program. So, if you have any questions, direct them our way."

"This little jaunt of yours was completely unauthorized; you realize that don't you?" Agent B added.

Agent B then pointed to Miriam and Daniel at the window.

"And who are they? Your girlfriend and her kid? Is this the security you run here, General? Giving free reign to outsiders and children? There is going to be a thorough investigation on this little episode of yours, Doctor Miles."

Sensing they were the object of their discussion, Miriam and Daniel looked back. Ben waved to them that it was fine. Somewhat relieved, they looked back out the window.

"Jack, who the hell are these pencil neck-" Ben started to say to Wellman, unable to restrain his anger any longer.

"Hold on, Ben. Just take it easy," Wellman said.

"I thought this was a DOD project."

"Not anymore," Agent A declared.

The general could see this train was about to go off the rails. He could not stop the NSA from taking over, but he still wanted to protect Ben, Sidesh, and the real program.

"There's a lot more to this than you know, Ben."

"Like what?"

"You of all people should have known the risks you were taking, Doctor Miles," Agent B said.

"Suppose you've altered events from this little trip of yours? You may have changed the future."

"Like we'd even know, moron," Sidesh mumbled under his breath.

Ben caught the words, but no one else seemed to. The agents directed icy stares to Sidesh who was casually fiddling with his cell phone.

"Is there something you'd like to add to the discussion, Doctor Kumar?" Agent A asked.

Sidesh looked up innocently. He acted as if he did not say anything. He rolled his shoulders and flashed a smug look of ignorance.

"How involved were you in this little...trip?" the other agent asked.

Sidesh seemed not to understand them for a moment. He then raised his hands and shrugged.

"Sorry?" he said in a suddenly very thick Indian accent. His smile was the innocence of a child. "I very brand new here. I just follow orders."

Sidesh turned to Ben and shrugged. He went back to his phone. Ben drifted over to him and glanced down. Sidesh's fingers tapped out a command: ERASE DRIVES AND SECURITY VIDEO - ENTER.

Ben patted Sidesh on the shoulder, and addressed the two agents.

"You know, I was not aware there's a law against time travel. In fact, I don't think there's anything illegal about anything we've done."

"We'll invent a law and back date it," Agent B threatened.

"I think we're done here," Agent A said.

The two agents pushed their chairs back and stood as one. They might as well have been joined at the hip.

"This program is now under the auspices of the NSA You all need to leave the premises. Now. And I'm sure we don't have to warn any of you about keeping quiet about this program, do we?"

Ben directed his eyes to Wellman.

The general shrugged helplessly. He did not like this any more than Ben did. He fought hard for hours with the President and the National Security Advisor. Regrettably, he was ultimately overrruled.

"You two at the window," Agent B said. "Hey! You two at the window. You need to come with us."

Miriam and Daniel turned around and stared at the agents. Agent B was still pointing at them. They looked to Ben, flashing alarm.

"We want to question the both of you," Agent A added.

Ben saw the stark fear in their eyes. He turned to Wellman with a pleading gaze.

Wellman nodded. He stood up.

"You have no authority over my people, gentlemen," he announced.

"They are not your people," Agent A said.

"They damn well are my people. They are under my direct command, which comes from the Pentagon. If you have a problem with that, I suggest you contact the Chairman of the Joint Chiefs. I can't stop you from shutting down this program, but I'll be damned if I let you harass my staff," he told them in no uncertain terms.

The two agents conferred. Then, they turned back to Wellman.

"Fine. But you all have to leave the building, right now," Agent A demanded.

"All right," Wellman replied reluctantly.

Agent B locked the front door after everyone had exited. They walked to the parking lot without saying a word. Miriam and Daniel stayed glued to Ben's side. When they reached Ben's vehicle, he looked back to the building. Wellman could see how despondent he looked. He had invested over four years of his life on the project. Now he faced with the task of starting all over.

"I'm sorry, Ben, but my hands are tied," he said.

"I understand, General."

Ben glanced at Miriam and Daniel. They were fascinated by his SUV. Daniel touched the polished metal and looked up at his mom with amazement. She shrugged, shaking her head.

"What do you think they'll do to the program?"

Wellman shrugged.

"Hard to say. Probably store it all with the Ark of the Covenant and our flying saucers," he quipped.

"Is your order for here, or to go, Miss," Sidesh mumbled to himself.

"Take it easy, Sid," Ben said, patting his friend on the

shoulder.

Wellman turned his attention to Miriam and Daniel. They looked to be the most lost souls he had ever seen. They focused their eyes on Ben, their one and only anchor in this new world.

"Hey, how about introducing me to your friends," Wellman suggested.

Ben turned to Miriam and Daniel. For the first time in his life, he realized he was going to have to be responsible for someone other than himself. He had never really been interested in pursuing relationships or thoughts of having a family. Responsibilities like that had a tendency to distract the mind. Now, whether he liked it or not, he knew he could not abandon them.

"General, this is Miriam. And this is her son, Daniel."

"Nice to meet you both," he said to them.

They nodded politely.

"They don't speak English," Ben said.

"No, I don't suppose that they would."

"You know, I think I'm going to need some help, General," Ben admitted.

"Yeah, I kind of think you will," Wellman agreed. "Well, why don't we start with some lunch?"

"Great. I'm starving," Sidesh said.

Ben looked to Miriam and Daniel, and rubbed his stomach demonstrably. They both nodded. Then he suddenly realized how famished he was. After all, he had not eaten anything in two thousand years.

"None of us have eaten in a while. Time travel really gives you an appetite, General," Ben revealed.

"Really. Very interesting," Wellman said. "I'd like to hear everything that happened."

Ben sighed, reflecting for a moment. Whatever their ultimate fate, he knew Faith and Charlie were now long deceased and buried these two thousand years. A sudden jolt of heartache struck him.

"That will take some time," he finally confessed.

"I believe we have a lot of that right now, don't we."

"Yeah, I suppose we do," Ben agreed.

CHAPTER XXII

General Wellman pulled up to the ranch style house set at the tail end of the cul-de-sac. He exited his car and strode up the long driveway that led to the garage at the rear of the house. While he was dressed in civilian clothes, anyone observing him would say he had a military background. About halfway up the driveway a ball flew out from behind the house and rolled up to his feet. He scooped it up just as a barking dog flew out from the back yard. The excited dog skidded to a stop and barked excitedly, wanting his ball back. Daniel, racing after his dog, came to a sudden stop when he saw the General. He saluted sharply. Wellman grinned and gave back the salute. He tossed the ball back to the smiling boy.

"Hello, Daniel."

"Hello," he replied.

"How are you?"

"I am very well, thank you," he replied in broken English. Then he grinned at Wellman's appreciative smile.

In the four months since his arrival, Daniel looked very different. He was clad in shorts and a t-shirt. His hair was cropped short. He had even put on a little weight. While before he appeared much older than his years, he looked quite a bit younger now, except around the eyes. His brown eyes still had that hard gaze he often saw in combat veterans. They were eyes that had seen and experienced hard times. The pleasant smile he flashed would never erase the harsh life he had endured so many centuries ago.

"Where is everyone?"

Daniel pointed to the backyard. He waved for him to follow. They walked up the driveway. The dog scampered alongside, jumping up and down at Daniel, trying to get the ball back.

"Down Argos. Behave."

Ben and Miriam were resting in lawn chairs enjoying the very pleasant Indian Summer. When they saw Wellman, they stood up and greeted him warmly.

Ben was clad in Bermuda shorts and a short sleeve Hawaiian shirt. Miriam wore a yellow sundress. Like Daniel, she had undergone a great transformation since she stepped out of the time displacement machine. She had a more modern hairstyle that suited her face. She wore no makeup. However, she did have neatly manicured fingers. However, like Daniel, she still had the exotic presence of someone from another place.

"Would you like a beer or lemonade?" Miriam asked.

She glanced toward Ben who nodded with approval. She beamed proudly at speaking properly. In the last four months, both mother and son had devoted many long hours to learn English.

"Yes. A beer would be great," Wellman said.

She went into the house to fetch the beer.

"Grab a seat, Jack. Take a load off," Ben said.

"Thanks."

Wellman grabbed a chair. He smiled mischievously at Ben in his wildly colorful clothes. They were very un Ben-like, at least for the old Ben. On the new Ben, they seemed oddly appropriate.

"Nice threads. Very chic."

Ben fought back a chuckle as he looked down at them.

"I can't take credit for them. Miriam picked them out."

"I like them," Wellman said.

"Thanks. You should see the rest of my closet. These are the tame ones."

Wellman laughed.

Miriam returned with the bottle of beer.

"Thank you, Miriam."

"You are welcome."

Miriam took the third chair next to Ben's. He took her hand. His fingers stroked it tenderly.

Wellman drank some of the ice-cold beer. It hit the spot.

"So, I hear you're making some progress on the new engine."

Ben shrugged, "Some. We're right back to square one. But I'm hopeful. Naturally, the security is intense now. I'm not sure they completely trust us."

"Well, can you really blame them?"

They turned to watch Daniel playing catch with his dog.

Wellman looked back to Ben. He was surprised at how quickly Ben had taken on the job of husband and father. He seemed quite content with his new responsibilities.

"You have a nice family, Ben."

"Yeah, I know."

Ben reflected upon Miriam and Daniel. Four months ago, the last thing on his mind was having a family, and now he could not imagine Miriam and Daniel not being part of his life. It was amazing how quickly a person's life could change.

"Any news about the 'you know what'?"

Wellman shook his head. He took a swig of beer, looking about to make sure there was no one else around. While he was not a paranoid man, he knew one could not be too careful these days.

"Nothing definite. But the rumor is it's been completely dismantled."

"Well it's probably for the best," Ben said whimsically.

In the months that followed their return, he had hoped that something might be done for Faith and Charlie. He soon realized they were lost to him forever. What were the lives of two people compared to National Security?

"I've been meaning to ask you something, Ben," Wellman said.

"What's that?"

"In the months since you've been back, have you noticed anything different?"

"Different?" Ben replied, knowing where he was going.

"Well, if the present was altered in some way by your trip, you're the only one who would know because you knew how things were before you traveled back. I wouldn't know. No one would know. Only you would know."

"Oh, you mean something like Russia landing on the moon

before we did?" Ben said casually.

"Russia landed on the moon first?" Wellman exclaimed.

Ben's hard expression cracked into a big smile.

"Funny, Ben. Very funny. You almost gave me a heart attack."

"Sorry. But the answer to your question is I have not detected any difference in the present. It doesn't mean there hasn't been any. It's big world. By the way, those men in black asked me that same question not two months ago," Ben revealed.

"Did they? You never told me they paid you a visit."

"Well, they threatened to cancel my Netflix if I told anyone."

Wellman set his beer on the grass. He leaned forward in the chair, setting his elbows on his knees. His voice dropped almost to a whisper. He sounded very enigmatic.

"Ben, how would you feel about taking your family on a little trip?"

Ben leaned forward now until only a foot separated them. He matched the guarded tone of the general.

"Trip? Where?"

"Oh, about halfway around the world," Wellman said.

"Can you be a little more specific?"

"Not really."

Ben sat back. He tried to read Wellman's face, but saw no answers in those reticent blue eyes. He glanced at Miriam who was only partly following their conversation. The last four months had been quite stressful and eye-opening for Miriam and Daniel; far more than it had been for him going back to their time. For the first few months, he could barely leave them alone. They stuck to him like glue. He became their emotional and physical anchor to their new existence. General Wellman had given every assistance he could, including acquiring new identities, from birth certificates to Social Security numbers. They received thorough medical examinations and a number of inoculations. He even provided a military translator to help immerse them in English. Literally, every moment for them was a new experience that was both thrilling and stressful. Observing them struggle day after day was an eye-opening experience for him as well. In the beginning, it was exhausting but over the weeks that followed, he underwent his own transformation. While he did this to satisfy an obligation to them, he soon found himself growing extremely close to Miriam and Daniel until he saw them as his wife and child.

"Do you think they would be up for a trip like that?

"They've never flown in a plane before, Jack. To tell you the truth, they're barely used to being in a car. A few weeks ago I gave Miriam her first driving lesson."

"Really? How did that go?"

Ben grinned. He had her drive in circles in an empty parking lot. There was no risk to anyone, but she still managed to scare the hell out of him.

"She's a work in progress."

Miriam, realizing they were talking about her, stared questioningly at Ben. He mimed turning a steering wheel. Her blush of embarrassment brought a grin to the general.

Daniel and Argo came over. They dropped down to the grass to listen in to their conversation.

Ben looked at them. He knew he could not protect them forever. They managed to survive in a far more hostile world two millennia ago. He took Miriam's hand, stroking her fingers.

"How would you like to go on a trip?"

"Trip?"

She thought about it and shrugged a yes. She turned to Daniel and asked him in Aramaic if he was up to it. He nodded eagerly. The boy was fearless.

Ben nodded to Wellman. Then he thought of a potential problem.

"Won't they need a passport?"

"I'll take of it," Wellman promised.

Ben gently rubbed Daniel's head.

"Okay. Let's do it."

***

The long flight to Israel was exhausting to Ben, but not to Miriam and Daniel. The two took turns staring out the window. One would point to something and the other would lean in and express complete wonderment. Naturally, when Ben tried to explain to them about flying halfway across the world, they were terrified of the very idea of traveling like a bird. For a while, Ben thought he would have to cancel the trip completely. He could have never made the trip by himself. They were not ready to be left alone for any appreciable amount of time. However, when Miriam saw how important the trip was to him, she agreed.

For most of the flight, Ben immersed himself in deep conversations with General Wellman about the new engine. Otherwise, they both slept as best they could. Even Miriam and Daniel finally dozed off.

After arriving, Wellman whisked them through customs with the assistance of several Israeli air force officers. Within thirty minutes they were traveling in a car toward Jerusalem. Naturally, the lay of the land had undergone drastic changes in the preceding two thousand years. Jerusalem, much larger today, had a population of nearly one million.

"Are you sure that's Jerusalem?" Miriam asked, gazing at the tall buildings, the multitude of cars, and massive crowds.

"Yes, it's the same city," Ben assured her.

Neither Miriam nor Daniel had still quite come to grips with the concept of time travel. They pressed their faces against the glass of the car searching for some common architectural or geographical feature that they might recognize. However, two thousand years had left few relics from their past existence. Those that still existed had become so ground down by time they would likely not recognize them.

About five minutes after leaving the city, the car rolled up a bare escarpment toward a host of tents and vans. Ben recognized the terrain now. Two thousand years had not worn them down completely.

The car pulled up alongside a dusty van. One by one they climbed out of the car. Ben pulled his safari hat over his head to block out the sun. Miriam had a sun hat, and Daniel a new Dodgers cap. General Wellman, in civilian clothes, dropped on a pair of aviator glasses.

All around them was an archeological excavation. Two large tents were off to the left, parked near three Chevy vans. To the right the actual archaeological work was underway. A number of ancient structures had been uncovered. The roofs had long since rotted away, but parts of the stonewalls still remained, even after two thousand years. Recently recovered artifacts covered several long worktables. One worker in dusty gray overalls was carefully brushing them of dirt before setting them on the adjacent table.

Ben looked left and saw a familiar sight. Several caves had been opened up and cleared of debris. Closer to the caves his eyes locked on the circular stone rim of the old well that served the community back then. Miriam and Daniel saw it too. They both pointed at it and talked back and forth excitedly. Although Ben had picked up a smattering of Aramaic, he could not follow what they were saying.

Emerging from the big tent, a deeply tanned, white-haired man appeared. He saw Wellman and waved as he approached.

"Shalom, Jack," he beamed.

"Afternoon, Paul," Wellman replied, shaking the man's calloused hand.

The chief archeologist quickly wiped his hand from a towel hanging from his belt.

"How was your flight?"

"For a long flight I prefer something a little faster. Like a Raptor," Wellman replied.

Paul Melnick was sixty, but could easily pass for early forties, even with his snow-white hair and bushy eyebrows. He had the steely gaze one associates with a military man.

General Wellman turned and introduced Ben, Miriam, and Daniel.

"This is Ben Miles. Ben, this is Professor Paul Melnick, formerly General Melnick of the Israeli Air Force. He's an old friend."

"Good to meet you," Ben said, shaking his hand. "This is my wife Miriam and my son Daniel."

They nodded politely to the professor. Melnick turned a directing glance at Wellman. The general's nod spoke volumes.

"It's a great pleasure to meet the both of you. You've come a very long way haven't you?" Melnick said in Aramaic.

Their faces brightened at hearing their language. Miriam nodded, understanding his meaning. The professor stood there, staring at the two as one might at a long thought extinct animal suddenly discovered to be alive.

"Come along. We have a lot to see," he said.

Melnick led them across the barren earth and into the first uncovered hovel. It now dawned on both Miriam and Daniel that they were actually standing in their old home. Of course, there was little to see after two thousand years of wind and water erosion. The walls had been well worn down until they barely stood a foot high. Whatever furniture it once possessed had long since disintegrated, or had been taken away by future dwellers.

Ben stood there picturing Faith and Charlie standing before him in their ancient garb. Even now, it seemed like something that happened several lifetimes ago. The place seemed so much smaller than he remembered. He looked to Miriam and Daniel. They were staring back at him. He could see they were reliving the same heart-rending memories.

"We believe these homes were originally for miners back in the First Century when they were excavating for copper in the nearby hills. When they were eventually played out, they were taken over by families," Professor Melnick related. "As you can see, people back then lived very simple lives compared to today."

Wellman and Melnick stared at Ben, Miriam, and Daniel who appeared to be only half-listening to him. They displayed melancholy, haunted expressions. Unlike Wellman, Melnick only knew part of their story. However, he knew enough to suspect what they were feeling.

"But then you know all about that, don't you?" Melnick said to Ben in English.

Ben nodded solemnly.

"At some point this place was renovated rather extensively. Several additional rooms were added about that time. We believe it might even have been a school of sorts."

"Why don't you show them what else you found," Wellman suggested.

"Sure. It's back over here."

He waved them toward several worktables covered with recovered artifacts. Most of the items were simple utensils, including old jars, rusted pans, and several hammers. Melnick went to the farthest table and turned over a large tablet.

Daniel showed no interest in that. He picked up several of the items and set them back down. He stopped when he came to a cardboard box filled with a number of miscellaneous items yet to be identified and catalogued. However, one item caught his eye immediately. He picked up the dusty, badly nicked wooden ball. He recognized it as the one he would toss to Argos. He flipped it in the air excitedly.

Miriam reacted with alarm. She grabbed his arm, and leaned in to admonish him.

"Don't touch anything, Daniel. Put it back."

Daniel frowned, squeezing the ball tight against his chest.

"But it's my ball, Momma."

Miriam stared at the ball again. She recognized it now. She

looked around and noticed everyone was too busy working to watch her. She slid the ball into the handbag hanging over her shoulder. She set her arm around her smiling son.

Professor Melnick brushed dirt off the ten inch by twenty-inch tablet revealing the writing carved into it. It was broken around the edges.

"When we first uncovered this, everyone suspected it was a practical joke by one of the team. Excavating ancient sites for weeks can be incredibly tedious."

Ben leaned in, but he was having trouble reading the chipping.

"What does it say?"

"Oh, it's in English," Melnick revealed with a sly grin.

"What?" Ben said.

He leaned over it again. He choked up as he read the words:

WE ARE BOTH WELL AND CONTENT. WE HOPE YOU ARE AS WELL. NOW DO YOU BELIEVE? FAITH.

"Whoever carved it wanted it to survive. It was buried several feet in the far corner of this home."

Ben pointed to the top of the tablet that was partly broken. Only some writing had survived the two millennia.

"What about that part there?"

"Well, as you can see edges have chipped away, or broke off, over the last two thousand years. However, it looks like a name to me. What do you think?"

Ben pressed his face right up to the tablet. He carefully ran his fingers along the chipping. He sucked in his breath, a tingle running up his spine. The words appeared to be:

TO BEN MILES

"What do you think it reads?" Melnick asked.

Ben stood up. He fought down a flood of emotions.

"As I said, we all suspected it was someone's idea of a joke. But one of the team did a little searching on the name Ben Miles. Not an unusual name, but I recognized it having read a little bit about your work in physics. And then, looking a little deeper, I saw you had a sister named Faith, who was married to a man named Charlie."

Ben thought for a moment. Then he turned to Wellman who flashed a knowing smirk.

"You told them to excavate in this area, didn't you?"

Wellman shrugged, "Well, I just suggested they do a little poking about where you said you arrived. To tell you the truth, I really didn't think Paul would uncover anything."

Ben looked back to Professor Melnick.

"Did you find anything else?" he asked.

Professor Melnick nodded.

Behind the excavation, in a shallow pit, they stood over two worn down mounds of earth. Both were about the length of a human being. One was a little longer and wider than the other was.

"When we found the bodies we stopped excavating," Melnick said. "But we did collect several DNA samples."

Ben found himself ready to lose it. His eyes misted over, his words choked with emotions.

"What do you know about them?"

"You mean other than they both had twenty first century dental work?" Wellman said, with a raised eyebrow.

"Well, it's a man and woman. We estimated their age to be in their seventies, possibly even eighties. They appeared to have died from natural causes. But that's just a guess. We did find this around the women's neck," Melnick said.

Melnick held out a rusted chain with a slightly bent crucifix hanging from it. He offered it to Ben. He stared at it, recognizing it immediately. With a shaking hand, he accepted it.

"Odd thing is people did not start wearing those until around the fifth century. Before that they wore only crosses. I'm guessing you'd probably like to keep that."

Ben nodded solemnly.

After the professor had given them a further tour of the

excavation, Ben returned to the two graves. He took one knee and stared at the twin mounds. Miriam and Daniel stood close by his side. General Wellman and Professor Melnick watched them from a respectful distance.

"You did it, Charlie. You saved her," he said. "Faith, maybe things did work out the way they were supposed to. Maybe."

Ben dug his fingers into the dry earth, grabbing a handful. The soil scorched his palm but he did not feel the heat. He slowly let it spill between his fingers and back onto their graves. After some reflection, the same hand reached up and gripped the cross hanging around his neck, squeezing it tight. Miriam and Daniel, pressing against him, set their hands gently on his shoulders. Looking up at them, the overwhelming sadness passed away when he saw the love in their eyes. He put his arms around them and embraced them.

THE END

Made in the USA
Coppell, TX
14 December 2021

68652110R00157